Forgive Me Never

a novel

DANIEL MARTINEZ

Forgive Me Never

For information about this title or to order other books and/or electronic media, contact the publisher:
Daniel Martinez Publishing (Costa Rica)
US Mailing Address: 6703 NW 7th Street
Suite # SJO-12708
Miami, FL 33126
dmpublishing@zoho.com

ISBNs: 978-0-9882677-2-5 (print)
        978-0-9882677-9-4 (eBook)

Printed in the United States of America
Cover and Interior design: 1106 Design

DEDICATION

To my mother

Maria Luisa Cisneros

(1925–1963)

Is it fair to expect love from a mother

Who never had any herself?

It is forgiveness to finally feel she gave us her best

From the empty cup her own parents had placed in her heart?

———————————

CHAPTER 1

Frida Cervantes appeared to be perturbed by something as she shuffled with her two children, ages nine and four, along Houston's Pebble Mount Motel's walkway to the small room she had just rented for the night. Of course, her face *always* showed some depression, but that afternoon a small part of her inner mournfulness had given way to a quiet but desperate anxiety about something.

Olivia, the older child, asked, "But, mamma, why are we coming to this hotel? I want to go back to our house."

Little Benito looked at Olivia and then shifted his sad gaze to his mother, as if he, too, expected some type of answer. But he was already used to being ignored and not getting any answers about anything. Too small, too young to have given up on life.

They continued their slow walk to meet their destiny, and that gave 24-year-old Frida a few more seconds to think about an answer to Olivia's legitimate question of concern. Not that the answer mattered at all.

"It's just something we have to do for a little while, that's all," was Frida's feeble response.

Olivia was not socially or interpersonally bright, but she knew that other poor families in their neighborhood often went into hiding when the parents had vicious fights — mostly mothers running away with their children. But not to hotels, or motels even. They fled to relatives' homes or stayed with friends. That was not the case here, Olivia knew, for there was no father at home, and no fight to speak of. As usual, the rent was overdue, but the landlord had not yet thrown them out of the miserable, dilapidated structure they all called home. It was a mystery. It was 1982.

At last, they all arrived at Room 121. Frida froze in front of the door with the key in her trembling hand, just long enough for the two kids to give her a puzzled look. She must have been contemplating something very carefully. They went in.

It was a cheap motel on the city's south side, and it smelled rather musty from the carpet's old age and from the room having been shut undoubtedly many days since its last rental. The drab-yellow walls clearly had not been painted in perhaps ten years; two picture frames with images of far-away sailboats were so faded that they could easily be mistaken for pictures of cloudy skies. There was what looked like a very old bed with its midsection sunk in, one chair, a black-and-white television with a rabbit-ears antenna, and a very small closet with one of its two doors missing. In the bathroom, the bathtub had a little bit of black and green mold, and the commode had no toilet seat, but it was working. Yet the kids noticed none of this because it was not too different from what they had at home.

Frida set her green purse on the small wooden chair and then sat on the edge of the bed without saying a word. Benito sat by her side, looking like maybe he wanted to say something but couldn't — just looking lost and unsure. It would have been normal for any mother to have taken the hand of her small child in this situation, but Frida just stared out the window and into space, her hands clasped together, practically indifferent to the presence of her young son. Maybe he sensed something; maybe he just needed to be held by his mother. But, even by age four, he had not developed the social skills to ask for love. It wouldn't matter anyway, for he would not be getting any, and he might have known that.

Olivia was still exploring the room as the quiet tragedy was unfolding at the edge of the bed. Didn't find more than an old coloring book that another unfortunate kid had left behind, maybe even years before. She quickly lost interest.

"Mamma, what are we doing here?" questioned Olivia.

Frida finally got up from the bed, walked toward her young daughter Olivia, and placed her cupped hand over her cheek. It was unusual for Frida to do that, to touch her children. Olivia placed her hand over her mother's to savor the moment, while Benito just looked from the edge of the bed, like a stranger watching life go by.

"I got to go to the motel office to get some coffee," Frida blurted out, matter-of-factly.

"Good — we'll come with you," added Olivia.

"No, you and Benito just wait here, and I'll be right back."

She picked up her purse, opened the door, and, before closing it, looked back and made direct eye-to-eye contact with Olivia and then with Benito. Her mother's grave look gave Olivia the chills, but she did not know how to interpret her feelings. Frida closed the door behind her.

After about twenty minutes, Olivia started to wonder why her mother was taking so long just to get coffee. By that time, Benito had already taken a position standing by the window — looking, hoping, wanting. Olivia had turned on the black-and-white television but kept running back to the window when she heard noises outside. Nothing. The look of anticipation on her face must have melted dozens of times.

Two hours later, Benito told his sister that he was hungry and thirsty. She gave him water from the bathroom sink, but she herself was feeling weak from lack of food. A couple walking outside on the walkway were startled when they passed by the window and saw the droopy eyes and forlorn faces of the two children inside. Secretly, Olivia was wishing that some angel had sent this couple to bring them food and drink, but no, the angel had not done such a thing.

They had been by the window for five hours — tears of desperation were beginning to flow down their cheeks. By that time, Olivia had moved the old chair to the window, sat on it, and placed Benito on her lap. He never gave up waiting for mamma by the window, until sleep overtook him later that night. Olivia carried her little brother to the bed and fell asleep next to him.

Next morning, they were awakened by a loud knock on the door. *Why would mamma knock if she had the key to the room?* Olivia wondered. She certainly was glad to hear that mamma was back, yet she also was confused as to why she had stayed out all night. And without telling them. They were scared, they were hungry, they were lonely.

But it was the police.

"Where's mamma?" cried Olivia. Benito, in a daze and wet with urine, took hold of her hand.

"We are here because it was reported that there were two unsupervised children in a motel. Are your mother and father here?" asked the officer.

Olivia explained all the details, with her heart pounding from the realization that something terrible might have happened to her mother. A quick police check of the surrounding areas revealed nothing — no cadaver, no mother at a bar. So Houston's Child Protective Services, also known as DSS, took Olivia and Benito and placed them with relatives.

It would be several weeks before Olivia would be told by her 26-year-old Aunt Jenny, who, by that time, had taken her and Benito in, that officers had discovered that her mother had been killed by a tractor-trailer on the highway in front of the motel, sending her body flying into a grassy, wet ditch nearby. The body was so badly decomposed when a highway repair crew finally spotted it a few weeks later, Aunt Jenny said, that it was later just cremated. Because of the unusual circumstances, and because the family was so desperately poor, there had been no funeral.

It was a devastating blow for Olivia, who had held out hope that mamma would still show up somehow. For two whole days, she was disconsolate — didn't eat, didn't sleep. She hid under the bed. She never quite recovered from the loss — she just learned to make believe that her life would return to normal. It was an unfortunate, but necessary, façade.

It was a most unusual case — police officers talked about it for a long time. *The Houston Chronicle* had picked up the story right away after the police showed up at the motel. They gathered all the facts, and the headline said it all:

MOTHER ABANDONS HER TWO SMALL CHILDREN AT SEEDY MOTEL

The police and the reporters had spoken to the motel manager, and, in no uncertain terms, he stated what he'd seen.

"Sure, I'll tell you. Yesterday afternoon, this lady and her two kids rented Room 121 — she paid cash. They all went to the room — I could see it well from this window. A few moments later, the lady came out all by herself, and, at this very corner in front of the motel, she boarded an intercity bus — the one going to Dallas/Ft. Worth. I figured another relative had come by to take care of the kids. Never saw her again."

Frida was not dead. She had deliberately lied to her two small children, taken them to a motel room, and heartlessly told them she was going to get some coffee. Innocently, they believed her. While they were eagerly waiting for her, she boarded the bus to Dallas and left them behind, all alone in a motel room, with no food or water. Their safety, their comfort, their happiness, and their future were none of her concern. They cried for her — they looked out the window for hours, yearning to see her face. They waited, and they waited, until they were overcome by sleep from the painful exhaustion. But mamma never returned.

CHAPTER 2

Nineteen Years Later

"You are two minutes late, Olivia!" barked 41-year-old Karl Williams of the Williams Circuit Components Company in southwest Houston. Every morning, he would stand by the employee entrance when it opened at 6:50 A.M. and closed promptly fifteen minutes later, as per his orders. Anyone coming in even one second after the 7:00 A.M. starting time was considered late. After the door closed, no workers were permitted to enter; they were sent home for the day with no pay.

"Sorry, Mr. Williams. I had to take my five-year-old daughter Gabriela to the babysitter's," groveled Olivia.

"That is not my concern, you lowly spic. That's your problem for having a daughter and no husband. But then again, that's part of your dirt-poor immigrant culture, isn't it? You will get two demerit points against your pay. Now get to your station before I decide to place you on toilet duty for the day."

"Oh, thank you, Mr. Williams. I will try to be better. Thank you, thank you."

In quiet tears and with a choking knot in her throat, poor Olivia Cervantes hurried to her circuit board soldering station, put on her work apron, and began her shift, as she had been doing for the last two years.

She was 28, very petite, about 5-foot-5 with shoulder-length dark hair and big, beautiful brown eyes.

It was 2001. Her family had moved to Houston thirty years prior, in 1971, from Monterrey, Mexico, to find work in the growing oil industry in Texas.

The drastic downturn in the market in the early '80s affected the family's meager income, and they never quite recovered after that.

Olivia had managed to find work at Williams Circuit Components in 1999, after having searched fruitlessly for a job for more than a year. She had had several small jobs here and there but eventually had to leave because the employers cheated all employees out of their pay, figuring correctly, that the employees had no recourse. At Williams Circuits, all the women who worked there knew that Karl Williams got some perverse enjoyment from asking them many inappropriate questions during the interview, questions the women were obliged to answer because of their desperate need for the job. Not only that, but he had a habit of ordering them individually to come to his office, where he would touch them all over. If they protested, he would place them on his blacklist and would make their lives so difficult at work that they saw no alternative but to quit. When Olivia had first applied and went for the interview, she had left his office in tears but was glad that she had been given a job which would help support her and her then-three-year-old daughter Gabriela. She had no husband and no boyfriend to depend on.

The company occupied about one-fourth of a block near the corner of Westheimer Road and Dunlavy Street, and employed 65 full-time employees in the production of circuit boards destined mainly for electronic components for the military. Since the job consisted mostly of assembly-line, repetitive work, it was an ideal position for workers with limited facility in English. The legendary rudeness and abusive managerial style of Karl Williams were palatable only because the work was steady and the pay reliable. Even so, most workers at Williams Circuits had to have supplementary incomes to be able to pay all their bills.

Olivia was busy soldering, her tears dripping onto the soldering platform, when her friend Sonia, who worked right next to her on the assembly line, whispered, "Don't let it get to you, Olivia — you have us on your side. We know he's a real bastard." Sonia gently squeezed Olivia's upper arm.

"Sonia, I don't think I can take it. I do my best, but Mr. Williams makes a big thing out of everything."

"Yes, he does." She suddenly went quiet. Then she whispered, "The creep is looking at us from the observation deck. We'll talk at 12 noon."

To Olivia's left on the assembly line was Rosalba, who became aware of the conversation. She told Olivia, "Wipe those tears! He's not worth it!"

Lunch break was a heavenly respite from the tedious work on the soldering line. Workers had to breathe in the lead, tin, and rosin fumes coming from the hot soldering irons, and that was in spite of the ventilation system installed just last year, after workers had complained of headaches, nausea, and other ailments. Fumes rose from the work area toward the extraction fans high up on the ceiling, but they had to pass by the workers' noses first.

Most of the workers brought their own lunches — sandwiches, tacos, canned soups. Some ate outside by the parking lot, but most went to the large eating area. Olivia and six of her girlfriends almost always all sat together, unless someone was mad for some unclear reason.

"What'd ya bring, Olivia?" asked 55-year-old Lizbet. "Oh, just a boloney sandwich."

"You still upset about this morning? You should know by now that he will always find something to complain about," commented Lizbet.

Glenda, 26, joined in. "What did you expect? He's a man, so he's a pure bastard."

Judith was married but had a boyfriend on the side because, she said, at age 46, she wanted sex all the time, and only single, irresponsible men are satisfying in bed. "Okay, girls, we could talk about something more important, right? Like did you have good sex last night?"

"You all are very supportive, I appreciate that. Maybe it was my fault I was late for depending so much on the buses around here," emphasized Olivia as she bit into her boloney sandwich.

And Rita, 22, who colored her black hair blond because she wanted to be a Texas *gringa*, put in her best shot at the conversation. "Did you all notice that cute, new Mexicano who's now on Row 3, Position 12? Wow, *Papacito* — he's so good looking!"

"Cool your engine, Rita, or you'll end up pregnant in no time, girl," admonished Lizbet.

Sonia arrived a few minutes late at the lunch tables; she signaled Olivia to join her at another table.

"Excuse me, girls — I have some personal thing to discuss with Sonia."

Olivia had known Sonia for several years and regarded her as her best friend. Sonia Minetti was 32, married, about the same height as Olivia, with long, brown hair and black eyes. She and her husband Matt had one six-year-old daughter, Esther. Everyone knew Sonia as a sensible, confident, headstrong, and moral person. In fact, when women at work had some type of personal problem, they all asked Sonia for advice, for she would tell you to your face what needed to be done. Because of this, she was well respected by everyone who knew her. Her greatest asset for the women at work, though, was her willingness to confront abusive boyfriends and husbands when the abuse took part in the work parking lot. Her mouth was unstoppable in savaging men who became aggressive with women — and on various occasions she had even called the police on them.

"Sonia, what's up? Did you want to talk about that Karl Williams some more?" asked Olivia, somewhat perplexed and a bit hesitant.

"My guess is that you don't read the newspaper much, right?" queried Sonia as she dug into her macaroni-and-cheese lunch.

"Just now and then. I just prefer the news on TV."

"On several occasions, you have said that your mother died way back in 1982, when you were nine years old — is that right?"

"I really don't want to talk about it, Sonia. My mother's death is still the most painful chapter in my life," stressed Olivia as she bowed her head and lost the gleam with which she had started the conversation with Sonia. That early episode with Karl Williams had ruined her morning, and now this very personal and painful topic was laying waste to her lunch and, possibly, to the rest of her day.

"And I know that, Olivia. I sense that half of your soul died with your mother, and that is why I am having this conversation with you." Sonia left it at that as they quietly continued with their lunch. Their usual friends at the other table kept throwing glances at them, perhaps wondering just what it was that they had to discuss that required a separate table. But there was sufficient space between the two tables to guarantee some privacy.

Olivia took about three minutes to compose herself after Sonia's surprise opening of the topic. Then she dared to continue. "So why are you asking now?"

"I've been thinking about something for two days — something I read in *The Houston Chronicle* recently."

"Oh, great. Don't tell me you read about some self-help group for adult women who lost their mothers when they were very young."

"Are you free tonight? Can I come over around 9 P.M.? My daughter Esther would be in bed by that time, and Matt can stay at home with her. I figure little Gabriela will be in bed, too, so we can sit by your table and have some coffee."

"Yeah, that sounds okay."

They continued eating and talking about other stuff associated with the bad treatment of the workers on the soldering line, especially the treatment of three women who had reported to Sonia that Karl Williams had forced himself upon them. One, Carmelina, was now pregnant. During her employment interview several months earlier, she had told Karl Williams that she was 22, but, in reality, she was 17, a minor. The abuses were getting worse, and the women thought they should be doing something about it, instead of just suffering in silence and gossiping about it during lunch breaks.

Work let out at 4 P.M., and, afterwards, Olivia rushed to Paloma's house, her babysitter, to pick up Gabriela. Olivia had already ritualized her entrance into Paloma's house, to make it more fun for her daughter.

After knocking on the door, she would say, "Heellooo, is there a little angel here who is missing her mamma?" Gabriela would run to the door screaming, "Mamma, mamma — I am your little angel. Give me a kiss!"

"My little angel, I missed you, I missed you! I promise I will always be here for you, for all eternity!"

Paloma, 60, and suffering from various ailments, had thought from the beginning that it was rather odd for Olivia to continually promise her daughter that she would always be there for her, no matter what. In Paloma's view of the world, normal children never even question the possibility of a parent not being there but that, on the contrary, they go through childhood feeling that parents are practically immortal, that they *will* be there for them forever. Well, at least when they are young and most vulnerable. Paloma felt that Olivia might not be fully aware of what she was doing, or even why. But Olivia's subconscious wounded soul knew.

"So, tell me, Paloma, how was she today?"

"Oh, she's never a problem. Today we did some drawings, and she drew a beautiful one of you and her — it's in the bag."

"I drew it all for you, mamma, because you are my best mamma in the world!"

"What is it, Paloma? You seem a bit sad or bothered by something."

"It's my son. You know, he's in California, and he told me he just broke up with his girlfriend. They had been going out for maybe five years. He's taking it pretty hard."

"Yeah, we've all been there, but he has friends who can give him support, right?"

"Yes, he does, but I would prefer that he be here so I could console him myself."

"Paloma, you're all heart. I would probably feel the same way, but he's a big boy now, and he'll get over it. Suggest to him to go on a vacation with some friends — it'll take his mind off it."

"Thanks, Olivia."

An hour later, Olivia and Gabriela arrived at their apartment building on Bissonet Street, near the corner of Beechnut. It had four floors — occupied mostly by poor folks, Mexicans and whites. They went up the stairs to their apartment, #207.

It had two very small bedrooms, and the living room was combined with the kitchen. The bathroom was designed to be a disaster, for it was so small that anyone taller than 5-foot-4 using the toilet had to sit practically sideways on the seat because one's knees would butt the wall in front if sitting properly. There was no window, so, with little ventilation, mildew was a permanent resident over all the fixtures, walls, and shower curtain.

And the cockroaches — the small German kind plus the Texas tree variety — those monsters! Olivia had almost given up trying to exterminate them. With so many unkempt apartments, the filthy creatures would just migrate temporarily to the next-door residents and then return, as if with a calculated vengeance, for the attempted genocide. Indeed, it was hopeless, for the cockroaches had fecundity, adaptability, a positive attitude, and time on their side.

But that is all Olivia could afford. She was proud that she and Gabriela were not receiving any government assistance, although she understood why so many of the people she knew were. It was only because of her extraordinary effort to always provide for her daughter that things were generally going in the right direction.

After dinner, Olivia read two stories to Gabriela, and then it was bedtime at 8 p.m. A little after that, when Olivia was doing some cleaning, there was a knock on the door. She quickly looked at the clock, but it could not be Sonia because it was not yet 9 p.m. Then it dawned on her that it was the beginning of the month, and the rent was due. She dreaded paying the rent.

It was Bull Garcia, the muscular and tall 35-year-old building manager from apartment 101 downstairs. "Well, hi'ya, Olivia — you know what time it is. Can I come in?" He came in before she could answer. He looked around quickly and asked, "She's asleep, right?"

"Look, Bull, here's half of the rent money right now. Take it, and I'll give you the other half next week."

"That's not the way it works, princess. You know Mr. Wickers, the owner, hates late rent payments. In fact, he's been real nice to you and hasn't thrown you and your little bastard girl into the street. Yet."

"I appreciate that, believe me, but I hardly spend any money on anything besides rent and food. Please understand."

"Last time, Mr. Wickers had already drawn up the eviction papers for this apartment. By now, you and the kid would have been sleeping somewhere else, in a one-bedroom apartment with 12 people from Guatemala. Quite nasty way of life. But I argued with him in your favor."

Olivia disliked — no, hated — Bull Garcia for the type of man he was, and because of how he always took advantage of the situation. His eyes were going up and down her body, and she knew the routine.

"Can you just be a decent man and help me out because I have a kid and I need assistance?"

"Help you out? Princess, I always help you out. How many months have I gone to bat for you when your rent was late? Mr. Wickers is a real bastard when it comes to money — he wants no excuses. Now, isn't it fair that you help me out, too?"

"Not this way, Bull. I have a small daughter. I'm trying to be decent. I have to give her proper moral examples, and this makes me feel like dirt, like a failure."

"But you're wrong, Princess. When you do this with me, you are doing what needs to be done to provide a roof over her head. She's happy, and she's growing up right." He moved closer to her and started stroking her arm and then her hair. She couldn't move away too much, for he already had her against the wall. By this time, some tears had already started rolling down her cheeks.

"So just give me a few days, not a full week. Maybe I can pawn a few things," pleaded Olivia, the sides of her mouth already drooping with an impending sob.

"Come on — it's not as if we haven't done this before when you couldn't pay the rent. Don't start getting virtuous on me all of a sudden. We both know what you are. You are a fucking whore who will do it for money. That's right, virginal bitch: When it gets down to the bottom line, you open your legs for money! You can't erase that! So don't give me a fucking hard time. You either pay the full rent now, or you let me make you feel good all over!"

Olivia was now covering her face with a dishcloth so as not to wake up Gabriela with her sobbing. It had been a valiant attempt, once more, to prevent Bull Garcia from taking advantage of her financial problems, but it had failed again.

Bull put his arm around her and led her slowly in the direction of her bedroom. "That's my princess. You are such a beautiful person. And you know me — I really am a very loving guy when you don't give me any trouble. I want you to know how much I respect you for making this sacrifice to keep a roof over your daughter's head. You are going to love this very much — it will make you feel so good all over. You'll see."

They entered her bedroom, and she closed and locked the door behind them. As usual, she used an empty pillowcase to cover her face completely while it was happening. She had learned more than a year ago that having his face so close to hers in that position was intolerably repulsive — it made her want to vomit. Besides, she wanted to prevent him from even trying to kiss her lips — they were sacred ground, she felt, to be defended at all costs; they were the lips she used to kiss her young daughter Gabriela goodnight, every night.

The same rule applied to her hands — the hands she used to hold Gabriela's little hands when they walked together. After placing the pillowcase on her face, she would clench her hands in tight fists to prevent him from intertwining his fingers with hers. She felt strongly about that. Yet, oddly enough, even though Olivia reluctantly submitted because her determination to be a good mother told her she had to do whatever was necessary under the circumstances to keep her apartment going, there was a subterranean element in her soul that described more fully what she might not have been fully aware of: "You can defile my body, but if you touch my hand or kiss my lips, I will kill you!"

When he finished, he got up matter-of-factly and said, "In spite of all your resistance and all that, I know that you really do have the money for the whole rent, but you tell me you don't because you *want* me to ravish you once a month. I know you well, Olivia. You seem to be unable to get a boyfriend who will satisfy you in bed, so you do this little trick on me. Well, don't forget now, one week for the rest of the money. Mr. Wickers does not like delays. And one more thing, Princess. I've told you before — get some damned lubricating jelly for next time — your pussy is always dry, like elephant skin. Comes with age, you know." He gingerly walked out and closed the door. She heard him whistling down the walkway.

Her pillow was wet with her quiet tears and her body robbed of self-respect by the monster who lived downstairs. Lying there on the wicked bed, she had to remind herself that she was doing everything possible to be a good mother to Gabriela, a mother who would always be there for her daughter, no matter what, no matter how ugly the challenge.

In the shower, she scrubbed and scrubbed to remove his essence from her body. She even used dishwashing liquid on her body to supplement the strong hand soaps she utilized for these repulsive occasions. Afterwards, she dabbed herself all over with diluted rubbing alcohol to further cleanse away any residual contamination from this animal.

She did the best she could to compose herself quickly, for Sonia was due to arrive in a few minutes. She forced herself to watch a short segment of a situation comedy, and it helped to get her mind off the event that had become a regular and regrettable part of her life. Then there was a friendly knock on the door that sounded like Sonia.

"Hi, Olivia, I stopped over at La Ojarasca Panaderia-Bakery and brought some of your favorite chocolate *conchas* and eggy *ojos-de-buey*. Mmm, smells like great coffee in there!"

"Hi, Sonia — come in. My favorite *conchas*!"

"Olivia, your eyes are swollen — looks like you've been crying. What's happening? Is Gabriela alright?"

"Yes, she's alright; she's sleeping."

For more than a year that these assaults had been happening, Sonia had never come over on the night when one had transpired. Olivia did not know how to react now that Sonia suspected that something was very wrong.

"So, can you tell me what happened?"

At that point, Olivia just broke down, and the floodgates of tears and sobbing exploded. She used the damp towel nearby to cover her mouth and face so as not to wake up or frighten Gabriela. Sonia put her arm around her and kept quiet as Olivia unleashed a torrent of painful tears. Her wailing and weeping frightened Sonia, who had no idea what awful thing Olivia was dealing with. The only comfort for Sonia was just knowing that Gabriela, the center of the universe for Olivia, was safe, sleeping in the adjacent bedroom.

Sonia hugged her tightly, held her hand, patted her shoulder, and offered a few comforting words. A few minutes later, Olivia's sorrowful bawling started to wind down, until it became just a few breathing spasms. With a few tissues, Sonia wiped Olivia's wet face and gave her a fresh one so she could blow her nose.

"Olivia, let me get you some of your delicious coffee — it will make you feel better."

The two women just sat there at the small dinner table, wordlessly sipping on their coffee slowly, Sonia's hand on top of Olivia's.

"I am sorry, Sonia. You caught me at a very vulnerable moment. I did not mean to unload my tears while you were here."

"You are my dear friend, Olivia, so it is never a bother. Do you want a chocolate *concha*? They're fresh."

Sonia wisely changed the subject to something lighter, like silly gossip from work, as they both enjoyed the genuine Mexican bread from the favorite neighborhood panaderia-bakery. Soon enough, Olivia's face improved, and she started to smile a bit over Sonia's attempts at being funny. But secretly, Sonia knew that she could not possibly bring up the subject that she had hinted to Olivia about at work that day. It was too heavy, Sonia knew, and Olivia appeared to be very fragile at the moment. No more floodgates tonight.

"Do you feel ready to talk about what happened, or do you want to just skip it?"

"Give me a minute, Sonia," mumbled Olivia, as she appeared to be searching for a way to say something. To make it easier, Sonia stopped looking at Olivia's eyes.

"I am afraid you will think I am a worthless person," sighed Olivia, as she, too, stopped looking at Sonia's face and looked down at the table instead.

"You seem to be implying that you are doing or have done something terrible or immoral, maybe even criminal, but, from what I know about you, I doubt you would do something like that — deliberately, that is."

"Maybe you should stop being my friend, Sonia."

"You are scaring me, and I am totally confused. We are talking without really communicating, Olivia. If you did something you now regret, well, haven't we all done that at one point or another in our lives?"

"Yes, I suppose so. I am so ashamed — very ashamed."

"Olivia, just say it, and we will deal with it together."

All sorts of scenarios were streaming through Sonia's consciousness. Maybe Olivia had stolen something from work, maybe she was getting into drugs, maybe she was bringing different men home every night, maybe...

"If you don't want to be my friend after this, I will understand."

"Olivia, if you have a moral aberration I am not aware of, then, yes, I will cease being your friend. But I cannot imagine you being a bad person at all! Have...have you done something to Gabriela?"

Sonia's question startled Olivia, and she quickly realized that her inner conflict about whether or not to tell Sonia what had just happened in the bedroom was producing unnecessary and harmful speculation on Sonia's part. Olivia had to come forward or close the door for now on that issue.

"No, I have not done anything bad to Gabriela. Please believe me when I tell you I feel so ashamed and dirty about this."

She remained silent for about half-a-minute. "I have been having financial problems for about a year now, so, when the rent is due, I'm not able to pay it in full — maybe just part." She hesitated again.

"The building manager lives downstairs, and he collects the rent from all the tenants at the beginning of the month."

Sonia started looking at Olivia's face again, although Olivia looked mostly at the floor.

"A year ago, he started threatening me with eviction. I got scared. Gabriela and I need to have an apartment." Olivia was wringing her hands, tears now flowing down her face.

After a long pause, which Sonia did not interrupt, Olivia got to the point. "So he said that, if I went to bed with him, he would rescind the eviction process." She looked away from Sonia and started to cry again.

"Is that all?" was Sonia's surprised response. "Olivia, do you realize how many of us women have had to use sex as a means when other options don't work? No, don't feel ashamed. It's part of life — both men and women sometimes have to do unpalatable things in life, just to get by!"

"Sonia, it's more like rape! I resist all the way because I detest the bastard! He drags me to the bedroom. I resist when he's taking my clothes off. I am totally dry, so he tears up my insides. I cover my face with a pillowcase! I am afraid of him!"

After about a minute, she calmed down and added, "Yet, I cannot say no and I don't call the police because I owe rent money — so he is entitled to my body."

Stunned by what Olivia had just confessed, Sonia asked in a whisper, "Olivia, how often does this happen?"

"Almost every month when the rent is due. Been going on for a year."

"Anything else?"

"He said I was a whore because I use my body to get money — rent money. He's right. I always wanted to set a good example for my baby. Now, I'm just a whore! I have failed, Sonia. I am just a whore!"

"No, Olivia, you are not that! You are a good woman. Stop talking that way."

Sonia was a good friend, but it was not easy for her to listen to Olivia's story of how she had painfully failed in some way. Sonia's mind started wandering back to some previous years, remembering how she, too, had had her share of moral failures, events in life she preferred not to willingly recall. Her history of hardships helped her to fully understand the moral anxiety and personal self-deprecation that Olivia was going through.

That Olivia only half-heartedly resisted Bull Garcia made Sonia feel that Olivia felt in her heart that she did not have the full right to her body, just as she felt that she had no right to dignity in dealing with Karl Williams at work — the boss had the full right to insult and denigrate her at will. Maybe Olivia, through the years, had developed an obsessive form of mothering — she had to do whatever needed to be done to be the perfect mother, even if she lost herself in the process.

Sonia chose her words carefully and then spoke. "Olivia, I have heard carefully what you have said, and I do not condemn you. I do judge you, as I judge everyone I please, and, in my judgment, you did not act out of malice or moral turpitude. We will fix this problem together."

"The fact remains that I have done what I have done. Maybe, underneath, I really *am* just a worthless person."

Sonia had enough experience in providing friendly advice to all the women at work to reach the conclusion that night that it might be fruitless to try to address Olivia's low sense of self directly. It might well be just one symptom of a larger constellation of problems deep within Olivia's soul, something that could better be addressed by the topic originally slated for that night and which had been pre-empted by Olivia's crisis. Sonia felt that there was nothing else to do at this point but to continue to provide support to her best friend.

Well, that was what she thought until Olivia added another dimension to the matter.

"I am also terrified that he might do something to harm Gabriela."

"Olivia, do what? What makes you say such a terrible thing?"

"That is another reason why I don't resist, Sonia. This animal gives her looks that make my stomach turn."

Sonia had a daughter of her own, six-year-old Esther, so this new revelation certainly hit home for her. This depraved serial abuser had to be talked to in no uncertain terms.

For the next two hours, they spoke about more personal matters, but, mostly, Sonia provided assurances to Olivia that she was a good person and a decent woman who had been victimized. Sonia told Olivia that the original subject had to be postponed for some other evening, and Olivia agreed.

On the way out, Sonia asked, "Oh, by the way, you did say that this Bull Garcia lives in apartment 101, right?"

"Yes — but don't write him any nasty letters."

"I promise I won't. Get a good night's rest, Olivia. See you tomorrow."

Walking down the stairs, Sonia was thinking of the best way possible to help Olivia handle the rape attacks. She quickly considered various options. Then she walked to her car, returned, and went to apartment 101. There was music playing inside. She knocked on the door.

With a big smile, she said, "Hi, you must be Bull Garcia, right?"

"Yes, baby — I am all yours!"

She pointed her police-sized pepper spray at his face and blasted him for about five seconds. Bull retreated, practically blinded by the burning liquid pepper in his eyes, and fell to the floor in pain. With her leg, Sonia pushed the door closed and turned the music up a notch. For the occasion, she had brought a medical safety mask, which she quickly put on, but, still, she was being affected by some of the fumes. Then she produced her aluminum bat, which she always carried in her car, just in case. She hit Bull several times on the shins and upper legs while he was writhing in pain on the floor and oozing abundant mucus from his nose and reddish streams of tears from his eyes.

"Shut the fuck up, you worthless worm! Shut up!" She raised the bat again.

"Okay, okay. I don't have any money here, but you can take the stereo and ten ounces of weed on the kitchen table."

"Shut up, you fucking parasite! Do you know why I am here to kill you?"

Of course, Sonia was not going to kill this cockroach, but she figured she had to instill the fear of fiery hell in him. He had to learn an unforgettable and painful lesson.

"*Kill* me? What did I do? I am just the manager of the building."

"Do you know why you deserve to die?"

"No! I *don't* deserve to die!"

"Yes, you do! You have been raping Olivia up there in apartment 207. Does that jar your memory a bit, you sewer rat?"

"*Rape*? No, she calls me up and asks me to sleep with her — that's all."

She hit him again three more times to increase the pain.

"No, please — no more. Oh, God, I'm hurt, I'm hurt. Okay, so I coerced her. Okay — I admit it."

"You didn't just coerce her, you raped her! Say it! Say it, you fucking amoeba!" She hit him again.

"Yes, I raped her, I raped her. Oh, it hurts, it hurts. Please, no more."

"She contracted our assassination group to give her protection. You will never, ever, ever again go near her or her daughter! Say it, you motherfucker!"

"I will never again go near Olivia or her daughter. Never, never — I promise! Oh, God, this hurts! Oh, God! I can't breathe."

"On one more condition, I might let you live."

"Please, yes — what is it?"

"You will pay her rent for one full year. You will have no more contact with her. Is that clear?"

She hit him two more times, once on each upper leg, full force. Both femurs might have cracked or broken.

"*Is that clear*?"

"Yes, I will pay her rent for one whole year — I will." He was definitely in a lot of pain.

"If Olivia ever calls our group because you are not honoring your part of the deal, we will come in a group and kill you with machetes. They will never find the pieces. Is that clear, you miserable lowlife piece of dog shit?"

"Yes, no problem! I promise! Thank you so much. I promise, I promise!"

"And don't try any smart tricks, you asshole. Olivia was smart enough to have installed a secret camera in her bedroom. It shows you raping her with her face covered by a pillowcase. We now have that video, and if this goes to the police, you will be put away for a minimum of 30 years, and dozens of hardened criminals in prison will have a joyful time with your butthole. Or we might just decide to chop you up into fine pieces. Just ponder that if you get any funny ideas."

Of course, there was no video, but he would always have to worry about that.

He started to throw up all over himself from the combined effects of the pepper spray and the shock of the blows to his legs. She took his wallet and extracted his driver's license from it. She closed the door behind her.

Sonia was actually trembling as she walked to her car, because never in her life had she done such a thing! This one time, though, it needed to be done, especially because Olivia had mentioned that she was terrified of the way Bull Garcia looked at little Gabriela. He had already shamelessly crossed a very important line — there was no sense in waiting for him to cross a second one, especially because, on several occasions, his eyes clearly indicated he might already have considered it.

After silently going over everything she had done that night at Olivia's building, Sonia concluded that she had acted properly under the circumstances. She placed her protection bat on the floor of the back seat of her car and drove home to kiss her own little angel.

CHAPTER 3

The following morning, Olivia made the effort to start the day earlier to avoid being late for work if there were any delays along the way. This time around, however, Karl Williams' wrath fell on two of the newer men on the soldering line who were caught talking with each other while soldering. It was easy to detect this, since, some months back, Williams had directed the sinister installation of hanging microphones and video cameras throughout the entire work area. Workers estimated there were no fewer than 23 microphones and 15 cameras. No prohibited conversation remained undetected. The two poor guys were indignantly chewed out in front of everybody and threatened with numerous pay demerits. It was just a matter of time, the workers thought, before clandestine microphones would be installed in the bathrooms. They weren't sure about cameras yet. Such was the draconian administrative philosophy of Karl Williams.

Olivia had had a night of fitful sleep — she had dreamt that faceless monsters were chasing her. After getting up, she had showered again early that morning, just in case, to ward off the bad vibes from Bull Garcia, and now, she was feeling much better at her work station. The talk with Sonia the previous night had given her a level of comfort, knowing that there was one decent human being on the planet who did not condemn her for her moral failures. That meant the world to her.

At lunchtime, the small group of women friends sat together again and whispered about the three women who had said they were either raped or seduced by Karl Williams. And the clock was ticking on Carmelina, the pregnant 17-year-old who was saying that it was Karl Williams' baby. According to informal and unofficial policy, pregnant women were shifted to a highly

19

toxic area at work. If they cared for their baby, they really had no choice but to quit. That suited the company really well. That would be happening to Carmelina real soon.

Lizbet was busy shoveling rice and beans into her mouth, together with piping hot corn tortillas, but she managed to pause for a moment, with her mouth full. "We just seem to talk about all these atrocities, yet we don't do much about them."

"Listen, Lizbet, we all desperately need this job. We have families, so, if we make waves, he can easily replace all of us. There are about 300 uneducated people waiting in line for each one of our jobs!" exclaimed Rosalba, who was now on a yogurt diet.

"In a way, we are like slaves. Replaceable slaves. But I agree with you, Lizbet. Maybe we should do something," suggested Sonia.

"You are all out of your minds!" exclaimed Rita, the wannabe blond *gringa*. "Most of us would not only lose our jobs, but we would also get deported! I will miss my friends and the great weekend dances at the Baile Caliente Dance Hall!"

"Well, I'm done with lunch — gotta wash my hands," quipped Sonia, as her eyes motioned Olivia to join her.

At the wash station, Sonia commented, "You are looking much better, Olivia."

"Oh, yes. Talking with you got a big load off my chest. Thanks for listening."

"The thing I wanted to talk to you about last night is very important. Couldn't do it last night, but do you feel up to it tomorrow night? I know it's a Saturday night, but this will give you an additional 24 hours to recover from last night's ordeal even more."

"Let's see. Yeah, that will be okay. Nine, again?"

"Perfect."

After lunch, everyone went back to their stations, and Friday quitting time quickly came: 3:30pm. That was when Karl Williams relished handing out paychecks personally to each worker. Everyone got in line, and each person was required to put his or her hand out, while Williams waited that extra second to hand out the check. The workers envisioned that he would have loved for each and every one of the groveling workers to say, as he was receiving his check: "Yes, Master, thank you oh so much for your Benevolence and Grace, oh Master! I am at your complete disposal, and do with me as per your wishes and desires, oh Great Master." His handing out the checks in that manner was another one of his sadistic power games to make the workers feel that he was in control, that he was the boss, that he was the one who was keeping them afloat in America! Everyone could see the megalomaniacal — almost orgasmic — joy in the grand but cynical smile he had when he did this. In his own eyes, he was God Himself! All the workers knew it.

On Saturday morning, Olivia and Gabriela visited Edeline Brunswick, who lived there in the same apartment building. Edeline was 81, widowed, lived all alone, had hair as white and as fluffy as cotton, and looked like one of those intellectual women in British movies from the 1940s and 50s. Even though she had a touch of Parkinson's and Alzheimer's, her mind was still sharp, so she continued to engage in her favorite pastime: Complaining about the culture and about politics all the time. Olivia didn't mind, for she thought it was her duty to help her out. She saw her twice a week, cleaned her apartment a bit, and did her grocery shopping.

In her quavering voice, she uttered, "Olivia, it's so nice to see you again. I see you have the little darling with you. How have you been, Gabriela?"

"Good, Mrs. Brunswick."

"Come over here, you little angel!" While still sitting on her usual cushiony seat, Mrs. Brunswick took Gabriela in her arms and squeezed her. Ever-obedient Gabriela just took it in stride and made faces to her mother to indicate that Mrs. Brunswick had again miscalculated the power of her arms, at least when hugging small, thin kids. When she was finally released, Gabriela let out a sigh of relief, and Mrs. Brunswick kissed her on the forehead.

Olivia sat next to her. "So, tell me, how have you been in the last few days?"

"You know the routine. I read and write a bit, mostly my memoirs, the last 75 years or so. But my hand tremors are making my writing illegible, so I can't read what I've written. Damned Parkinson's! Mother Nature is winning the power struggle I have with her. I would like to think that I am the master of my fate, but she spits in my face and declares that no one can live outside the rules of nature. I guess I need to learn how to accept that rule gracefully, but, damn it — I won't surrender to Mother Nature, the bitch! Oops! Sorry — I forgot Gabriela was here."

But Gabriela was busy looking at Mrs. Brunswick's hundreds of ancient figurines and knickknacks all over the walls and tables.

"Been sleeping okay?"

"That's the best part of my life!"

"I take it you still hate TV programs?"

"Worst trash since the beginning of civilization, Olivia! They dull the mind, which is what the government wants. It's almost as if the government were saying, 'Don't think — just obey the law and shut up!'"

"At least you keep busy with one thing or another."

"And you, Olivia — you okay?"

"Mostly, yes. Going to work, taking care of Gabriela, reading a little bit. Yes, I'm okay."

"Oh, Olivia, I can see it in your eyes — something is on your mind."

"Very perceptive, Mrs. Brunswick. One of these days, I will have to tell you a lot of things."

"Those eyes don't fool me — this has to do with men, right? You're looking for a husband, and it's a tough selection out there?"

"Well, yeah — that's part of it. And I can't figure them out. Some are real animals."

"Yes, Olivia, but there are good and bad women, too. It's not just that some men are bad — it's that the human race is rotten at the core, for the most part. My mother used to beat me for no reason throughout all my childhood. If I said a bad word by accident, she would force a hot spoon into my mouth — most of the time I had painful blisters all over my tongue. Damned sadist! I can say I hated that damned woman up until I was 60 years old. Then I just gave up on that, and I went to visit her grave — first to spit on it and then to forgive her."

"Sorry to hear that, Mrs. Brunswick. I guess you might say I have love/ hate feelings about men, just like you had for your mother."

"Look dear. I'm 81. I was married to the same man for 55 years — he died just a few years ago. Throughout those years, I often thought that men and women were not meant to marry and be together forever and ever in perfect bliss. What a damnable lie we throw upon the young people of today! We are two different species, almost!"

"So how come you two stayed together?"

"Well, it's not because you *get* a quantity of happiness when you have a husband. The real truth is that, in getting a husband, you are simply *avoiding* one of humanity's great miseries, and that is loneliness. My husband didn't *make* me happy — my work and hobbies did. But had I not had my husband, I could not have enjoyed those things that truly made me happy."

"Seems almost like a contradiction in itself. Hard to understand, Edeline. So am I wrong in wishing I had someone — you know, like a real boyfriend or husband — because I want to be happy?"

"Olivia, you are young, you are full of hormones, your body yearns for the closeness of someone you feel loves you. It is wonderful to be madly in love, but it doesn't last — it never does. Well, that fiery and passionate phase lasts just long enough to fill your house with babies — that's the way nature designed it. And that's okay, too. Listen, we'll catch up on this some other day, honey. Feeling tired and dizzy."

Olivia helped Mrs. Brunswick to her bed and covered her with a light blanket. She and Gabriela put away some groceries and tidied the place up a bit. They locked the door on the way out.

Walking down the several flights of stairs, Gabriela blurted out, "Mamma, I like Mrs. Brunswick. She sounds like she's smart."

"Oh, so you think she's smarter than me?"

"Well, no, you are smarter. But she's very smart. I love to hear her talk."

Next on Saturday's agenda was a visit to Olivia's aunt, 45-year-old Jenny Cervantes. Jenny had taken in nine-year-old Olivia and four-year-old Benito back in 1982, after Olivia's mother Frida abandoned them at that pitiful, flea-infested motel. Jenny did not have the heart to tell young Olivia and her brother about the abandonment, so she had concocted that story about Frida having been killed by a tractor-trailer on the highway in front of the motel. She had intended to wait a few years, until they were a bit older, to tell them the truth, but the lie became part of their lives and the family culture. With each passing year, it became increasingly more difficult to go back to correct what had become the official history of the Cervantes family. Jenny felt it would do more harm than good to tell them the truth.

Frida and Jenny were the only two children of Tomas and Florencia Cervantes. Well, officially, anyway, because Tomas was known to go out with the ladies, especially after spending long hours at Mexican cantinas. There were rumors of one or two women who let it be known that they had borne him a child — one in Mexico, and another there in Houston. Never proven, just rumors, but Florencia knew about them, and it added to her dysthymic depression. Looking at her face, one would think that she had never had a happy moment in her entire life — her face was like a lifeless and boring photograph from the 1800s. Yet, Tomas didn't seem to care about her expressionless face; it might have suited him better for her not to have any opinions about anything. Or at least it seemed that way on the outside.

Tomas and Florencia Cervantes had moved from Mexico to Houston in 1971, when Frida was 13 and Jenny 15. Two years later, Olivia was born to Frida, then 15 years old. In spite of being strict Catholics, the family was not particularly revolted by one of their daughters giving birth and not being married. It was said that the child's father was an unemployed teen laborer who quickly returned to Mexico upon learning that Frida was pregnant. She never claimed to even love the boy. Unfortunately for Frida, five years later, when she was 20, she gave birth again, this time to Benito. She confessed that it was a different father, a boyfriend who had never been presented to the family, one who also left after learning of her pregnancy. This one followed the seasonal harvest workers to Oregon. He never contacted her again. Frida's parents didn't seem to care either way.

Frida's sister, Jenny, was a very young woman when Frida went through her two pregnancies — she was 17, then 22. She must have been adversely affected, for she never had or wanted a boyfriend and, as an adult, never expressed a desire for a normal romantic relationship with a suitable man — she had, in fact, no children and had never been married. In many ways it could be said that poor Jenny was a slightly less tragic version of the chronically depressed personality of Florencia, her mother. Yes, Jenny's soul was depressed, maybe even damaged, and she had weird thoughts she dared not share with anyone, but, like a chameleon, she could hide these and feign laughter to suit any joyous occasion. Not that she was trying to be dishonest with people; she was simply and honestly trying to convince herself that she was enjoying life like most everybody else. Yes, Jenny had her own demons that were knocking on her door, increasingly louder, demanding to be acknowledged, while she desperately pushed back on that door to keep it shut.

She didn't live too far from Olivia and Gabriela's apartment — a small house that had been home to Olivia from ages 9 to 21, when Olivia moved out and got her own apartment on Houston's south side. Jenny was about two inches taller than Olivia, a bit thinner too, with short, black hair, and pretty, honey-colored eyes. All her adult life, she had worked as a seamstress out of her home, something that suited her well, considering that her inner disturbing thoughts and depressive mood required solitude to manage halfway decently. The truth was that any person who spent a few continuous hours in her presence would come to see how, at some moments, Jenny appeared to be distracted by some unseen internal activity — maybe intrusive thoughts, perhaps whispering voices, maybe even some other, secondary personality slowly trying to take dominion over her. Having lived with her for years, Olivia knew about Jenny's internal distractions, and paid little attention, for she considered it as part of Jenny's natural character. Besides, Jenny always treated her and Benito courteously and provided the security and stability that Olivia and Benito never really had when they lived with their mother Frida. In spite of all of Jenny's peculiarities, no person could ever say that Jenny had done them wrong.

When Olivia and Gabriela arrived at the house, Jenny was busy doing several dress alterations for an upcoming Mexican *charro* wedding — she had to somehow attach *crinolinas* to the underside of dresses to make the bottom half expand like umbrellas.

"Hi, Aunt Jenny — we thought we would drop by to see you."

"Good to see you, Olivia, Gabriela." Gabriela gave Jenny a kiss on the cheek, but Jenny did not really pay that much attention to her.

Jenny's workroom was filled with hundreds of interesting things, beginning with the 500-or-so spools of colorful threads neatly arranged on a wall. There was a huge table in the center, on which were rolls of exquisite fabrics, maybe ten different types of scissors, a box of shiny thimbles, maybe two-dozen dress patterns, and ribbons, ribbons everywhere. There were also four mannequin dress forms by the corner, and, of course, Jenny's old, reliable Singer sewing machine.

"So how are you doing nowadays, Jenny?"

"Yeah, okay, I guess. Good thing I got lots of work, so it keeps me busy. How's it going at the circuit company?"

"I don't mind the work, but our boss is a real jerk — can't stand him."

"Sorry to hear that. I work alone because I can't stand people in general."

"Don't you get lonely sometimes?"

"Lonely was when I used to live with mom and dad. No, I shouldn't talk about that. Why did you just say that? I didn't mean to. I'm a real fool. Sorry."

Olivia was perplexed by that semi-confession and apparent confusion that came out of nowhere. "I don't get it, Jenny. How can you feel lonely living with your parents? Seems impossible."

Jenny was quiet for a few seconds; she seemed to be clenching her teeth. Then she said, "Look, Olivia, I am real busy right now. Come back tomorrow, Sunday, and we can sit down for some coffee. Might be a good idea to leave the kid with a babysitter."

Olivia was sorry that they had caught Jenny at a bad moment, a very bad moment. For years, Jenny had had episodes of confused speech, but Olivia had gotten used to them when she was living with her. Jenny's doctors had prescribed medications and had spoken of terms such as "bipolar," "borderline," and "multiple personalities" but had never referred her to a psychologist — if she actually ever needed one, that is.

Gabriela and Olivia gave Jenny quick kisses and left. They spent the rest of the day at the park and doing some light grocery shopping.

When 9pm came around, Olivia was almost too tired from the day's activities, wishing that she had not made that appointment with Sonia. Gabriela was already in bed. Olivia got the coffee brewing, and there was a knock on the door.

"Sonia, glad to see you, come in." They hugged at the doorway.

"On the way here, I stopped at the *supermercado* and got you this box of La Abuelita Mexican chocolates. I know that Gabriela loves the way you make your hot chocolate."

Olivia loved this brand of hot chocolate, but it was the thick document file that was in Sonia's hand that caught her eye. *Was this that serious?* she thought.

They chitchatted and prepared coffee together; Olivia got the Maria Cookies from the shelf. The topic for the night was ready to explode.

"Okay, Sonia — I have been worrying about what you have been wanting to tell me for a few days. I fear the worst, but let's have it."

"From my understanding of you and your life, I feel this will be a life-changing discussion for you, Olivia, and for the better. With pain, but for the better."

"What can you possibly tell me that will change my life? As long as Gabriela is safe and healthy, my life is okay."

"Because I knew that this will change your life, I researched it first, to make sure we were not dealing with theories or suppositions. I would not want to tell you something that, later, will prove to be untrue. Are we clear on that?"

Olivia was getting visibly unsettled by Sonia's ominous preamble. "Yes, I know you would not want to hurt me."

Sonia reached across the table and held both of Olivia's hands. "I believe, Olivia, that your mother was not killed the night you and Benito were left at that motel." Sonia waited for Olivia's reaction.

Olivia's face was one of consternation, of confusion. "Sonia, you are terribly mistaken. Everybody knows that mamma was killed that day, on the highway in front of the motel."

"Well, that is what you have been telling us at work, but who was it who told you that your mother had been killed?"

"My Aunt Jenny, a short time after we went to live with her." Olivia bowed her head. "She said that highway repairmen had found her body days after she was killed — of course, badly decomposed, so she had to be cremated."

Olivia let go of Sonia's hands. There was a long silence. Olivia could not bear to believe what Sonia was saying, but she also knew that Sonia would never play lightly with facts, especially those of this nature. Her face and her breathing were showing the inner struggle of these two competing realizations within her soul. It was boiling. Small beads of perspiration appeared on her upper lip and on her forehead. She started breathing as if she had just run up several flights of stairs.

"So, does this mean she did not die that day, as Jenny told me? She died some other day — is that it?" asked Olivia, with the sides of her mouth starting a painful frown.

"No, Olivia, your mother, Frida, did not die. She boarded a bus in front of the motel and left for Dallas."

"That is ridiculous, Sonia. How could mamma just board a bus and leave Benito and me abandoned in that terrible motel room? That is just not possible!" cried Olivia as tears started to trickle down her cheeks and her breathing got shallower and faster. "Why are you telling me this, Sonia? I thought you were my friend."

"After I read about this case, I thought about it a long time before I decided to tell you. If I were in your shoes, I would definitely like to know the truth about my mother. Do you feel I would ever try to hurt you?"

"Right now, I am feeling that way. Besides, Sonia, how do you know that my mother boarded a bus to Dallas that day?"

"I would never make this story up, just to hurt you. The police and newspaper reporters interviewed the motel manager, and he declared that he saw your mother board the bus right in front of the motel. Later the bus driver was located, and he said he remembered picking up a young woman, about age 25, wearing a flowery dress, at the motel corner. You know that your mother was 24, and you can attest to it that your mother was wearing a flowery dress that day."

"Why should we believe that motel manager? Maybe he killed her, buried the body somewhere, and then made up the story about the bus to Dallas."

"And the bus driver's testimony?"

"So many people get on and off buses, he could easily be mistaken."

"The newspaper story classifies this case as a missing-persons case. If there had been a pedestrian accident on that highway on that day or soon afterwards, the body would have been identified as that of your missing mother. But there was none, and the police currently maintain your mother's disappearance as an active file. There never was a dead body. All that is contrary to what your Aunt Jenny told you."

Olivia was now in shock; she appeared to be in a daze. She still could not readily believe what her reliable friend Sonia was telling her. A large number of scenarios were going through her head, generated by the remote possibility that what Sonia was saying was actually the truth. She was even entertaining the possibility that Sonia was lying — that the evil Karl Williams had threatened to fire her if she did not carry out such a fiendish plot against her.

Could Sonia be susceptible to such intimidation? Or, perhaps she was paid. Nothing was too diabolical for Karl Williams. *Besides, all friendships have a limit, however moral the friends may be,* she thought. Olivia was a mess of confusion. Her mind and her heart were unable to evaluate properly what she was hearing. She was trembling, perspiring, breathing irregularly. Her eyes were open really wide, as if to evaluate a threat more efficiently. But where was the threat?

Sonia opted to remain quiet for a while, letting the information sink in. After about five minutes, she bent over and retrieved a large manila folder from her purse, which was on the floor. Without a word, she strategically placed it on the table by her side without opening it. It was rather bulky; Olivia kept looking at it, afraid to ask what it was, because, in her heart, she knew it could only contain documentation about the events elucidated by Sonia. Finally she built up the courage to confront the contents.

"Are those the reports of the things you've been saying?"

"I would never lie to you, Olivia. I made a large photocopy of the motel story published by *The Houston Chronicle* two days after your mother failed to return to the motel. Are you ready?"

Olivia took a deep breath and then nodded her head. Sonia placed the photocopy on Olivia's side of the table:

MOTHER ABANDONS HER TWO SMALL CHILDREN AT SEEDY MOTEL

Olivia was transfixed by the screaming headline that had appeared on page 2 of the newspaper way back in 1982, when she was but nine years old. All these years, the headline had been there, at the newspaper's headquarters, waiting for Olivia to read it, but she had not even been aware of it. She didn't blink, and she didn't take her eyes off of it. Her lips continued to tremble slightly, but otherwise, her posture was almost catatonic. Sonia knew she had to keep silent as long as Olivia was in that state.

About fifteen minutes elapsed, and Sonia noticed that Olivia's lips were trembling more and that tears were starting to stream down her cheeks, dampening the photocopy on the table. The forehead muscles that had maintained her eyes wide-open were relaxing, so her eyes were looking droopy. Then, as Sonia had feared, Olivia exploded with a blood-curling wail that scared the seasoned Sonia so startlingly that she, too, began to cry alongside Olivia. Sonia put her arm around her, and, again, gave her a dishcloth to cover her mouth so as not to wake up Gabriela. But Olivia was wailing from the bottom of her heart. Uncontrolled sobbing. Sonia was beginning to worry about the wisdom of having told such a painful truth to her best friend. Maybe she had overstepped her bounds or duty as a friend. Maybe it should have been a relative who told her the truth. Then again, it was the relatives who were all part of the lie conspiracy. And an unspoken conspiracy it was, spontaneously created after Frida had gone missing, since it suited some that Frida be considered conveniently dead and out of their lives. If Frida were deemed to be just missing, some relatives, perhaps even Olivia, might, at some point, decide to search for her and ask her some questions which might have produced some very disturbing answers. Definitely, for these relatives, it was far better for Frida to remain dead.

Olivia had cried for about 30 minutes and had quieted down. She wasn't saying much. Sonia asked Olivia if she wanted her to spend the night in the apartment with her and Gabriela. Olivia nodded yes. Sonia then called her husband Matt to advise him of the situation and to let him know she would be spending the night at Olivia's. She asked briefly about Esther, and Matt replied that she was sound asleep.

Sonia took Olivia to her bed, and she immediately got into a fetal position; Sonia covered her, and then she took a quick peek at Gabriela, who appeared to be sleeping soundly. She brought the sofa cushions into Olivia's bedroom and made a bed for herself on the floor. Throughout the night, Olivia woke up a few times, but Sonia was right there to comfort her. Finally, at around 3 A.M., Olivia fell into a deeper sleep. And so did Sonia.

Olivia got up late Sunday morning and went to the kitchen. She saw that Sonia had already fed Gabriela some pancakes.

"I am making some *huevos rancheros* with hot chile for both of us. You hungry, Olivia?"

They had a quiet breakfast, after which Sonia took care of the dishes.

"Olivia, I got to get going pretty soon. Will you be okay?"

"I just need time to decide how I feel about all this. So confused. I'll be okay. Thanks for staying the night."

"Sure. Oh, I almost forgot to tell you. Good news. That animal, Bull Garcia, well, he won't be bothering you ever again. And, he promised to pay your full rent for one full year. Just stay away from him."

Sonia kissed Gabriela and Olivia. "Call me if you need me. See you tomorrow at work."

Olivia spent the rest of Sunday at home with Gabriela. She called her Aunt Jenny to let her know she would not be able to see her that day — "...Not feeling well...," she told her.

CHAPTER 4

The following week was a blur for Olivia — all the women at lunch break commented that she was looking strange or maybe a bit sick. The truth of the matter was that Olivia was consumed by her inner thoughts concerning her mother and the motel event 19 years prior. It was as if she could not concentrate on her surroundings, on her work, because her mood was being directed by very powerful emotional reactions to the thoughts about her mother. Anger, joy, confusion, hope, anxiety, fear, rage, betrayal — these took center stage in Olivia's emotional life that week, when she was trying to put everything in perspective. One minute she was angry, and the next she was hopeful that she might again see her mother. Then again, she asked herself why she should look forward to perhaps seeing her mother, when her mother had so callously and heartlessly betrayed her and four-year-old Benito. That certainly was an unforgivable sin perpetrated by mamma. And if the bitch wasn't dead, maybe she deserved to be, for that betrayal alone. Yes, Olivia became emotionally unstable in trying to deal with the avalanche of thoughts. She even felt that the pain and the betrayal she had already suffered entitled her to kill mamma, if she ever saw her again.

On Wednesday of that week, Sonia caught up with her in the locker area at work. "Olivia, I know you are dealing with a lot right now, so I brought you the file I had with me last Saturday at your house."

"More good news, Sonia?"

"No, these are photocopies of other child-case stories that appeared in the newspaper in the last several weeks. A reporter by the name of Jason McDougall specializes in these family-interest stories. A month ago, he researched your mother's 1982 case and wrote a story about it. I noted his phone number at

The Houston Chronicle near the headline. It might be a good idea to give him a call — he might help you understand your case a bit better."

"Okay, thanks. I'll think about it."

An unfortunate and innocent victim of Olivia's new roller-coaster emotional state was little Gabriela. Olivia became very impatient with her, using a nasty tone of voice most of the time.

"Gabriela, I told you that your dinner is on the table. Come now, or I will throw it in the trash."

"But, mamma, I am on the toilet. I can't hurry any more. Please don't throw away my dinner."

"Well, that is your problem, you little bitch!"

Almost immediately, Olivia regretted her words, for never, ever had she used that terrible word to address her young daughter. With tears rolling down her cheeks, she went to the bathroom and knelt to hug Gabriela as she was still sitting on the commode. Gabriela already had tears of her own.

"I am so sorry, my little angel, for using those terrible words. Please forgive me."

That would have been the end of it, except that Olivia could not help herself, and her fury continued to come to the surface at the slightest provocation.

"Damn it, Gabriela, why are these fucking shoes all over the floor? I asked you five minutes ago to put them away! Why are you such a lazy little pig?"

"Mamma, I am not a pig — I am just a little girl." Her voice cracked as she continued, "Please don't call me 'pig,' mamma."

After several similar episodes over several days, Olivia wouldn't even think of apologizing once more to her daughter, for Olivia was already thinking of herself as a hypocrite, as a mother on the verge of failure, as a woman who had failed in almost all areas of human endeavor. And it only got worse.

Gabriela had been sleeping in her own room since she was about six months old, with no problems, but Olivia's new emotional state and coolness toward her was having an effect on her sense of security. One night, when Olivia was already asleep in her own bedroom, Gabriela quietly walked into the bedroom. Olivia woke up. "What do you want?" Olivia cried out, icily.

"Mamma, can I sleep in your bed with you?"

"No! Now go back to your bed, and don't bother me!"

In the morning when Olivia got up to go to work, she opened the door that led from her bedroom to the living room and discovered Gabriela sleeping all curled up on the floor, right against Olivia's door. Poor Gabriela had slept there all night, with her little body up against her mamma's closed bedroom door. Sadly, that was as close as she had been permitted to get to her mother, at a time when Gabriela desperately needed her the most.

The sight of Gabriela all curled up on the cold and bare floor — and the realization that the child so desperately had wanted to be held by her mother that night — felt like twin daggers into Olivia's heart. Crying and sobbing, she immediately sat down on the floor and picked Gabriela up, taking her into her arms, rocking her, and asking, once more, for forgiveness.

"Oh, sweetheart, I am so, so sorry that I told you to go away. That was wrong, what I did. Please forgive me, please forgive me — you are precious. God, please help me!"

Olivia must have spent about fifteen minutes holding, kissing, and rocking Gabriela in her arms, there on the floor. She must have apologized a dozen times. But Olivia also knew that it was not just a matter of regretting and apologizing but of being able to consistently refrain from acting in that callous manner toward her innocent young daughter. She was aware that her moodiness and hostility were worsening and that she had to talk to Sonia about it before something really tragic happened. Yes, Olivia had become deathly afraid that, on the unrestrained impulse of the moment, she might hurt Gabriela. No telling how bad that would be. After that, apologies wouldn't even matter.

At work, the employees were still talking among themselves about what to do concerning Karl Williams and his "I-carry-the-big-stick-around-here" mode of administration. While Olivia still wanted to contribute to the group effort, she was overwhelmed by the multiplicity of feelings inside her concerning the newfound information about her mother's death or disappearance and her own, personal concerns about her volatility of her emotions and behavior toward Gabriela. She was able to catch up with Sonia after work one day.

"Sonia, hi. I've been meaning to talk to you about something."

"I've noticed you looking stressed out, and I know why."

"No, it's not just from what you said about my mother. I am still trying to sort that out. It's about my abilities as a mother. I think I'm failing, Sonia." A few tears rolled down her cheeks.

"What exactly do you mean by 'failing'?"

"I've become very impatient and intolerant toward Gabriela. Almost everything she does bothers me, and I yell at her. I have never been this way."

"We all get irritable when we are suffering about something, so we can't really be perfect mothers."

"Oh, I'm sure I am far from perfect now. A few days ago, I called my daughter 'pig,' and I yelled at her to get out of my bedroom when she wanted to sleep in my bed. That is unforgivable, Sonia."

"But understandable, Olivia. It would be unforgivable only if you didn't care about your failures."

"Sometimes I am afraid I might even hurt her." Olivia started to cry, but softly, so as not to draw the attention of other co-workers in the area.

Now Sonia started to look more concerned. "In what way do you think you might hurt her?"

Olivia didn't answer. She looked at the floor.

Sonia added, "Would you want Matt and me to take her for a few days? It'll give you time to heal yourself."

"Thanks, but I am not at that point yet."

"Olivia, why don't you go talk to Don Chago, in your old neighborhood? Didn't you say that he's been like an informal spiritual advisor for you and Aunt Jenny since she took you in?"

"Yes, he's the only man I have ever trusted — the only one who has treated me honestly and with respect. Not that I deserved it."

"Go talk to him and let him know how you feel about all this. He might have just the right words to help ease your pain and doubts."

Olivia thought what Sonia was suggesting was a great idea. She immediately called Don Chago, and, after a little bit of superficial talk, she made the appointment to see him that very night in south Houston. Sonia agreed to pick up Gabriela at Paloma's. The two girls would enjoy playing together that evening.

Don Chago, 78, was old-school Mexican. He had worked in a *hacienda* in Mexico as a young boy, sometimes 18 hours a day, to please his *patron*, who demanded complete loyalty and servitude. His family had moved to Houston when he was 25, and the break from servitude caused an unusual change in his perspective. In Houston, he found menial jobs where his bosses treated him inhumanely, something he was acutely aware of and despised with a passion. So he became a shoe repairman — with *no* boss. The excellent quality of his work became well known, so his business grew rapidly. Perhaps more importantly, his customers appreciated his commentary and his views on life. He seemed to have acquired a sensible yet incisive understanding of the "… principles of life…," as he called them, from having worked with the humble village people in his native Mexico.

He had a huge Pancho Villa black mustache as his trademark and was a bit paunchy, but his body was hard and still muscular from all those years in the northern Mexico desert sun. His hands were enormous, thick, and full of calluses from working the leather in his shoe-shop. They weren't even leathery, but more like the dry hide of a rhinoceros who's been out in the sun too long. Don Chago had been married once, but his wife had died many years earlier from uterine cancer. After that, he said that his new family were all his customers, and their families. He said he was happy that way.

Olivia arrived at the shop, and there he was, working even at that hour. The smell of leather permeated the area, and there were literally hundreds of shoes on tables, racks, on the wall, and in various stages of repair. Don Chago was hunched over at his worktable.

"Olivia, my child — is that really you? Oh, my God — you have turned into a beautiful angel! Come over here!" Don Chago gave her a warm hug and kissed her on the cheek.

"I feel happy that you agreed to see me on such short notice, Don Chago. You are looking good yourself. Strong as an ox!"

"Well, you are very kind, but I am feeling my age nowadays. But, no complaints. I feel that, after age 60, I had beaten the odds, so this is icing on the cake! So what are you doing for work? Are you married now?"

"I do soldering at a circuits company there on Westheimer Road, near Dunlavy Street. Not great, but it helps me pay the bills. No, not married yet. As you know, I do have a five-year-old daughter, Gabriela."

"And your Aunt Jenny? Haven't spoken to her for a long time. Is she alright?"

"That's the big story, here, Don Chago. I was hoping that you might give me a little advice."

"Oh, Olivia, my child, come, sit over here. I'll just get the coffee brewing."

Olivia started thinking that, with the strong odor of leather in the air, plus the pungent smell of the bottles of liquid leather stains, she would not be able to appreciate the aroma of freshly brewed coffee. *Well*, she consoled herself, *I've come here for the advice, not for the coffee.*

"I have some old chocolate *conchas* here. Kinda' hard — bought 'em about ten days ago — but they're still good."

"Just the coffee, thanks."

"Very well. What is the problem?"

"You knew that my brother Benito and I went to live with my Aunt Jenny when our mother died back in 1982, right?"

"Very tragic story."

"Apparently, according to police reports and several reporters at the local newspaper, my mother Frida was not killed on that highway that day. They say she boarded a bus for Dallas at that corner."

"Incredible! Are you sure of that?"

"I read the articles. Yes, I tend to believe that. There never was any funeral, either."

"It is inconceivable that your mother would have done that!"

"Yes, hard to believe — even harder to live through it. But several independent sources have given testimony to that effect."

"So, what we have here is child abandonment? Your mother just deserted both of you at that motel?"

"That's what the bitch did."

"You know, Olivia, I did not know your mother very well. She had come to me several times for some shoe repairs. We talked a bit. I sensed that she was a very troubled woman."

"Do you have any idea?"

"She never did want to talk about herself, but she was sour on life, on her being a mother. So how does that make you feel — this thing about abandonment?"

"I preferred it when she was dead."

"You had already adjusted to the idea of your mother having died. Well, to some degree, I am sure your soul did not finish getting the mothering all girls require — you were nine years old, if I remember correctly."

Don Chago's last statement hit Olivia in her heart. Yes, Olivia had not finished getting all the mothering that is necessary for children to develop confidence, security, and a yearning for healthy independence. She was like a creation-in-progress stopped too soon, like a loaf of bread taken out of the oven five minutes too early, like a little birdie abandoned in the nest before it had grown feathers to fly on its own. It was clear that Olivia was wounded. She just had not known it.

"Yes, I was nine. My Aunt Jenny helped us out, but now I've learned that she lied to us by saying that our mother was killed. She knew it was a lie."

"So, now you feel betrayed, and you don't know how you should feel about the situation?"

"I feel upset about this."

He took another sip of his very hot black coffee as he looked into space in deep thought. Then he stroked his huge mustache to help him organize his ideas.

"My child, it would seem to me that you would be more than just 'upset.' Are you being honest with yourself about your feelings?"

"I do have this short fuse."

"You get angry or upset easily?"

"Yes, sort of. Especially toward my daughter Gabriela."

"How do you lose it with her?"

"I scream at her — even for little things that never used to bother me."

"Think about it. Are you really angry at her for whatever she did, or is that the hidden rage you have against your mother?"

Olivia started thinking that Don Chago's insight had brought to the surface a very important point. Olivia had turned poor Gabriela into a convenient target for her aggression. But there was a more profound, hidden motive.

"You have a point. Maybe I am more than just upset. I am angry at my mother — the bitch, the lazy pig. She didn't want the trouble of raising us, so she just left."

"The only way to work your way back to betterment, Olivia, is to acknowledge the life of your hidden emotions, many of which you might not be entirely aware of."

"Over the last several days, I have been wishing that I wouldn't have to deal with my mother being alive. I knew that I was coping a lot better when she was 'dead.' Maybe the useless whore should remain dead. But, then, I also feel I need her, and that makes me feel like a victim, which I don't want to be."

"What a jumble of emotions. Probably a bit worse than having a love/hate relationship with someone — no?"

"Yeah, that spills over into my relationships with men. Can't trust them, but, once they start making moves on me, I feel helpless — a strange feeling, like they have a right to do to me whatever they wish, like they own my body. I resist, but it is futile — no courage."

"Would you like to meet your mother?"

"If I saw her, I would kill the bitch! I would kill the bitch! For 19 years, I've been without a mother, and Gabriela has spent all her life without a grandmother! I would kill the damned whore!"

Olivia's face had turned red, and her neck veins had pumped up to give her a rather hideous look that Don Chago had never seen in her.

"I thought you were 'just a little bit' upset," quipped Don Chago, provocatively.

Olivia herself was rather surprised by her expression of anger or rage. Afterwards, she settled down; she felt a bit embarrassed.

"You are right, Don Chago. I should recognize my subterranean emotional life and that what I feel is a rage against Frida — the bitch who left her children at that seedy motel! Fuck the whore! She really should have died that day!"

Don Chago let the conversation stand at that point; he was quiet. He wanted Olivia to cool down a bit. But he was glad that Olivia was expressing a desire to hurt her mother, for that would be the healthiest emotional response, given what Frida had done to her children. Any other, less-intense response would encompass a certain degree of repressive pathology, which would provide for a generally quiet state of affairs in the present but would signal serious mental-health issues for the future.

He detected that Olivia's mood was changing.

"But I feel guilty about saying those things about my mother. It is not right to judge one's mother."

"Olivia, you must learn this rule: feelings are never wrong. Feelings may be detestable and even immoral, but they are never wrong."

"I don't understand what you're saying. It is always wrong to feel like hurting someone."

"More accurately, Olivia, it is wrong to *hurt* someone, but it is not wrong to feel that you want to do that. We can't deny that we have unwanted feelings."

Olivia was trying hard to understand the distinction that Don Chago was trying to make. "So, what you're saying is that it's okay to feel you want to kill someone?"

"Think of feelings as windows into your soul; you can hardly blame the window when you see something unpleasant inside, right?"

"Well, I never thought of it in that manner, but you're right."

"Now, let's get back to what you said about your daughter Gabriela — that you scream at her for little things that didn't used to bother you. Do you realize that she's become a convenient target for your rage against your mother?"

"Yes, yes — you are right."

"And I bet that, after you scream at her you, become overwhelmed with guilt and remorse?"

"I am ashamed of it."

"The remorse is a signal from your true mothering soul that you have stepped out of the normal, moral limits of your disciplinary standards. In effect, you have been screaming at your mother."

"Don Chago — so what do I do? I can't continue on this path — I'm afraid I might hurt my daughter in a more horrible way!"

"It's clear to me, my child, what you must do."

"Name it — I trust your advice."

"You must search for Frida, assuming that she's still alive."

"But what will I do even if I find her?"

"She's probably depressed with shame for what she did, while you are rightfully angry at her. My guess is that she won't ask to be absolved — that she knows she did wrong, that there is no forgiveness. But your expressing your rage at her, without physically hurting her, will heal 50% of the relationship. You must find her, Olivia. If not for your sake, then for Gabriela's. Her life might well be at stake."

"One more thing, Don Chago. Is it right for me to judge my mother? That question came to my mind because I am judging her, because I have so many negative opinions of her now, and because it occurred to me that I would not want Gabriela to judge me when she is an adult — for her to say I had been an inferior mother. I am doing the best I can."

"It is folly to think that parents are infallible simply because they are one's parents or to think that one's mother occupies some holy ground, above reproach. If you are to be a better mother to Gabriela than your mother was to you, then you must judge your mother mercilessly, so that you don't follow her wayward and painful footsteps. You must prune the tree your mother planted in your soul when you were a child — remove all the dead leaves and broken branches, and water faithfully the good parts, for this is the only tree you will pass on to your own daughter. If you close your eyes to your mother's failures, then the hidden hand of your wounded soul will be your only guide in the darkness, and you will end up hurting your daughter in the most egregious manner. Not because you don't love her, but because, in trying to be a good mother, you would be blindly following in your mother's footsteps, those she left when she was lost herself, when she was trying to find her way in her own darkness. As a child, you had no way of knowing that she had lost her way. So open your eyes and judge, Olivia. Your own daughter will judge you many years from now — as she should — if you take the wrong path now."

On the way out, Olivia thanked Don Chago and promised him that, the next time she came for advice, she would bring fresh chocolate *conchas* for both to enjoy with his excellent and aromatic Mexican coffee.

CHAPTER 5

It was late that Friday night when Olivia picked Gabriela up from Sonia's house. At home, they had barely enough time for a quick snack, and then it was time to put Gabriela to bed. Olivia hugged her for a long time.

"What's wrong, mamma? You hugged me too long."

Olivia was taken aback by her daughter's comment; it made her think that Gabriela was very much in tune with what was happening. It made her think that Gabriela was absorbing the good and the bad in her surroundings and that this was the nature of the tree that Olivia was planting in her little daughter's soul. It made her think that she needed to do the right thing, for it was her duty and responsibility — even if Frida had done the wrong thing with Olivia and little Benito.

In fact, in spite of it.

After she made sure that Gabriela was sound asleep, Olivia sat stoically at the kitchen table with a cup of coffee, mulling over all the information she had at that point, considering what she really wanted to do. There was a sense of jubilation in the expectation that she would again get to see her dead mother — she would again have a mother and Gabriela would have the grandmother she had known only in stories told by Olivia. But what kind of mother would abandon her two children? Her feelings kept changing by the minute. Maybe she needed more information to form a better opinion of the matter. It was time to call that reporter Sonia had suggested, Jason McDougall. Certainly, he would have many more details. But tomorrow was Saturday.

Olivia waited until 9 A.M. on Saturday to call the number Sonia had scribbled on one of the photocopies of his stories.

"Yeah, McDougall," he uttered, as if someone had asked for him. Olivia could hear his busy fingers on the computer keyboard.

"Excuse me — is this Jason McDougall?"

"Yeah — who's this?"

"Well, my name is Olivia Cervantes. My mother abandoned us at that motel in 1982."

The keyboard clicks stopped. Olivia waited for his reply.

"Is your mother's name 'Frida'?"

"Yes, unfortunately."

"So, you read my stories on your case?"

"I wouldn't be calling."

"I would like to talk with you about the matter. You are the unknown factor in this case. But what is your personal reason for calling?"

"You have some details that I need to locate my mother. Is she alive?"

"Can you come over to our central offices, on Texas Street, right now?"

"I have a five-year-old daughter. Do you have an appropriate space there in your office where she can play while we talk?"

"Absolutely. I'll advise the security desk at the front door that you are coming."

Olivia packed some toys for Gabriela and took the bus for the short trip to the downtown area.

Once inside *The Houston Chronicle* building, Olivia and Gabriela were escorted by security to office 412. The door was already open.

"Hi, I am Olivia, and this is Gabriela. You are Jason?"

"Come in, Olivia and Gabriela. My, my, you are a very pretty girl. And how old are you now, Gabriela?" With her fingers she indicated "five." "Wow, that means you are getting to be a big girl very quickly."

Gabriela smiled.

Jason indicated to Olivia the little corner of the office farthest away from where his desk was. Olivia situated Gabriela there with toys and a coloring book. Then she and Jason sat by a coffee table next to his desk. He had already brought two soft drinks for them and one apple juice for Gabriela.

His office was meant to be a working office, so it really did not look neat or ordered. There were newspapers and clippings everywhere; stick-on notes decorated most of the working wall. Books and photocopies of other writers' articles were on tables and on the floor. This reporter wallowed in information.

Jason McDougall was 34, and had been working for the newspaper since he'd graduated from the local campus of Rice University with a degree in journalism. About 5'9", he was stout and muscular, with brown hair and brown eyes. As can be expected from a reporter who deals with details and facts, he was intensely dedicated to researching his raw information before he wrote his stories, for never once had he been asked to retract any facet of any of the stories he had written through the years.

"Olivia, I have to tell you that I am very happy you called. About a month ago, I wrote the story of your mother Frida and the 1982 event at that motel. Well, that and other things, because there are many cases of children being orphaned or abandoned, and I thought they would be good public-interest stories, so people can get to know how many children suffer."

"So what we have here is that I answer your questions so you can write a story about our suffering, and, in return, you give me information about the whereabouts of my mother Frida?"

"Olivia, you make it seem so cold, so heartless."

"So how would you describe what we are about to do, Jason? I came here for your help."

"Look, Olivia, I am very familiar with the Frida case…"

Olivia interrupted him. "Really? Did you know that, up until about one week ago, I believed that my mother had died, that I suffered without a mother for 19 years and counting?"

"I am sorry to hear that. How was it that you were not aware that your mother had taken that bus to Dallas?"

"I was told a few weeks later, by my Aunt Jenny, that our mother had been killed on the highway right in front of the motel. It was a devastating blow to my brother Benito and me."

"So your Aunt Jenny made that story up?"

"Well, it looks that way at this point, and I do not know why she would have."

"And your brother, Benito — how is he doing?"

"I'd rather not talk about that — ever."

"Alright, we'll skip that. Writing these stories encompasses interviewing the affected children, many now grown up. But if it bothers you…"

"Yes, it bothers me, at least until I can get to trust you."

"Fine. I interviewed various people for the Frida story that I wrote and which appeared in our newspaper about one month ago. There is no doubt at all about the facts."

"And these are?"

"Your mother Frida left you and Benito in that motel room. Several minutes later, she was seen by the motel manager boarding a Dallas-bound bus. The bus driver corroborated the story. There were no reported pedestrian fatalities at or near the motel for the month beginning the day your mother disappeared. There were no unidentified or unclaimed female cadavers at the city morgue fitting the description of your mother."

"So, in your view, my mother abandoned us at that motel — she did not die at that time?"

"That is correct. I have no reason to lie to you, if not simply because I do not like to hurt people: I also have my professional pride in reporting only that which I have found to be absolutely true."

They had been talking for a few minutes when Gabriela shuffled over to where they were sitting. "Mamma, I'm tired. Can we go home?"

Jason responded before Olivia could answer. "Oh, Gabriela, your mother and I were just finishing our little conversation. Would you like to go to an interesting restaurant where they have a giant fish tank?"

"No, Jason, that will not be necessary. I appreciate your help, but we'd better just get going."

"Mamma, I wanna see the fishies. Okay, mamma?"

"Olivia, really, this is no bother. It's about a ten-minute walk from here."

It was called *Mi Tierra Linda* — an upscale Mexican restaurant catering to the white-collar office and financial crowd in downtown Houston. After they were seated by the *maitre d'*, Jason took Gabriela in his arms and showed her the giant aquarium with the dozens of tropical fish. Gabriela's face was lit with pure delight. Back at the table, she just would not stop talking about all the wonderful fishies.

"Is this where you bring all your prospective interviewees before you squeeze them for information?"

"Olivia, look. From the moment that we met face to face back at the office, you have shown nothing but a hostile attitude toward me. It would be very natural and understandable for me to respond in kind toward you, since you certainly would deserve it, but I make the effort not to — I try to be civil. You came to me — keep that in mind."

"Aren't you being hostile by mentioning that you are trying not to be hostile?"

"Well, my intent is to get us on the right track, away from subtle aggression."

"I expect that anyone who is nice to me wants something from me."

Juanita, the waitress, came to their table and took their order. Olivia went for the massive *Enchiladas a la Veracruzana*, Jason for *Pollo en Mole Poblano*, and Gabriela for the smallish refried beans with flour tortillas. Gabriela was busy looking at the hundreds of decorations on the walls and those hanging from the ceiling: *sombreros, molcajetes, petates, guitarras,* colorful dresses, *charro* outfits, horse saddles, *chicotes,* and multicolored *pericos* with huge beaks.

"You mean that, ideally, the only person you would accept with no hint of suspicion would be an altruist — somebody whose mission in life is to give, give, give, with no expectation of receiving something?" asked Jason, somewhat facetiously.

"You make it seem there is something wrong with my attitude."

"In my view, an altruist is a sick person, maybe some type of masochist. I am sure you wouldn't want to make friends with such a human being, even though on the surface, knowing such a person would appeal to you, Olivia, because he or she would meet your requirements."

"Oh, so now you are saying that I'm sick or something. Do you analyze your wife in this same manner?"

"I don't have a wife or girlfriend, but, if I did, I would want to talk about our feelings and expectations."

"You are too analytical. Maybe that's why you don't have a wife."

There was a pause in the conversation. Jason's face showed some disappointment. He started to look at the decorations that Gabriela had been admiring for a few minutes. Just about then, the food arrived, together with a big *molcajete* full of ground red chile, and a *sombrero*-shaped container full of piping-hot corn tortillas. The silence was troublesome, perhaps only to Jason.

He started thinking that they had gotten off on the wrong foot, that Olivia was not a very introspective person, so going in that direction had been a mistake. Her continued hostility was evidence that she always expected men to take advantage of her, and her last comment about him not having a wife was an outright attack, perhaps indicating that she was feeling defensive and angry about his comments. Finally, she broke the thick sheet of ice that had fallen upon their table.

"Look, Jason, you are probably a very nice guy. Please understand that I have had bad experiences with men, starting with Gabriela's father, who left us. And I am sorry I said that about your wife."

"But I told you, I don't have a wife!"

"So then you have nothing to be sore about!" She made a funny face at him, hoping to make him laugh. It worked. He got over the slight about his non-wife and gave Olivia a big smile.

Olivia and Gabriela were eating almost non-stop. Jason helped to spread the refried beans on another flour tortilla for Gabriela. By that time, the resident *Mariachi* musicians had spotted them as a family and had gathered around their table, offering to play a *serenata* tune. Jason whispered something into the lead musician's ear, and the seven-piece *Mariachi* band, with brass, strings, and vocals, rendered a slow and beautiful romantic song, *"Esclavo y Amo,"* to the delight of everyone in the restaurant, especially the young couples. It did not escape Olivia's imagination that the central phrase of the song — "I don't know what it is about your eyes that has captivated my soul" — may have been a subtle message from Jason, who, after all, had whispered this selection into the lead musician's ear. Interesting, too, was that Jason just gave her oblique glances as the music was in full bloom. For Olivia, it had been an unforgettable experience, and she almost cried thinking that, for once, a man was admiring her eyes and not her body. It was almost an epiphany of sorts, because she always felt that she was not meant to have a decent relationship with a man, since she was essentially not worth any man's effort — that she was, in Bull Garcia's stinging words, just a whore. But this pleasant experience with Jason opened the door to something more decent, but just a crack — it could still be all part of her wild imagination.

After the music ended, the magical moment was definitely brought to an end when Gabriela blurted out, "Mamma, why is that guitar so big?"

"It is a bass guitar, honey — it makes bigger, lower notes." Then, in her best voice, Olivia tried to reproduce and hold a very low note, but her beautiful soprano voice made that impossible. So Jason said, "Let me try it," and, with his baritone voice, he produced a highly contrasting low note. "Now that is a low note, Gabriela!" They all enjoyed their operatic efforts and had a few more laughs about them.

"Jason, thanks for the *Mariachi* music piece — it was beautiful."

Still noticeably uncomfortable about it, he responded, "I thought you might like that...tune."

After the *Mariachis* retreated to another table, the waitress came over and asked if they wanted anything sweet. Olivia did not hesitate. "Do you have chocolate *conchas*?"

"Sure we do! And lots of other goodies, including those delicious, eggy *ojos de buey, campechanas, marranitos, cuernitos,* and maybe a dozen other things for your delight."

Olivia and Jason ordered the *conchas*, with coffee, and Gabriela ordered a *cuernito* with milk.

Once they had finished and were just outside the restaurant, Jason suggested to Olivia to just think about what they had talked about, and, at their next meeting — if she wanted one — they could talk specifics. Jason kissed

Gabriela goodbye on her forehead and, not wanting to appear too forward, gave a more formal handshake to Olivia.

With a quick bus ride, they arrived at their apartment building, and, as they were entering the large garden area in front, Olivia saw Bull Garcia dragging a large trashcan, which seemed a bit of a chore for him, given that he had braces on both knees. Olivia thought that maybe the creep had fallen off a ladder doing some apartment work. *Serves him right*, she thought, *for being a servant of the devil.*

She figured out quickly that he was working on the walkway that led to the stairs they needed to take, and that would put them uncomfortably close to him. But when he finally saw them, he opted to promptly move to another area not in their path, clearly trying not to look at them in their eyes. More importantly, Olivia noticed that, this time, he did not make any attempt to look up her skirt as they were going up the stairs. *Sonia must have given him a good scolding*, Olivia thought.

But not all was positive. As they got to the second-floor walkway, Olivia glanced quickly in his direction and caught him giving them a hateful sneer, although he quickly looked away. It bothered her a bit, because she wondered if his undercurrent of hate had intensified. No telling what he might do.

That night was different from many other nights before it. With Gabriela sound asleep in her own bed, Olivia started thinking about the life-changing events of the last week. Her main focus was the revelation that her mother did not die near that motel in 1982 and that she still might be alive. Understandably, Olivia was feeling an approach/avoidance conflict about a possible search for her mother. She asked herself many questions. Did she love her mother? Does one really love someone who has been dead many years, or is one in love only with the memory of that person? Does she need to forgive her mother for abandoning her and Benito, or is this terrible act basically unforgivable? If it is unforgivable, what does that imply about a future relationship with her mother? Is it her parental duty to make the effort to try to forgive — for the sake of providing Gabriela with a grandmother? Is Frida even capable of being a good grandmother? What possible reason would Frida have had to make her act of abandonment justifiable, or at least understandable? Is it *ever* morally justifiable to leave children in a motel and willingly take off on a bus forever? One gnawing feeling that Olivia had to contend with, on top of everything else, was that her mother abandoned her because she was not worth anything as a child, as a person. Her fear and suspicion of this materialized inside her soul as her mother's voice telling her, "You are worthless,

Olivia. Better to throw you in a garbage dump, because you are worthless, Olivia — worthless, worthless..." It was an irrepressible feeling, and, yes, it even felt like her mother's voice.

Too much to deal with. Maybe it was better to just let Frida stay dead?

Olivia certainly had many questions to consider — good ones too, but few answers. She thought hard about what Don Chago had advised her — that, to be a better mother, she had to improve on her mother's shortcomings. But didn't Aunt Jenny play the role of mother after Frida disappeared in 1982? Hadn't Aunt Jenny imbued Olivia's soul with good feelings and thoughts, as well as crazy ones when she had those long mental spells? Olivia had spent more years with Aunt Jenny than with Frida, but the ones she spent with Frida were the formative ones — the ones in which the mother plants the tree.

She was also thinking about Jason, as she had had a very pleasant time with him at the restaurant, in spite of the rough start at his office. Hours later, she was still feeling flutters in her heart about the romantic *Mariachi* song that he had requested, and silent tears flowed down to her pillow because he made her feel like a person — not like a body to be used for pleasure, as others had done before, and as the despicable Bull Garcia repeatedly and savagely had done, too. "Yes, Jason, you...may touch my hand," she whispered to herself as she fell asleep.

CHAPTER 6

By the time they had finished breakfast on Sunday morning, Olivia had already decided that she would make every effort to locate Frida — if she was still alive, that is. But, first, she had to talk to Aunt Jenny, for surely she knew more about the matter than what she had told Olivia over the years.

Olivia called Sonia and asked her if she would mind accompanying her to visit Aunt Jenny later that day. Sonia agreed to do it. But first Olivia and Gabriela made a quick stop to check up on Mrs. Brunswick on the top floor. Olivia had already done some shopping for her during the week, so that would not be a problem. "Hi, Mrs. Brunswick. We stopped by just to say hello again."

"Oh, Olivia — thank you, darling. Happy to see you."

She had been listening to the radio in bed, but Olivia thought she should move around a bit more. "Mrs. Brunswick, I've got to get you out of bed. Walk a bit. Come on."

"I would have died a long time ago if it wasn't for you, Olivia."

"No, ma'am, you are still strong, with a sharp mind."

Olivia held her by the arm while they walked around the apartment slowly. Since the bedroom smelled a bit stuffy, she changed the sheets and set a fresh blanket on the bed. Then she figured that it was best to give Mrs. Brunswick a bath, too. After the bath, Olivia applied English Rose talcum powder over most of Mrs. Brunswick's body, dressed her, and sat her by a window with a large-type magazine.

"You know, Olivia, that English Rose makes me feel young again. My husband gave me an English Rose Talcum Kit as his first present when we first started going out. We were young and romantic. Thank you very much."

"I knew you would feel good about it."

47

After checking her fridge for basics, they said goodbye to Mrs. Brunswick, and they both hurried to the street corner to meet Sonia and her daughter Esther. Once in Sonia's car, the two girls started playing joyfully, as they always did.

"So how did it go with that reporter, Jason? Any good info?"

"He said pretty much what you had told me, and I have no reason now to doubt either of you. Please forgive me for acting hostile toward you."

"It was understandable, Olivia; that was a hard revelation to accept. So does that mean you will try to locate your mother?"

"I've given it much thought, and, most definitely, yes — although I still do not know how I'll feel when I see her for the first time. In a sense, she will not feel like my mother, but more like just another woman. When I spoke to Don Chago, he suggested that I most definitely confront her about her actions."

"And, Aunt Jenny — does she know why we are going to see her now?"

"No, but I have a feeling that she knows more about this than just that my mother left us."

"I seem to remember you telling me once that Jenny sometimes gets these strange episodes, like she goes into deep thought about something."

"More than that, Sonia. I now believe that she listens to voices. Up until about one week ago, when you told me about the newspaper stories concerning my mother, I used to think she was just unusual. But ever since this crisis broke out, I have been reading a lot about similar cases and about mental problems and such. Aunt Jenny struggles to keep going when her mind starts to split — can't say it any other way."

"'Split'? What are we talking about — like 'split personality'?"

"Last time I spoke to her, she was arguing with herself. Something about feeling lonely when she was living at home with her parents — my grandparents, Grandpa Tomas and Grandma Florencia."

"That's serious stuff, Olivia. So, how can we really believe anything she will say today?"

"I don't know, but I do know that she manages to keep her small business going, so she must be in contact with reality."

Sonia was about to make a right turn in Aunt Jenny's neighborhood, but Olivia corrected her. Two minutes later, they arrived.

"Hi, Aunt Jenny. You remember Sonia and Esther, right?"

"Yeah — they were here several months back. Hi, Sonia. Hi, Esther. By the way, Esther, that is a lovely dress, lots of cross- and double-stitching. Nice."

Gabriela promptly looked at her own dress and asked Olivia, "Mamma, does my dress have double-itching like Esther's?"

"It's called 'double-*stitching*,' honey. No, it doesn't, but it has a beautiful floral pattern. Here, both of you, come and sit here and make good use of these puzzles."

Apparently, Aunt Jenny was in a good state of mind — not smiling much, but not frowning, either. That was a good sign. Olivia suggested that maybe Aunt Jenny show Sonia some of her working tools there in the main room. Jenny thought it was a great idea. She motioned them to join her at the kitchen table, where they chit-chatted about her current backlog in dress alterations and such. The coffee was ready, and there already was a generous bowl of beef *barbacoa* with a large plate of hot flour tortillas on the table. Gabriela and Esther were served on a separate, low table that had been placed near their play area. It was a delicious delight for all.

"Aunt Jenny, remember that, over the phone, I had mentioned to you that I wanted to talk about something very important?"

"Yeah — spit it out."

"About one week ago, I learned something very disturbing about that day in 1982 when the police came to get us at that motel. Would you like to tell me something about that, or would you just prefer that I tell you what I discovered?"

Jenny stopped chewing, though her mouth was full. She looked intensely at Olivia and then at Sonia, as if they were conspiring against her. Her neck muscles stiffened, and a small tremor traveled down her body. She slowly finished chewing but pushed her plate away. No one said a word. Jenny's eyes became glassy, but the rest of her face was expressionless, like a cadaver's.

"Maybe I should get the girls situated in the adjoining room," suggested Sonia as she got up and moved Esther and Gabriela. When she returned to the table, Jenny had a creepy smile and was playing with a dangling curl of her hair; she was still deep in thought.

"Jenny, Olivia asked you if you want to offer some details about 1982, or if you prefer for her to tell you what she now knows."

Aunt Jenny composed herself a bit, moving as if trying to shake off something. "Well, Olivia, you are now almost 30, so I guess it's time to get to the real truth about what happened at that motel."

She winced, as if vividly recalling something.

"You seem to know something about your mother, so I'll just confirm it. Yes, your mother did not die in front of that motel in 1982. She took a bus to Dallas."

Olivia and Sonia already believed that to be the case, but, still, the truth coming from someone who knew about it firsthand had an impact.

That creepy smile came over Aunt Jenny's face again, and she was looking intensely at the surface of the table, as if there were something there. She gestured as if she were about to say something, but the effort evaporated in a few seconds.

"I better not say more, or I'm gonna get hit with a rope."

"Who will hit you with a rope, Jenny?" whispered Olivia.

The creepy smile disappeared, and Jenny made eye contact with Olivia.

"Oh, nothing — I was just saying silly things, that's all. So now you know the truth. Sorry I lied to you when you were younger — I was trying to protect you and Benito."

"Is she still alive?" asked Sonia.

"I know some people in Dallas — long-term clients and friends of friends. A few years back — maybe five — I inquired about Frida, and I was told she was still alive. But now, I don't know."

"Okay. So, Aunt Jenny, do you know why mamma found it necessary to abandon us?"

Jenny began to move her body slightly, in a bizarre manner, like the undulation one normally sees in a snake that has just swallowed a large prey. It required nerves of steel for Olivia and Sonia to remain at the table, for neither had ever witnessed Jenny or any other person move in that horrible manner. Then, Jenny raised her head and cleared her throat.

"It is personally painful for me to tell you what I think the reason was that your mother left you."

"Painful to you because you suffered in some way at that time?" asked Olivia.

"Painful because I...was...lonely...living at home with my parents — your grandparents."

Sonia interjected, "So, why did Frida leave her two children?"

There was a long silence. It appeared that Jenny was trying to say something, but, somehow, she couldn't open her mouth. She kept moving her head backwards, as if avoiding some unseen thing that was covering her mouth. Sonia and Olivia were scared and remained silent.

Then, in a strained voice, Aunt Jenny managed to utter a few words. "Frida was shamed and broken." She continued to struggle to get the words out. By this time, Jenny was perspiring profusely; the collar of her white blouse was completely wet.

"Jenny, why was mamma 'shamed and broken'?"

In a guttural tone, Jenny added, "Because your father is your grandfather."

Olivia and Sonia were left speechless, while Jenny was hyperventilating. They calmed her down and let what she had said sink in. The three women just looked at the surface of the table without saying a single word. Olivia's head was whirling with the ramifications of what she had just learned. Finally, she spoke.

"So not only did the bitch abandon us, but she left us with a profound shame in our hearts. Just imagine — my Grandpa Tomas is really my father, and my Aunt Jenny is really my sister! Damn the bitch! Damn the fucking bitch!"

Sonia held her hand, but Olivia was not crying. No, she was livid with hatred, with rage against Frida for leaving her with this familial damnation, a legacy which could never, in any manner, shape, or form, ever be erased. *A hellish and ever-lasting punishment*, Olivia thought.

Just about then, Olivia's face turned greenish-grey, and she ran to the toilet to vomit. She threw up for about three minutes, and, then, she washed her mouth and face, and came back to the table. Sonia was still stunned; Aunt Jenny was in a daze.

"But it happened to me, too," whispered Jenny, playing with her hair once more.

"What, exactly, happened to you?" queried Sonia.

"Oh, nothing. I was just saying that things happen."

"Jenny, did Grandpa Tomas touch you in a sexual way?" inquired Olivia.

She was clearly struggling to tell them, but she also kept referring to "the rope."

"He will hit me with a wet and hard rope. It hurts more. Yes, I love it — hit me again, father! No, don't hurt me."

Olivia was trying to prevent her stomach from acting up again, while Sonia was trying to make sense of what Aunt Jenny was saying.

"It happened to me, too," whispered Jenny again.

Sonia ventured a risky question. "Jenny, were you raped, too?"

"Yes, yes, yes, yes, yes — it happened to me, too! To me, too — yes, yes!" Jenny was trembling but not actually crying; Sonia held her hand as well as Olivia's.

Two minutes went by.

"That was brave of you to finally talk about what happened to you and to Frida," offered Sonia. "I am sure that has been bothering you for years."

Aunt Jenny began crying, but in a muted tone, as if trying to hold it back. Maybe she was embarrassed. Olivia was still in shock, still in "angry" mode.

"Sonia, has that ever happened to you?" asked Jenny, not really expecting a "Yes" answer.

"No, Jenny. I've lived through a lot of hardships — but not anything like that. I am sorry this happened to you."

"What are we going to do about this? Damn the bitch!" raged Olivia, directing her gaze at Sonia.

"I don't know what you mean, but the first step is just to talk about it more to get all the details. Let's not be too hasty," argued Sonia.

Olivia got up from the table, called the girls, and they all went to the large backyard for a walk and a look at the butterflies.

Sonia stayed with Aunt Jenny, still trying to comfort her, but Sonia began having some serious doubts about her ability to sustain her supportive role with Olivia — and, now, with Jenny, too. She knew that a friend is supposed to be there when others need help, but her reserves of compassion and empathy were being depleted at a fast rate by the two women in crisis. And this was only the beginning, since they barely had gotten to the details of what had actually happened during those terrible years when Frida and Jenny were in their early teens and were being repeatedly raped by their own father, Don Tomas — Olivia's grandfather. Besides, Sonia had her own husband and daughter who needed her love, understanding, and compassion; if she was all worn out by the time she got home, her own family would suffer. Sonia seriously asked herself if she was able to maintain these friendships, given the great need these two women displayed. Maybe it was humanly impossible — maybe it was time to recommend professional help for them.

When Olivia came back from the backyard, Sonia gave her the suggestion that maybe Jenny should get a psychotherapist, given her state of mind. Olivia didn't even need to think about it — she readily agreed. The plan was to get Jenny to a therapist the following day, and, for the moment, they would call one of her long-time clients who was friendly with her, to come spend the night with Jenny.

After Jenny's friend came over, Olivia, Sonia, and the girls were ready to leave. Olivia took Jenny over to a quiet corner and asked her, "Just so that I am perfectly clear on this, Jenny: You are saying that my grandfather Don Tomas is also my father?"

"Yes. When Frida was 14 and pregnant with you, she told me that the father of her baby was Don Tomas, our own father. He is also your brother Benito's father. This came from your own mother's lips. She never recovered from the profound shame she felt. And when she disappeared in 1982, I said that she had died because I was trying to shield you from the damnation and family wreckage your mother left behind. Forgive me if I did the wrong thing."

"I appreciate that you were trying to do the right thing. And Grandma Florencia? What was her role in this? Did she know her husband was raping their two daughters?"

"She has never said anything, but she knew what was happening." Aunt Jenny paused. "I just don't feel like talking about it anymore — makes me sad and angry."

Olivia squeezed Aunt Jenny's hands, kissed her on the cheek, and said goodbye.

The ride back was quiet, as both women were deep in thought over what to do concerning the new revelations. It seemed that Olivia's history was littered with sexual and moral sin, and neither woman knew exactly what needed to be done, if anything. Olivia was as determined as ever to locate Frida, to confront her about the abandonment, but, now, also to ask her the specifics of the rapes and her two shameful pregnancies. It would not be a pleasant visit.

And, Sonia — well, she was worried about Olivia and Jenny but also about herself, for she was feeling the strain of holding up what had unwittingly become a one-sided relationship with Olivia. In fact, it made her feel guilty and selfish. *Aren't we supposed to help our friends in need?* she thought. Before this, yes, she believed in that. But the current crisis had exposed that as just a fluffy theory, an ideal, a delusion that we all believe in to feel that we are wonderful people when we help others. Yet we all have limits on how much we give in a relationship. One would have to be a fool to be in a giving relationship or friendship where one does not receive much in return. Yes, ultimately, all relationships must have a give-and-take structure, for, if not, then they would be composed of a masochist and a parasite. *Not a very healthy proposition for either side,* she thought.

In the meantime, Gabriela and Esther happily played a guessing game in the back seat, fortunately oblivious to the serious issues that were in the minds of their mothers in the front seat.

After Olivia and Gabriela were dropped off, they went grocery shopping and then spent the rest of Sunday quietly at home.

CHAPTER 7

On Monday morning, Olivia was busy at her workstation, soldering the circuit boards as fast as she could on the moving production line. Judith and Lizbet were fanning the conversational fires concerning Carmelina's contention that the father of her unborn baby was none other than Karl Williams, their monster boss. Glenda, the man-hater and the more-mellow Rosalba were cautioning that the group had better not take any action unless Carmelina was 100% sure that Karl Williams was the father. This involved asking her some very personal and intimate questions, which she was glad to answer because she, too, detested the man. Rita participated but was not of much help, since she seemed to have been getting a kick out of the whole intimate thing. Once Carmelina told them the details, all the women in the group were confident that, indeed, Karl Williams was the father. At that point, there was no need for a clinical paternity test, since Carmelina assured them she had not had sex with anyone else. Then, they had to devise a method of how best to deal with their tormentor — they all needed to hurt him because of the way he treated everybody at work. Besides, Carmelina would be needing financial help in raising her baby. The fact that she was underage would also work to help her case.

Olivia participated in the discussions because she hated Karl Williams in her heart, although, when he scolded her about some matter, she would turn into a cowardly putty and could not defend herself. It was one thing to voice her opinions in the group of women and quite another when faced with a threat.

She felt a light tap on her shoulder. It was one of Karl Williams' assistants, notifying her that she was being summoned to the boss's office. She immediately knew it could not be good. Her friends wished her well — with their eyes.

She got to his office and was ordered to close the door behind her. "Sit down, Olivia," said Karl in a commanding and cynical tone.

"Yes, sir. What do you need me for?"

"I have become aware that you have been saying some nasty things about me and the company." He walked slowly around Olivia's chair, like a cocky inquisitor.

"No, sir. I only say things like I wish there were fewer tin and lead fumes in the workroom, but that's it." She wondered just how he had come to know about her criticisms. Were there spies among the workers, traitors who yearned to ingratiate themselves to The Tyrant?

"You and I both know that you are a lying spic bitch. Do you always lie, Olivia?"

"No, sir — not usually. I mean that I am telling you the truth. I have not been saying bad things about you or the company."

"Tell me, Olivia Spic Bitch, what would you and your little bastard girl do if suddenly you were out of a job?"

"That would be very bad for us. I need the job to support us."

"So, you wouldn't want to jeopardize that, right?" Williams moved closer to Olivia from behind while she continued to look forward.

She was becoming apprehensive about his standing right behind her, where she couldn't see him. She didn't feel she could just turn her head to look at him, for fear of antagonizing him. He was, after all, the boss.

Olivia started thinking about the larger picture here. Not only was she weighed down by the recent revelations concerning her mother — plus the problems with Bull Garcia — but she also had to contend with the increasingly aggressive posture of Karl Williams. Why did life have to be so difficult? Why couldn't her life be more like Sonia's, who had decent parents, a loving husband, a family, and the courage to defend herself? Why was it that Sonia had a happy life, while she had essentially a miserable one? Why had God permitted her mother to die when she and Benito were so young? But now — as she knew more accurately — why had God permitted her mother to abandon them at that motel and for them to grow up painfully motherless? Why had her mother not provided her with a father? How was it that Olivia ended up as a single mother? Why had she not yet developed a decent and stable relationship with an eligible man? Was God trying to punish her because she was born out of irredeemable sin? Was she so worthless that even God would forsake her?

It was this constellation of corrosive and toxic self-doubt that practically paralyzed Olivia when she was confronted with offensive and aggressive situations, especially those created by men. That is how she had had a series of superficial boyfriends in high school who had promised her love but who had just used her for sex. That is how Gabriela's father had convinced her to lower her guard, while having no genuine intent to marry her. Her need to be touched and held were overwhelming to the point that it compromised her ability to use reason and moral judgment to guide her behavior and her normal defenses. And the looming advance by Karl Williams was bringing all that to the forefront, once more.

So after a brief, contemplative silence, she meekly answered his rhetorical question. "No, I wouldn't want to lose my job. I appreciate all you've done for us."

But, by this time, he was already rubbing her shoulders, standing behind her. She felt uneasy; she remembered all the bad things she and her group of women friends would say about him at lunch break — he was a brutal sadist, a heartless abuser of women, a cynical and deplorable human being, a cold, sexual predator. She could have gone on, mentally listing all his contemptible personality traits, but something felt shamelessly soothing about his smooth, gentle, and caressing touch.

Her heartfelt feelings about what was right or wrong didn't seem to matter, because he had cleverly connected to her wounded soul, the part of her that desperately needed to feel wanted and desirable, even loved. She never had gotten enough mothering and certainly no fathering — twin weaknesses that made her tragically vulnerable to attention and physical touch. Ever devious and stealthy, Karl Williams knew it, and he capitalized on it.

It was almost as if she couldn't help herself — practically a reflexive surrender to his deceptively gentle but ultimately exploitative touch. He was gentle with some women, rough with others — whatever worked to get him what he wanted. It could be said that he enjoyed having the moral and ethical flexibility of a true Machiavellian — an interpersonal manipulator not constrained by silly social rules and mores meant simply for the inferior classes of humanity. In essence, he just needed a warm body to ravage.

At about that moment, Williams gently slipped his hand inside her bra and began to fondle her breast. She gasped — but not out of fear or surprise.

She knew he had just nudged her onto the beginning of an unethical slippery slope, one that was comforting, reassuring, and pleasurable, but an unethical slippery slope nevertheless. She felt good, she felt guilty, she felt protected, she felt disgusted. Olivia wasn't resisting, not even in the half-hearted way she did when the filthy and uncouth Bull Garcia would force her to submit. But what of the moral values she had planned on teaching Gabriela when she became of age? What of the chaste, modest, and Catholic ideals she envisioned for her daughter? Wouldn't she be just a shameless hypocrite teaching those ideals to her daughter when she was letting herself be ravaged all over the carpet by her boss — her married boss? Those thoughts didn't make her feel good, for they obliterated her self-esteem as a mother.

Yet, something else inside her protested against any thoughts of hypocrisy that might have been trying to surface. Given her very deprived childhood and her essentially loveless life as an adult woman, wasn't she entitled to this small moment of intimacy that would make her feel wanted, valuable, secure, and desirable? Or was she condemned to live a loveless life as an adult — on top of her loveless life as a child?

Olivia knew Williams was just a snake, yet it didn't matter, as long as she had those comforting, good feelings inside. It was almost as if she were pleading with him: "I know you don't care about me, but could you please hold me and pretend for a moment that you love me?" Wasn't poor, unloved Olivia entitled at least to that?

So, there she was — love-starved Olivia, in the grip of the smooth sexual predator, slowly sliding down the slippery slope, getting ever closer to her point of no return, doing battle not against him, but within herself. Two major, decisive forces of her personality were bitterly struggling for supremacy at this one moment — her desperate need for touch and her ailing self-respect. *But what good is self-respect if the rest of my life is not worth living?* she must have thought.

Some other primal spiritual force within her came to life and provided her with a moment of deep insight and clarity. Had her mother Frida struggled for years with similar, conflicting inner doubts and forces before finally succumbing to the incessant need to flee, to escape, to obliterate her old, wretched life, at the expense of her children, born covered with blood, shame, disgrace, and dishonor? Wasn't that the same trial by fire that was confronting Olivia in Karl Williams' office? The wrong decision now would eventually affect Gabriela and Olivia's capacity to mother her in an honest and ethical manner — with pride, not shame. As Don Chago had warned her, she needed to be a better mother than Frida ever was, for her behaviors as a woman and as a mother were inextricably connected.

And with that as her newfound ethical inspiration, she set her needs aside — maybe just for the time being — and she jumped into action. She grabbed Karl Williams' grubby hand from inside her bra, yanked it out, and bit hard into it with indignant passion, exploding, "Don't you ever touch me again, you filthy scorpion, or I'll make sure your little empire here goes down in flames! You really don't know what I can do to destroy you, you worthless maggot!" She let out an agonizing scream, and with her white, cotton blouse still fully unbuttoned, she ran screaming out his door onto the observation balcony and down the stairs to the first-floor work area. All 55 pairs of eyes and ears on the soldering lines followed her every step and her screaming run into the women's locker area. They all saw Karl Williams' door close slowly.

Rosalba, Lizbet, Glenda, Judith, and Rita began whispering among themselves, for it was clear what had just taken place in Williams' office. Or, at least, they imagined the worst. They all felt that, maybe during the lunch break, they could all get their chance to talk personally with Olivia, to give her support. But that plan quickly evaporated when soon they all saw Olivia talking to the floor manager and then taking the exit door. Was she quitting, or was she gone only for the day?

The first thing Sonia did after work that day was to call her. "Olivia, are you alright?"

"Hi, Sonia. Thanks for calling," said Olivia, quite calmly.

"I can hear just from the tone of your voice that you seem to have recovered pretty well. Do you want to talk about what happened today?"

"The bastard was up to his usual games. He didn't rape me, but he had his hands all over me. I finally got the courage to bite one of them and scream. You saw the rest."

"I must say, you appear to be getting courage from somewhere, because you sound stronger about defending yourself. Is that accurate?"

"Yes, Sonia. I finally worked up the courage to fight back, but I should've done it much sooner. I hardly protested when he started."

"Well, you probably were afraid to take that risky step."

"Thanks for believing in me, but it was worse than that. I didn't stop him sooner because, to my horror, I was *liking* it, Sonia — I was *liking* it! Damn, I'm all screwed up!"

"You are only a woman. It's normal to feel the need to be touched or held — but, obviously, only by the right man."

"It took every bit of courage in me to fight back, and I'm glad I did."

"So, did you take the rest of the day off, or did you quit?"

"Well, I told the floor manager I was too upset to continue and that I needed to go home for the day. Let's hope that I don't get the toilet detail tomorrow. I might even get fired, but I can handle it."

"Wow! That *is* an improvement! I like that, Olivia!"

"I appreciate your support, Sonia. Please do me a favor and call our parish. I want to put Aunt Jenny in contact with the counseling office there. She really needs help. I would appreciate it."

"Sure, I'll take care of it. What's the latest with you trying to locate your mother?"

"Tomorrow, I will call Jason McDougall again, at the newspaper, and maybe go see him about what he knows of my mother's latest address, in Dallas or wherever. He might know something."

"Are you controlling your temper a bit better when you deal with Gabriela?"

"Thanks for asking. Well, I have bad moments when I feel overwhelmed by so many difficult things in my life, and, as is usual these days, I tend to get hostile toward her, even though I regret it immediately. So, I apologize."

"It's good, though, that you recognize it when you are being hostile."

"Really, Sonia — it was better when my mother was dead."

"Remember, I told you, when I found out about your mother through those newspaper articles, that I had to think really hard whether I should tell you or not?"

"Yeah, I have mixed feelings about that, still."

"I considered that, too, but I still feel it was the right thing to do. And if you come to hate me, well, that is the course you must take, but my conscience is clear. I did what I had to do for a friend, with the best of intentions."

"How're Esther and Matt?"

"Oh, they're fine. They're still at the museum downtown. Listen, the offer still stands for us to take care of Gabriela if you want to go to Dallas to search for your mother."

"It's looking as if I will be taking you up on that offer. What my mother did was wrong and unforgivable, no matter how good her reasons could have been. I have a very big score to settle with her. I am afraid of what I could do."

CHAPTER 8

Olivia found out at work the next day that she had not been fired, which was great. *Or was it?* she thought. It was not beyond Karl Williams' evil character to extract revenge in a clandestine manner, especially since he had come to work with a highly noticeable and humiliating bandage around his hand. A very proud and arrogant man, he was sure to do something that would be ten times as painful to Olivia. He would know just when to strike — firing her would be too easy. Other than that, the day seemed normal.

At lunchtime, she put a call in to Jason at the newspaper. "Hello, this is Jason McDougall. How can I help you?"

"Hi, Jason. It's me, Olivia Cervantes — remember?"

"Oh, hi, Olivia. Nice to hear from you again. What's up?"

"I think I am ready to go find my mother in Dallas. Can you help?"

"I am glad you feel ready. But let me remind you that, when I did the research for the article, I was able to track down the address she went to when she took the bus to Dallas in 1982. For purposes of the article, I didn't need to go any further. It's anybody's guess where she could be now. We don't even know if she is still alive."

"I've never tracked down anybody before. Will you help me?"

"Sure, Olivia. I know this means a lot to you. Can you come over to my office after work?"

Olivia felt apprehensive for the rest of the workday, for now the search for her mother was real, and she would be entering the unknown. But her anger and a new sense of loss were the engines that propelled her forward with her mission.

After work, Sonia graciously agreed to take Gabriela. Olivia arrived at Jason's office in downtown Houston.

"Olivia, you're looking pretty. Come in." He lightly hugged her and motioned for her to sit down. His secretary brought in two coffees and some chocolate *conchas*, Olivia's favorite. "You are looking a bit distressed. What's going on besides the mother issue?"

"You know my life, Jason. Why even ask? I've got lots of stressors. Yesterday I bit my boss on the hand when he started to fondle me in his office. Today I went to work and discovered that I was not fired, so now I worry he is devising some sort of terrible revenge."

"Yes, you did mention to me some time ago that this guy abuses the women employees. Why hasn't anybody put in a complaint?"

"No way! Most workers are illegal, and an investigation would be bad for everybody. That's just the way it is — we all suffer in silence and hope for the best. In fact, one of the girls there is a minor, and she claims it was he who impregnated her. But she, too, is an illegal."

"Well, we'll devote more time to that later. About your mother: Here is what I have."

Jason took out some old files and research notes he had written months earlier. "When your mother Frida took that bus to Dallas, she went to live for a week in a cheap boarding hotel in the downtown area, and then she moved to a small, one-bedroom house at 2307 Rancho Street. Apparently, she lived there a few years and then moved, but my newspaper colleagues in Dallas couldn't pick up her trail after that."

"So, does that mean I have to go there, to her last address, and ask neighbors if they know something?"

"Yes — shoe leather from that point on."

"Jason, I am feeling angry, but mostly I am feeling hopeless. Insecure. It's a big job ahead of me, and I am afraid. Would you come with me to Dallas?" She looked at the floor. "I am feeling terribly lonely — like the world is collapsing. I fear that I will end up being a failure, like my mother, and that my daughter Gabriela will be the new Olivia."

Jason did not immediately answer. His eyes wandered about the office as if he were looking for an answer somewhere on the wall or the ceiling, maybe even on the dusty floor. He was used to writing about people's problems, like the plight of children who are abandoned — the theme of his article that turned Olivia's life upside down. But he was not a social worker. Then he thought, *What good is writing articles about people's problems without actually doing something about it? Isn't it hypocrisy to write as if we care but then do nothing to actually help a real person in need?*

"Yes, I will go with you to Dallas, Olivia!" was his emphatic response.

Her eyes watered. "Thank you, Jason, thank you! You are an honorable man." Her heart spoke other words that never left her lips: *And I should have met you when I was 18.*

"So, when do you want to do this?" he asked.

"As soon as possible. I need to meet the bitch face-to-face. Can we do that tomorrow?"

"It's about 250 miles to Dallas — that's four to five hours' driving time, one way. Yes — let's do it!"

"Great. I'll call in sick and arrange babysitting with my friend Sonia. Pick me up at 7 o'clock?"

When Olivia arrived to pick up Gabriela, she asked Sonia about the favor, and she graciously agreed. Sonia told Olivia that she was glad that she finally had made the decision to go to Dallas, for it was a personal problem of great magnitude that needed to be addressed.

But things would not work according to the plan set in motion, for when Olivia arrived with Gabriela at their apartment, she saw an official-looking note on the door:

> THE TEXAS DEPARTMENT OF SOCIAL SERVICES (DSS)
> HAS RECEIVED A COMPLAINT OF POSSIBLE CHILD ABUSE
> AT THIS ADDRESS. SINCE THE SOCIAL WORKER DID NOT
> FIND YOU AT HOME, YOU ARE ASKED TO CONTACT OUR
> OFFICE AS SOON AS POSSIBLE AT THE NUMBER INDICATED
> BELOW TO SET UP AN APPOINTMENT.

The notice was signed by Greta Haroldson, Social Worker I.

Olivia was stunned. *Child abuse?* Were they referring to the instances when Olivia had screamed at Gabriela? What else could the notice be referring to? Gabriela was properly fed and taken care of. And just who submitted the complaint to DSS? Was it a neighbor listening through the walls? There obviously was some mistake. Even so, Olivia went into a panic, for she had heard many horror stories of other Latinos whose lives were practically ruined by self-righteous and over-zealous state social workers who saw child abuse in everything the immigrant families did. Olivia knew there was no child abuse, but that may not matter much now that DSS had her in its sights. It was another nightmare about to unfold. Olivia had no idea that it would be as if Satan had knocked on her door.

She immediately called Sonia.""Hi, Sonia. Sorry to bother you, but when we got home, I found a note from DSS saying they want to talk to me about child abuse. I am horrified!"

"Calm down, Olivia. Any details?"

"Not really — just that the social worker came around and left the note when no one answered the door. Why would they say that someone reported child abuse at this apartment? Oh, my God!"

"Besides your losing your temper with Gabriela, the way you described it to me, is there anything else? Be honest, be thorough."

Olivia gave her a few more details, but nothing substantially different from what Sonia already knew.

"Look, Olivia, they are cold, heartless bastards from what I hear. My understanding is that they are not truly interested in kids' welfare — it is the power they exercise over defenseless families that turns them on. The only other agency in the whole country that is worse is DSS in Massachusetts — a sort of State Gestapo that terrorizes families legally."

"So, I need to call them, right? Or can I just ignore this notice?"

"No! Do not ignore that notice, or you will lose your battle even if you did nothing wrong with Gabriela. Like Massachusetts, they operate on the principle of guilty-until-proven-innocent-by-a-preponderance-of-evidence!"

"So what will happen when I call them?"

"Who's the social worker?"

"It says here, 'Greta Haroldson, Social Worker I.'"

"I know some people who are familiar with the system, so I will ask them about this social worker. When you call her, she probably will want to set a speedy appointment at your apartment. She will want to see and talk to Gabriela."

"I've heard horrible stories about that, Sonia. She will turn my daughter against me, right?"

"You know how children are impressionable and can be led to say things. Unfortunately, she will ask to have time alone with Gabriela to ask her some questions. I suggest you do not coach Gabriela about anything, for it might work against you. These child welfare social workers are masters at looking only for the evidence they want and ignoring everything else."

"Oh, Sonia, Sonia — I am going out of my mind! This is horrible, horrible! I've never been through anything like this before!"

"Just calm down. I'll try to help you."

"Bull Garcia! He must have done it! He must have been the one who called DSS and made those accusations!"

Olivia was just guessing, but Sonia immediately knew that it was a real possibility, especially after the beating he suffered when she visited him at his apartment. If that were the case, the accusations were probably more serious than Olivia screaming at her daughter. Bull Garcia would go for blood, real blood. Perhaps he was hoping that a devastating loss for Olivia would make her move away; then, he would not have to pay her rent for the next 11 months.

"It's possible, Olivia. But another suspect is Karl Williams. That man has no limit on revenge."

"I can't handle this, Sonia. Everything is collapsing around me. My life is worthless! Worthless!"

"I'm sure you feel like just running away, right?"

"Yes! Yes! Run away from all this misery! Very, very far away! I can't take it!"

As soon as those words leapt from her mouth, Olivia realized the deeper meaning of what she had just said. It was another one of those moments when something suddenly becomes crystal clear in a confused person's mind. Sonia's question had been more than just a simple question about how Olivia was feeling at the moment — it had been a masterful stroke to help Olivia see that what her mother had done was an act of desperation, a decision taken when there were no better routes available. Olivia had just come face-to-face with the crossroads where her mother had been 19 years earlier. Frida had taken the road of abandoning her children because the only other way was unbearable and would have led to her inevitable suicide. And at this very moment, Olivia's heart was anguished and under the threat of terror. She was looking at her options at that intersection, yearning to take the one that would allow her to flee from the unbearable dread. Her words had made that clear. It was an epiphany of sorts.

"Sonia, I can see how you are trying to help me see how or why my mother made the decision she did. And it makes me angry."

"Angry that I am trying to help you?"

"No — angry that, for a moment, I got the feeling of just running away, just like my mother did. So how the hell can I then be angry at her?"

"Getting that desperate feeling — I think it's a human problem, not just a peculiarity of your mother."

"So I *shouldn't* be angry at her — is that it?"

"No, you *should* be angry, because her actions affected you adversely and because it was her duty and responsibility to provide you with love and care, even if she was not feeling up to it."

"So, it means she failed!"

"Yes, Olivia, she failed. But not because she was a bad or uncaring person. She failed because her difficult situation exceeded the limits of human tolerance of stress, anxiety, shame, trauma, panic, and hopelessness. She was a mother, but she was just a *human* mother — not an anointed messenger from God, endowed with a limitless ability to endure pain and suffering in her duties as a mother to you and Benito. So, not only was she suffering because of the origin of her pregnancies, but after she fled to Dallas, she had to contend with the toxic realization that she had failed as a mother and that she ultimately abandoned her children. I can't think of a more destructive force against one's feelings of self-worth. If she left because she was trying to avoid suicide, she may have only worsened her predicament. And if she is still alive, Olivia, your mother is probably just a walking corpse."

"It sounds like you're just trying to understand her — like you're on her side."

"No, I am on *your* side, Olivia, but I believe *you* have to understand your mother so that you can, ultimately, have a basis for rebuilding your relationship to her. Of course, until then, you are fully justified in raging against her."

"Even if I come to eventually understand her, I will *never* forgive her — never!"

"That is fine. What she did was unforgivable, but we are not yet at the point of even considering forgiveness."

"It's so easy for you to say that since you are not involved in this horrible situation."

"You are right. But back to your other current crisis. First thing tomorrow morning, you will call that Greta Haroldson at DSS to set up an appointment. We'll see what she wants."

"Yes, I'll do it, even though it feels like I will be calling Satan. This is the most horrible thing ever in my life."

CHAPTER 9

Late that night, Olivia called Jason to advise him of the new development and to cancel the 7 A.M. trip to Dallas the following morning. He said he would try to help her in any way he could.

Early next morning, Olivia called in sick at work, since she expected that the DSS appointment would be for that day. The floor manager told her she had only two sick days left for the year, so she had better get well soon.

At home, she sat by the phone, thinking about her life, and dreading to make that call to the social worker.

"Hello, my name is Olivia Cervantes. I got a note on my door that I am supposed to contact Greta Haroldson to make an appointment."

"I will connect you."

Thirty very long seconds passed. "This is Greta Haroldson."

"Hi, Greta. My name is Olivia Cervantes. You left a note on my door asking me to call you."

"Don't you ever call me 'Greta' again. To you, I am 'Ms. Haroldson.' What's the case number at the bottom of the notice?"

"'Case number'? I didn't know I had a case with you."

"Just answer my question, and don't interrupt. Case number at the bottom," Greta insisted, almost caustically.

Olivia nervously searched for the number in the now-crumpled, detested notice.

"Case Number 14528-2001-TX."

"Yes, I see it. Olivia Cervantes. Report of emotional and sexual abuse of a child. Available appointment is 3:00 P.M. today, at your residence."

Olivia was in shock. Where did this come from? "Emotional and sexual abuse" of Gabriela? *There must be a mistake; they are confusing me with someone else; the papers must have gotten mixed up; the person who took the report by phone must have heard wrong! But, in any case, this must be the end of the world!* A million thoughts were speeding through her mind.

"No, Ms. Haroldson — there is a mistake. There is no emotional or sexual abuse here. My daughter is a happy child. Please believe me!"

"Yeah, that's what they all say, including those detestable pedophile parents. I will see you at 3 o'clock. Make sure the abused kid is there."

Click.

For Olivia, it felt like Greta Haroldson had already made up her mind that Gabriela had been abused — in fact, she had called her "the abused kid." It appeared that the appointment would only be a formality. The wheels of tragic destiny were in motion, she felt.

Throughout the day, Olivia could not think of anything but the dreaded arrival of Greta Haroldson at 3 o'clock. She couldn't eat, couldn't do any housework, and even though she felt she needed to just sit and hug Gabriela, her full attention and thoughts were captives of the impending threat at the door, so much so that, as much as she wanted to *express love* to her daughter, she could not bring it to the surface of her heart. Yes, she could place Gabriela on her lap, and yes, she could wrap her arms around her. But she could just as easily have been a stiff and cold mannequin, for the warmth of a mother's love was just not there. No, under the circumstances, spiritual, motherly love was secondary, for a full defensive alert had appropriated all of Olivia's emotional and cognitive resources.

In the afternoon, things got worse as Olivia's hands began to exhibit slight tremors. She had begun to obsess about the stories in the Latino community concerning run-ins with DSS and its tactics. Sure, there were some cases of real child abuse that needed to be addressed, but there were far more where draconian measures broke up families and needlessly traumatized children by forcibly removing them from their homes, thereby causing irreparable damage to the parent-child bonds. And Olivia trembled at the thought of Greta Haroldson's hostility toward her over the phone. That alone made her feel as if she was about to deal with a demon disguised as a social worker. Her stomach churned excess acid, and she was urinating frequently.

It was 3:05. There was a firm knock on the door. *God help me*, she thought. She walked slowly, and then she opened the door to her nightmare.

"Hello. My name is Greta Haroldson. I'm from DSS."

"Yes, Ms. Haroldson. Come in, please."

"Are you Olivia Cervantes?"

"Yes, I am."

"And is this Gabriela Cervantes?"

"Yes. She's my daughter."

"I asked you if the kid's name is Gabriela Cervantes!"

"Yes, her name is Gabriela Cervantes."

Greta Haroldson was about 27, never married, no children, about 5'8", slightly thin, auburn hair pulled back in a French bun, skin as white as snow, full lips enhanced by dark lipstick, and immaculate facial makeup. She was dressed very nicely in a silk, low-cut crimson blouse with half sleeves and black A-line skirt that reached just below the knee. Her outfit included round-toe black shoes with 3-inch heels. Olivia felt diminished just being in the same room with her.

"Please, Ms. Haroldson — come sit over here at our table."

As Greta walked the short distance to the kitchen table, she looked around with disdain at the walls, floor, ceiling, cabinets, and meager furnishings. Before she sat down at the plastic-covered chair, she checked it and brushed the surface lightly. Gabriela stood by Olivia's side, grabbing on to her skirt. She obviously found the pretty woman threatening.

Greta took out a file from her oversized purse. "You know why I'm here. We received a report indicating that you have been emotionally and sexually abusing the kid, so we need to conduct a full investigation. After the investigation is complete, we will make our recommendation to the court — it may well include removing your daughter from here and placing her in a foster home. Do you understand what I have just said?"

Those words pierced Olivia's heart like nothing ever had, not even the supposed death of her mother when Olivia was nine years old. "But that is not possible. I do not abuse my daughter. I love her very much. I take care of her! Why are you doing this?"

"I really don't care what you think — and I asked you a question!"

"Yes, I understand what you are saying," mumbled Olivia as she felt the panic start to rise again inside her stomach, her arms, her soul. *How can I defend myself and my daughter against this vile adversary who has the full resources of the government on her side?* she thought, as the panic spread over her body.

Greta then proceeded to ask her many questions concerning the history of the family, doctor visits, inoculations, and the like. Then came the more difficult questions.

"Now I need to ask you more personal questions, so just answer them truthfully — or you will be prosecuted for lying to the government. And do not interrupt me. Do you understand?"

"Yes, I understand."

"In the few moments that I have been here, I have seen more than 10 cockroaches. Do you clean this place frequently?"

"Yes, every day. But in this building…"

Greta interrupted her with a nasty tone in her voice. "You are a good liar. Just look how you keep this place. It's a garbage dump. And you claim to love your daughter! Sure!"

"Please believe me…"

"Don't interrupt me!"

Greta got up and walked toward the old stove. She took a paper towel from the dispenser and passed it over the stove. "Look at this! How dare you call yourself a mother when you keep the kid in such an awful, dirty environment!"

"Ms. Haroldson, it's an old stove. I clean it, but some of the grease just does not come off."

"Excuses — that's what you are made of. A mother has to be clean, dutiful, and moral, and pretty, but it's starting to look like you don't qualify."

"Look, Ms. Haroldson — I can clean the floors and the stove again. But please don't say that I am a bad mother," pleaded Olivia, now on the verge of crying.

"Show me the bathroom."

It also was a very short few steps. Greta entered, now with a frown of utter disdain on her face. "Just look at that green stuff on the bathtub. How on earth would you put your daughter in there? Do you even care about her?"

"Those are permanent copper stains from the pipes. The bathtub is 100% clean and disinfected with a chlorine cleanser. I would never put my daughter in a dirty tub, never, ever!"

"Yeah, sure. And the ring in the toilet? How can you live like this?"

"Sorry, but, yes, that needs a little bit more cleaning. I will take care of that," said Olivia, almost in a whimper, as she was beginning to feel run down by the barrage of attacks from Greta.

Then, without asking permission, Greta opened the medicine cabinet and checked all the bottles there. "Aha! You are taking Zoloft, an anti-depressant. Not a good sign for a mother of a young kid. And what's this? Looks like birth-control pills. You took the one for today. Didn't you say you were unmarried and had no boyfriend? This is not looking good for you. Explain!"

Olivia had placed herself on birth-control pills to avoid a pregnancy from the monthly rapes by Bull Garcia. She had taken the one for that day because she still was not fully convinced that he would not suddenly show up again. But how to explain that to the interrogator from hell?

Concerned about the adult nature of the subject getting to Gabriela's ears, Olivia proposed, "I can explain that, but I'd rather wait until you finish checking the other rooms so we can place Gabriela in her bedroom, and you and I can return to the kitchen table to talk."

"How dare you tell me how to conduct in-home interviews! I have a university degree, I am certified by the State of Texas; unlike you, I come from a good Texas-born family, I been doing this for seven long years, and I know my job. And you? What are you? You are an invader, you barely know how to read English, and you work soldering little wires all day long. And on top of it all, you are immigrant scum! *You* are telling *me* how to do interviews? How dare you!" growled Greta, with a positively ugly, hateful sneer on her otherwise pretty face.

Olivia was stunned by Greta's hostile rebuke and the ferocity of her words. She just bowed her head, knowing that she was losing ground by the minute. Yet, surprisingly, Greta did not insist on an answer right away and moved on to Gabriela's bedroom.

It was a very modest but beautiful bedroom, adorned with lots of stuffed animals and with bright posters all over the walls. But Greta made a beeline to Gabriela's bed and took off the blankets to look at the bed sheets and then the mattress. "It looks to me like this mattress has urine stains. So she wets the bed, eh?"

"No, she does not. Those are old urine stains. I bought it used at a garage sale. I disinfected it several times before I let her sleep on it."

"We'll see about that." And again, without asking permission, she started opening the dresser drawers until she got to the one holding all of Gabriela's panties. One by one, Greta visually inspected the underwear crotch area, presumably looking for anything unusual, such as stains. Gabriela, witnessing something she had never before seen in her life, silently tugged at her mother's skirt as a sign of discomfort or concern. Olivia could only squeeze her hand and embrace her with one arm. In a sense, it felt like another rape of privacy.

"Okay — show me your bedroom," Greta commanded.

"When was the last time you painted this room? It looks like a hell-hole!"

"We don't have enough money to paint anything, but, if you want, we can ask some friends if they are able to help."

Greta then opened Olivia's closet and quickly scanned practically everything there. "I see that you have four pairs of shoes, but yet you have no money to paint this dump. Poor priorities. Will work against you in the investigation."

"Ms. Haroldson, I bought two of those four pairs at a tag sale. Each pair cost me 50 cents for a total of one dollar. I couldn't paint this room with that amount."

"Tell that to the judge when he asks about how you splurge on yourself and let the kid go wanting."

In another bizarre and unusual move, Greta removed the blankets and the sheets from Olivia's bed and stared at the sunken middle section of the mattress. "Is this where you do your dirty business?"

"I am sorry, but what do you mean by 'dirty business'?"

"Don't act like an innocent virgin here, Olivia — you have 'slut' written all over your face! You know what I mean."

Then Greta lowered her nose to the mattress and snarled, "It definitely smells like fresh semen here. You lied to me when you said you have no boyfriend. If you have no boyfriend, then you must be a prostitute! This is not a healthy environment for the kid!"

"No, no, that is not true! I did not lie to you. I can explain this — please, give me a chance to explain!" wailed Olivia as she was getting closer and closer to a complete collapse.

It was looking hopeless for Olivia, and, to make matters worse, the real tough questions had not yet begun. She was no match for the cunning and shrewd Greta, who could turn anything she wanted into evidence against anyone she pleased. Olivia felt she was a good mother most of the time, but Greta's interrogation was making her appear to be a monster not suitable to mother even dogs. *Why does mothering have to be so difficult?* she thought to herself. *Why does everybody want me to fail?*

"Very well, now back to the kitchen — if you can call it that — for some final questions."

Maybe Greta had no sense of this, but Olivia felt that she should send Gabriela to her bedroom to play. She closed the door.

At the kitchen table, Greta gave Olivia a stone-cold stare and spoke. "Olivia Cervantes, the report says that you bring different men to your bed for sexual intercourse and that you leave the door open so your daughter can watch while you're doing it. It also says you are contemplating permitting these men to have sexual contact with the kid, to raise money, perhaps. That's the whole complaint. What do you say?"

It was a devastating accusation. Not only was it not true, but it tore through the core of Olivia's being to think that someone believed that to be true and had submitted a complaint to DSS. Who could have done that? Could this accusation be a cynical and perverse embellishment of the monthly rapes by Bull Garcia? But just how many people knew of these? Did Bull Garcia spread the word around about it? Besides Olivia, only Sonia knew that Bull Garcia was giving Gabriela suspicious looks. *She wouldn't have done this — would she?* But maybe someone at work had overheard their confidential conversations, some spy for that hated Karl Williams. Maybe those hanging microphones at the soldering lines had picked up some wayward comments. Or maybe some other worker who wanted to be in good grace with Karl Williams had offered tantalizing information for money. Given the situation, that would have been a gold mine for Karl Williams. Even more anguishing was that, now that the accusation had been made, how was Olivia going to convince DSS that nothing had ever happened and that there was no danger or risk to Gabriela? These and many more questions bombarded Olivia's soul as she faced her formidable adversary across the table. Yes, once more, Olivia felt that the demons were getting too big to handle and that she needed to run far away.

"Ms. Haroldson, I am shocked at that accusation. It is absolutely not true. You said that my mattress smelled like semen, so I will explain why. Up until recently I was the victim of monthly rapes by our building manager, Bull Garcia, and..."

"Monthly rapes? You are not serious, are you?"

"I know it sounds odd, but that is the plain truth. I didn't have money to pay the rent so he would force himself upon me. He..."

"You not only are a bad liar, but you also fail to see that you have been working as a prostitute. You just hate to admit it. You are a hooker — plain and simple!"

"No, that is not true!" Olivia started to cry, but those words reminded her that Bull Garcia had said the same thing about her. *Two people concurred, so it must be true,* she thought. She was just a lowdown shitty hooker that men visit, not to hold her or to love her, but to satisfy their basic animal instincts. And just as they quickly leave the toilet after defecating, they promptly leave her soiled body on the bed after satisfying themselves with it. It was no different. So her value as a person was fast approaching zero. *What's the use in living, anyway?*

Then, with a wolfish look on her face, Greta asked, "Assuming that what you are saying is true, were those the times when you would leave the door open so the kid could watch?"

"No, no, no — oh God, no! When I knew that the rape was inevitable, I would close the door. Gabriela would be in her room sleeping. Absolutely, she never witnessed any of the rapes."

"So you would tell the rapist, 'Hold on a minute before the rape. Let me close the door first.'? Now, does that sound like rape to you? No judge will ever believe your wild story. You are just a hooker. It's worse when you can't even recognize it. I am sure that our psychologists will have a field day with you when they do their personality testing."

"What 'testing'?"

"It's just part of the investigation. We need to know that you are not unbalanced, that you are not a threat to the kid. Of course, I already know you are!"

Olivia received those words like a knife to the throat. There was nothing she could say to improve her image in the eyes of Greta, the DSS demon from hell. But it just got worse.

"Okay, I now need to talk with the kid, alone. You can just wait outside the door. *Now.*"

Olivia complied even though she had a death knot in her throat knowing she was placing her daughter in the hands of a very evil woman who was hell bent on destroying their relationship. But Olivia had no option; she knew from neighborhood stories that the child-welfare authorities move with SS lightning speed when parents don't comply. She just waited outside, quietly weeping, letting her tragic destiny run its course.

"Hello, my name is Greta. What is your name?"

"I am Gabriela, and I am five years old."

"That is a very pretty name."

"I know. My mother chose it for me."

"I came here to help you and your mommy."

"I call her 'mamma,' not 'mommy.'"

Greta snarled and thought that Gabriela was just being an insolent kid. But she held back her displeasure.

"Okay, we'll call her 'mamma.'"

Greta continued with a few more innocuous questions to create a devious rapport with Gabriela and perhaps win her trust. Then, like a vampire, she went in for the kill.

"When mamma bathes you, does she scrub your whole body with a cloth or sponge?"

"Yes. She uses a yellow sponge, but sometimes it's blue."

"And I am sure she washes your private parts, too, sometimes — right?"

Gabriela was a bit embarrassed at the question, so she hesitated in answering, eventually responding with a "Yes" after a few prods from Greta.

"I remember when my mother used to wash me when I was your age, and sometimes I felt a tingle in my private parts. I am sure you do, too, right?"

Without answering verbally, Gabriela just nodded her head. That elicited a wicked, triumphant smile out of the vampire that had so far not smiled at all.

She then moved on to the next line of attack.

"Sometimes mothers feel lonely, and they get a boyfriend who comes to their house for a visit. Does your mamma have a boyfriend who comes here?"

"Yes, but only a little bit at night."

"Your mamma is very pretty and very popular. I am sure she has lots of boyfriends who visit her here — right?"

With a big grin, Gabriela nodded her head in agreement. "Yes, my mamma is very pretty."

"And when the boyfriends come around, does your mamma just take them to her bedroom to play?"

"Yes, but they don't talk — they just make noises." By this time, Greta was getting high on all the evidence she was collecting. This was definitely a case of child sexual abuse, and she had cracked the case with her usual, erudite line of questioning. In her view, there was no one better in the Houston DSS bureau than she. Her boss, balding 51-year-old Antonio Guerra, was sure to be very pleased, for they needed to justify their gargantuan budget to the state finance committee.

"And I am sure that sometimes you have seen your mamma in her room with one of her boyfriends — right, little angel?"

Gabriela nodded her head, but with no particular expression on her face.

Determining that she had enough information, Greta decided to end the interview.

"Hey, kid, you can now go back to your bedroom to play with your rag dolls." She summoned Olivia from just outside the apartment door. "I'm done here for now. I will recommend that we do a complete investigation, including a thorough physical/medical examination of the kid…"

"'Medical exam'? Why would you want to do that? There is nothing wrong with her!"

"I told you already not to interrupt me! I will have to write on the file that you have been an uncooperative and hostile parent! Now, as I was saying, we will also request a complete psychological workup for you — to see what types of mental pathologies you harbor in your head. There is reason to believe that this kid has been abused and that you were in the process of renting her out for sex. Once we have all the results, we will have a court date to determine if the kid should be placed permanently in a foster home. Is that clear?"

It was shock upon shock for Olivia. She was speechless and could not believe that this woman Greta was making all these accusations against her. In a matter of seconds, she was numb.

"I asked you if what I stated was clear to you."

"Yes, it is clear," she whispered.

"I'm done. Here's my card with my direct line. You will be contacted soon." Greta closed the door behind her, because Olivia did not even get up from her chair.

Olivia was in an almost catatonic shock, staring at the vinyl cover of the kitchen table, for never in her life had she experienced a threat so vile, so catastrophic, as that which Greta had unleashed when she came into their modest home. Sure, she was not a perfect mother, but she was also not doing the heinous things that Greta had accused her of. And from the tone of the interview, Olivia knew that Greta had already made up her mind and that the so-called investigation would be no more than a sham, a required formality. At stake was her relationship with her daughter, who might very well be taken from her. From Olivia's humble position at that little table in the kitchen, it felt like Greta was omnipotent, or, at least, very powerful, with the entire resources of the government of Texas behind her. Indeed, Greta was like a vampire adversary coming to take away Olivia's only child.

And ruthless she was, this Greta. It was common knowledge in the huge DSS building in downtown Houston that, for some reason, Greta's cases usually ended up with the kids removed from their homes and placed in foster care. Even though DSS administration assigned new cases on a rotational basis, it usually turned out that Greta's cases presented the worst, most uncooperative parents and the kids with the most despicable abuse. Maybe she was just clinically perspicacious, because she had an uncanny ability to identify parents who were not at all fit to have children at home. On the other hand, some of her colleagues whispered how it could be that Greta professed a deep concern about the welfare of children in general, yet no one had ever seen her hug a child or even hold his hand. Worse, she had the unkind habit of referring to a child as "...the kid..." — she never called children by their real names.

But like other social workers at the child-welfare office, Greta had her own agenda, her own set of conscious and subconscious motives. The premier goal for Greta at DSS was to appear glamorous, efficient, cooperative, clinically intelligent and insightful, and non-expendable in helping the department justify its bloated workforce and budget by bringing in more "customers" — children and families who would be on the road to Sodom and Gomorrah without DSS intervention, no doubt. But the most outrageous motive for her latent anti-family perspective was that she was secretly in love with her boss, Antonio Guerra, a dyed-in-the-wool bureaucrat who had been boss at Houston DSS for about fifteen years. He was happily married, he said, but did not actively discourage the lusting Greta from over-extending herself to please him, especially in how she handled her case investigations to provide overwhelming clinical evidence in court that supported DSS contentions that the family was corrupt and that the children had to be permanently removed. Antonio Guerra relished it with a perverse passion when DSS prevailed in court, which was almost always, irrespective of the evidence, and Greta basked in feminine glory as his irreplaceable woman partner who could deliver the goods and make him feel like a successful boss, like an untiring champion for the welfare of children, like a king, like a real man — things that his wife possibly was not able to deliver, as far as Greta could tell.

So not only was Olivia in trouble because of the several unfortunate pieces of her life that were unsavory and which provided DSS circumstantial ideas on how to build a contrived and imaginary case that would appear unimpeachable and rock-solid in court, but also because she had to deal with a cold-hearted and perhaps sadistic social worker who had never been married and had never had a child to love. Olivia did not know it, and, so, she could not think of it as such, but how could a childless social worker ever empathize with the real-life hardships of parents who had to struggle to support their children? And wasn't it a central tenet of social-work ideology to be able to empathize with those who are suffering? Clearly, as a human being, Greta was operating outside of her privileged league. Yet, this minor detail was apparently irrelevant in the eyes of DSS operating philosophy. To top off Olivia's woes, Greta was obsessed with her boss, and she would do whatever was necessary to prove to him, once more, that she was his best social worker, ever. Ever! And — as a woman — far superior than even his wife.

It was late afternoon, perhaps almost 6 o'clock, when Olivia garnered enough emotional energy to force herself to get up from the chair in the kitchen. Still numb, she went to Gabriela's room and found her sleeping in her bed, so she shuffled back to the kitchen with the intent to fix supper. She gave the kitchen cabinets a bleak look from the hallway and opted to just drop onto her bed. She fell asleep almost immediately.

CHAPTER 10

When Olivia woke up in early morning, she quickly realized that a nauseous feeling of dread and doom was coming over her whole body and soul. She was hoping that she could just go back to sleep and perhaps not even wake up anymore — the real world was far too ugly. Yet, at the very least, she had to give Gabriela her breakfast. No work today either, as she had one sick day left from the hell-hole job.

Gabriela was already playing with her dolls and coloring books — she knew not to wake mamma up unless it was an emergency. When Olivia entered her room, Gabriela quipped, "What's wrong, mamma? You look strange."

"I just don't feel too good today — that's all."

"Did the bad lady scare you yesterday?"

"What makes you say she was a 'bad lady'?"

"Her eyes, mamma — she had the eyes of an angry wolf. I didn't like her."

"Well, we will have to see her again, I think, just so you know."

"But why, mamma? You don't like her either — I can tell."

"Somebody told her that I am not taking good care of you, and, since she works for the government, she has to see if that is true."

"I don't like her, and I don't like the government."

"Come, I'll make you some delicious pancakes with chocolate sprinkles."

While Olivia was making the pancakes, she tried to interact more with Gabriela, but her mind and attention were being conscripted by frightful, intrusive thoughts about what was about to come from DSS and that Greta woman. To Olivia at least, it seemed that life had come to a standstill while the matter was hanging over her head. The final outcome could be catastrophic for their life together, she felt. She would then have no option but to commit suicide.

"Mamma, do you still love me?"

Gabriela's innocent words brought Olivia from the fires of hell back into the kitchen, and, with spontaneous tears in her eyes, she knelt before her and hugged her tightly with full affection and motherly warmth.

"Oh, baby — yes, of course, I love you. I have always loved you and always will, always, always. You are my sweetest sweetheart forever and ever. What ever gave you the idea that I did not love you?"

Olivia pulled back a little from the strong hug to look at Gabriela's big eyes, which, by then, had tears, too.

"I remember the night you told me to get out of your room, and then you shut the door. I just wanted you to hold me," said Gabriela, with shuddering sobs.

"Oh, sweetie, I am so, so sorry. I should not have done that. That was hurtful of me, and I was wrong. I will never do it again. Please forgive me. You know you are my little treasure! I will always love you!"

Olivia just could not release Gabriela from her arms. She was the reason Olivia endured hardships and even abuse and insults. She was the reason Olivia avoided the dating scene. She was the reason Olivia felt it was her duty to submit to the ugly monthly rapes. Gabriela was just an innocent little flower that needed love and care, and Olivia was feeling remorseful that her mothering responsibilities had begun to deteriorate ever since Frida had come back to life. And Greta The Social Worker From Hell had arrived to make things worse, much worse. Olivia's debilitating feelings of panic and doom in response to her frightful situation were understandable, but, there, on the kitchen floor with her daughter Gabriela in her arms, Olivia resolved that she would never use her difficult situation as an excuse for any future failures in mothering and that, as Don Chago had advised her, she would strive to be a better mother than Frida ever was.

After a few minutes, Gabriela piped, "Mamma, I think your pancakes got cold!" A few minutes later, mamma and daughter had a happy time eating warmed-over chocolate-sprinkled pancakes. Then the phone rang.

"Hi, this is the DSS office downtown. Are you Olivia Cervantes?"

"Yes. Who's this?"

"My name is Susie Drake, Greta Haroldson's assistant. She put in an order for a medical exam for your daughter, Gabriela Cervantes. We were able to squeeze her in for tomorrow at 2:20 P.M. with Dr. Krodovic at the Ayers Clinic on Bummel Road. Can you make it?

"That's not her doctor. I can take her to our clinic, if that's alright with you."

"I'm sorry, but Dr. Krodovic is on contract with DSS to perform these exams. Be there tomorrow at 2:20 P.M."

Click.

Olivia had thought that maybe DSS would give her a week or so to prepare psychologically for this medical intrusion, so this was extraordinarily fast. As well as she could, she prepared Gabriela for the exam. Olivia herself did not know exactly what a medical exam on a child suspected of being a victim of emotional and sexual abuse entailed, but she feared that it would include an examination of her private parts. She explained to Gabriela that it may well include that very uncomfortable aspect.

"But, mamma, why does the doctor have to do that? I don't want him to!"

"I know, sweetheart, I know, I don't like it either when I go to the doctor and he has to do that to me, too. But maybe it will take only a few seconds, and it will be over quickly."

There was no easy way to help Gabriela understand or accept what was to come at the doctor's clinic. Olivia's revulsion at the idea colored her explanations, so she did not sound too convincing. It would be a terrible experience for both. Not sure of what to expect, she decided to again visit her friend Don Chago. Talking to the women at work would have been more appropriate, but they would all be busy on the soldering line. Besides, Don Chago was easily accessible — surely he would be there at his shoe-repair shop.

The bus quickly took them there. "Don Chago, here we are again! I see you are busy as always."

"Olivia, nice to see again so soon. I am sure there is something going on with you. And hello to you, too, little angel," he said as he patted Gabriela on the head, which she always liked. Olivia gave him a package with the freshly baked chocolate *conchas* she had promised him last time. But she was too upset to enjoy them with him.

After a little bit of small talk, Olivia explained, "Look, Don Chago, I need your advice again."

"I've learned a few things through all my mistakes and sufferings in life, Olivia. Will be glad to share that with you. What is the problem?"

"DSS came to my apartment. They said they received a report of child abuse, but I know it cannot possibly be true."

"Are they saying you did it or that it was someone else?"

"Both. The social worker is a nasty person who I feel has already made up her mind that something did happen. Now Gabriela and I will undergo some testing. Tomorrow I am due to take her for a physical examination at the clinic, on their orders. I am a ball of nerves. Any suggestions?"

"You have crossed paths with The Beast, my dear, and you have to prepare to do battle with them so that they don't get their way."

"That is not what I wanted to hear."

"DSS might have been created with good intentions as a response to community concerns about children who were being neglected. But you know how bureaucracies are. It grew and grew and started inventing its own rules on how to deal with families. Now it's a cauldron of politics, big egos, power grabs, jealousies, and revenge. From what I've heard, DSS has the meanest, most power-hungry personnel of any government agency. How ironic that they project an attitude of concern, love, compassion, and caring. Ha!"

"Yes, that is all good, but what can I do to protect myself and Gabriela? The mean witch threatened to take her away!"

"Information and courage. You need to learn very quickly some basic psychology, medical terminology, and social-work principles. You need knowledge so you can interpret the charges they will be leveling against you."

"But, Don Chago, do you mean I need to take a university course?"

"No, just go to the public library, check out some books, and read all you can over the next several days and weeks. You need to go to war against these fascists, or they'll legally take away your daughter for some fabricated reason! Contrary to what they profess, they really don't give a hoot about the kids."

Those words stuck in her mind: "You need to go to war against these fascists." So, for the rest of the day and the following morning, Olivia read articles and chapters on the subjects Don Chago had recommended. She was mesmerized by the incredible theories in child development and also by what some critics had to say about child-welfare agencies overstepping their power, especially DSS in Massachusetts. But that is all the time she had for the moment. It was time to head for that dreaded exam.

They arrived at the Ayers Clinic on Bummel Road a few minutes ahead of time, with great apprehension. After Olivia filled out a few forms, they were asked to sit in the waiting area, and, within ten minutes, the nurse came with an update.

"The doctor is in Examination Room 12, and he will see you now."

Olivia knocked gently on the door, and a voice asked them to come in.

"Hello, Dr. Krodovic?"

He was about 60, a bit rotund, with a harsh, Eastern European face. Had big ears but very thin lips. His white lab coat was starting to look not so white.

"Yes. The little one must be Gabriela Cervantes. Right?"

"Correct, and I am her mother, Olivia Cervantes. We are really stressed out about this, doctor. My daughter has never had this kind of examination."

"There is nothing to worry about. I do this routinely, but I must ask mommy to please wait outside the examination room."

"What? No, I feel I have to be here to provide comfort and security for my daughter. She already feels very apprehensive as it is."

"It's just routine. I know what I am doing. Please wait outside, and close the door."

Olivia responded with flared nostrils. "To hell with that, doctor! I am not going to leave my daughter alone on such an invasive and disturbing exam. She's only five years old! What the hell is wrong with you?"

Olivia was surprised at her defensive reaction to what the doctor was suggesting. She credited that to her having read something or other about physical exams.

"I am sorry you feel this way, but, okay, you may stay. Here is a child-sized gown. Take her behind the curtain, and dress her only in this."

It took about two minutes, and then they emerged from behind the curtain, with Gabriela holding on tightly to Olivia's leg.

"Set her on the table, lying down on her back."

"Mamma, I am afraid. I don't want to do it, mamma."

"It's okay, honey — it will take only a couple of minutes, and I am here to hold your hand."

"No, mamma! I don't want him to touch me!"

"What's all the fuss about? I see on your file that you are from those low-rent apartment buildings on Bissonet and Beachnut. We get a lot of those abused kids from those projects here for exams, so I gather that the touching and all that shouldn't be anything new to your daughter, if you know what I mean," mumbled the doctor callously.

"Doctor, are you going to look at her private parts?"

"It will only take a few seconds. I've done this hundreds of times for DSS."

As the doctor lifted Gabriela's gown to begin the examination, Gabriela, now full of tears, again pleaded with her mother.

"Mamma! No, mamma! Don't let him touch me, mamma — don't let him touch me!"

Even though it was uncomfortable for Olivia to watch the actual examination, she forced herself to keep on looking, just in case, especially because she thought it odd that the doctor was not wearing the customary latex gloves. More terrifyingly, he had a small stainless steel rod with a sharp hook at the end resting on the examination table. It reminded her of the amnihook that obstetricians use to sometimes rupture the amniotic sac in a delivery, but this rod was thinner and the hook appeared razor-sharp both on the inside and outside curves. What in the world was this ominous tool doing near Gabriela's knees on the examination table? Dr. Krodovic may have looked up twice at Olivia while he was performing the exam, but he said nothing.

Her face totally wet with silent tears, Olivia kept holding Gabriela's hand and reassured her that it would soon be over. They mixed their tears as mamma brought her cheek in contact with Gabriela's, and they wept together.

"Mamma, tell him not to touch me. Help me, mamma!"

As Olivia was holding on to Gabriela tightly, a very disturbing thought came to her mind: *Am I holding her to give her some reassurance, or am I restraining her?*

About a minute later, the doctor spoke. "Okay — it's all over. There really was no reason for all the hysterics," the doctor charged. "I do this all the time for DSS."

Olivia and Gabriela were still holding each other tightly as the doctor wrote some notes in a file. "You may get her dressed now. Throw her gown in the trash — she got it all sweaty. Besides, her living in that low-rent building probably means she has some head lice, too." The doctor then discreetly placed the mysterious hooked rod into a drawer; since Olivia had kept her eyes on it throughout the entire examination, she knew that the doctor had not used it on Gabriela, although she had already planned to question its purpose the minute he picked it up.

While tear-drenched Olivia was getting Gabriela dressed behind the curtain, she got a sickening feeling in the gut of her stomach. Had she just facilitated the emotional rape of her five-year-old daughter? Had it been proper for her as a mother to have ignored Gabriela's desperate pleas to prevent the DSS doctor from touching her? Almost sick with disgusting nausea, Olivia knew the disturbing answers to these two questions. An unforgivable lapse of judgment in her duty to protect Gabriela, she felt. The knot in her throat was further proof that she was sick with guilt and regret. *And just this morning, I promised myself I would be a better mother,* she thought. Gabriela's little voice kept reverberating inside Olivia's soul like an internal dagger, repeatedly stabbing her heart for her new mothering failure: "Mamma! No, mamma! Don't let him touch me, mamma — don't let him touch me!"

Oh, my God, how could I let this happen? It was horrible! Horrible! was her thought and her feeling.

Dr. Krodovic finally looked up from where he had been writing. "I will have to write in the report that you exhibited a posture of extreme paranoia and that you became hostile and aggressive, maybe because you are trying to hide something concerning the identified victim."

But Olivia was now morally energized by her profound regret and guilt over what she had just done and did not take the doctor's comments sitting down. She remembered Don Chago's advice: "You have to do battle…"

"And how about you, doctor? How is it that you specialize in these very intimate examinations of young children? Are you a latent pedophile, getting your pleasure in a socially acceptable way by providing a medical service but feasting on their little bodies and touching their private parts as you secretly salivate? In medical school, you could have chosen to specialize in cardiology, or even internal medicine, but no, you went for pediatric urology, which gives you a culturally respectable legal license to touch little children in their private parts all day long! Eh? Answer that, you sick, motherfucking pervert! I dare you to quote me on your report, you creep! And if you don't, I surely will, if and when we all end up in court, you vile degenerate!"

The doctor was taken aback by Olivia's incisive and aggressive rebuttal, yet he did not answer her question — he pretended to be busy writing in the file again. Olivia took sweat-soaked Gabriela in her arms and stormed out of the clinic. Gabriela clung tightly to her mother on the bus ride back home.

With that spontaneous rant, Olivia knew she had drawn a line in the sand and declared war on DSS — but especially on Greta Haroldson. She was glad, but she was scared to death about the reaction DSS would have when they heard of the news from the doctor, who undoubtedly would take revenge on Olivia for calling him a "latent pedophile." They initially had wanted her daughter, but now they would be looking for blood. How dare a puny Hispanic mother contradict what mighty, omnipotent, and omniscient DSS wants to do? Both mother and daughter would have to pay an unacceptably painful price, if for no other reason than to teach them, and other parents taking note, that one does not go against the wishes of DSS.

At home, Gabriela just sat in front of the television without saying much; she had calmed down, but apparently too much. Noticing this, Olivia sat down beside her and continued to talk to her about what had transpired in the examination room. She also encouraged her to talk about how she felt and was able to achieve a bit of success. The rest of the evening was spent on the sofa, with Gabriela sitting on her mother's lap. Destiny's wheels were moving in an unpleasant manner.

CHAPTER 11

$\mathcal{E}$arly Saturday morning, Olivia woke up with more panic than usual, so she called Sonia and suggested that maybe all the women friends from work could meet at Sonia's for lunch. Olivia said she really needed to be in the company of people who were not her enemies. Sonia readily agreed to help Olivia out.

Before leaving the apartment complex, Olivia and Gabriela visited Mrs. Brunswick to make sure she had adequate groceries and chatted with her a bit. As usual, she needed a few things done, so Olivia took care of those. Then, they were off to catch the city bus to Sonia's house.

It was a small but beautiful little house, there in Houston's southwest section. It was so immaculately clean that it made Olivia wonder just how Sonia felt when she visited Olivia's relatively dumpish apartment. Six-year-old Esther had her own bedroom, and there was one to spare — in case they wanted to have another baby. And the living room had two sofas and several cushioned seats, all now occupied by the girls from work.

They all greeted Olivia and Gabriela with unusual warmth, making Olivia suspect that they already knew of her terrifying situation.

"Olivia, we missed you at work, honey!" exclaimed Rosalba. "I felt there was a big emptiness to my right there on the soldering line."

Lizbet added, "Yeah, and we missed a lot of gossip when you weren't there at lunch time!"

"Gossip? I am sure she's been storing lots of goodies for us girls! What's lunch without hearing from Olivia!" exhorted Rita, with a quick glance over to Matt, Sonia's husband.

"Thank you all for coming. I just needed to get out of our apartment for a while. It's been a difficult three days," explained Olivia.

After sending Gabriela and Esther to one of the bedrooms to play, the women got down to more serious talk.

"Well, Olivia, we heard about the DSS problem. How serious is it?" asked Judith.

"More serious than the usual case. I know for a fact that nothing bad has ever happened to my daughter, and I certainly have not abused her, but that terrible social worker who came to our apartment three days ago appears to have made up her mind that I am a terrible housekeeper and neglectful mother."

"You mean that, with no real evidence, she's already concluded that there's been abuse?" fumed Glenda.

"Yes. But the most horrible part was the medical exam that Gabriela had to endure yesterday with that creepy Dr. Krodovic at the Ayers clinic. He insisted that I leave her alone with him in the examination room, but I refused. He certainly didn't like it."

"Good for you, Olivia. I've heard all sorts of horror stories about these doctors who specialize in treating children. Seems rather weird to me," opined Lizbet, with a wrathful look.

"Olivia, do you still not have any idea who might have filed that report with DSS?" queried Sonia, as Olivia gave her a look in mid-sentence to indicate the sensitivity of that issue.

Still looking at Sonia obliquely, Olivia responded, "My guess is still that evil Karl Williams. I know that it affected him that I just ran out of his office screaming when he was putting moves on me."

Sonia got the drift and did not mention anything about that animal Bull Garcia, even though she sensed that it could have been him, for Karl Williams had too much to lose in getting involved in a court case, where other unsavory stuff might come out into the open. Then Olivia changed the course of the conversation.

"Another thing that scares me is that I blew up at that Dr. Krodovic, who did the exam on Gabriela. I was furious that he was so unsympathetic toward her apprehension about the exam. When he finished, he said that we were just being hysterical."

"Imagine that! So unprofessional, too," exclaimed Rosalba.

"You said you blew up at him. What did you say or do?" asked Glenda, always ready to relish any attacks on men.

"I simply told him he was creepy, that he was a latent pedophile, and that I questioned with concern why he chose to specialize in pediatric urology."

"Damn, Olivia! I have never heard anything like this out of you. You destroyed the pervert!" praised Judith with a wry smile.

But, with a concerned look, Rita added, "So I bet that he will report your remarks to the case manager, that awful social worker you mentioned?"

"She's a real witch, so I really am concerned about what she will do. I've been doing some reading on state child-welfare agencies and such, and I've learned that DSS has a fascist attitude. They don't want anyone questioning their actions — not even the courts! My comments to that degenerate doctor are, in effect, a declaration of war! Puny me, how can I go to war against The Beast? I'm just a poor solderer, barely making it!" Olivia was near tears.

Lizbet took Olivia's hand. "I've known mothers who have lived the nightmare, so I know it won't be easy. But you have us, Olivia — we all are on your side." Pointing to each of the women, she continued, "There's Rosalba, Rita, Judith, Sonia, Glenda, and me. Each of us individually may be small potatoes, but all of us put together can exert a powerful force in your favor. We're here when you need us."

"Thanks, Lizbet — and thank you all for being on my side. This will be one horrible battle that I dread fighting."

It was just about lunch time, so Sonia brought out the *carne guisada* along with rice, beans, lettuce, tomato, and warm flour tortillas. It was a big job preparing it, so some of the women had arrived early that day to help Sonia out. Sonia's husband Matt had gotten up very early anyway to work on his specialty — pork and beef tamales. All the women praised him for the delicious side dish and told Sonia how lucky she was to have her own master chef in Mexican cuisine. Gabriela and Esther, who had joined them at the table, kept saying that they were the best tamales they had ever tasted!

After a little kitchen cleanup, the two girls were sent to the bedroom again, while the women served themselves coffee and Mexican sweet breads in the small living room. The conversation skipped from subject to subject, based on each woman's burning gossip of the day. Then it got more practical.

"So, what are we doing to help Carmelina? Her pregnancy is proceeding normally, she says, but I just wonder if this should have been promptly reported to the police. She's a minor, so that means what Karl Williams did was rape," cited Judith, who immediately got a sly look from Rita.

"Okay, Rita — what was that look all about?" complained Judith.

"Nothing. I just find it funny that you are criticizing Karl Williams for his sexual behavior when you are running around with a boyfriend behind your husband's back."

Like a comet, Glenda jumped in to defend Judith. "Rita, you are too young and inexperienced to understand that men like Karl Williams use women for pure sexual release. Whatever Judith is currently doing may not be morally defensible in the bigger scheme of things in life, but she is a good person overall."

Sonia then took control of the situation. "Look, Judith has a valid point. We have to think about helping Carmelina — she's too young and naive to know what to do. Any ideas?"

"Let's be sensible, too. This problem can potentially sink Karl Williams and the company. We would all be out of a job. So, in the process of sinking him, we would all go down with the ship. There are no jobs out there, not even in San Antonio. Think of our families," suggested Lizbet.

"Let me see if I understand what you just said, Lizbet. Are you saying that we should cover up the rape of this innocent and now-pregnant Carmelina just because it will hurt us financially?" challenged Rosalba, getting ready for battle.

"You said it very well. That is what I mean. And don't forget the truly fatal weakness of most of our co-workers: Many of us are illegal. We cannot ignore that, in our attempt to uphold the moral principle of helping a pregnant woman, we would be violating several other moral standards and producing pain for dozens of families."

Rita intervened, almost casually. "So what's the big deal with her getting pregnant, anyway? She can get help at the welfare office. Come on, girls! Get over it — she'll be fine. As soon as she gives birth to the little rat, she'll be out dancing again."

Olivia was listening, and she knew it would be a difficult choice. "Maybe there is a way to help Carmelina without jeopardizing everyone's job," she offered. All eyes were on her.

So Judith spoke. "Okay, Olivia — spit it out."

"We can form a small committee among us — and others — and approach Karl Williams to let him know that Carmelina is pregnant and that she'll soon be filing rape charges against him. That she's a minor would make it even worse. Since the rape charge will most likely lead to his downfall and imprisonment, we'll say that we would like to keep the company going since it feeds all our families. To facilitate this, we'll suggest that he transfer the ownership of the company into a trust that all we employees will own, and we would even hire him as the general manager as long as he abides by the new rules to be created by the new owners — that is, all of us."

"Why would he give us the company if he's going down anyway? Out of vengeance, wouldn't he just prefer to see it close rather than having us as the new owners?" asked Sonia.

"Yes, that might be his first reaction to this shocking proposal," explained Olivia. "But we would slowly lead him into making an alternative suggestion."

There was a moment of silence as everyone wondered just what that would be. Glenda spoke. "Alright — and what are we talking about?"

Olivia explained. "When he first shoots down our proposal, we can put the ball back in his court. 'Well, Mr. Williams, when Carmelina files soon, the rape charge will be coming your way. That's a first-degree felony with prison time and the requirement to register as a sex offender for the rest of your life. Most likely, you will lose all your company's military contracts. We are sure your family, especially your wife, would suffer greatly. But if you're not happy with our proposal to save the company, what would you suggest instead to save your hide?'"

"Olivia, that's brilliant! I didn't know you had it in you!" exclaimed Glenda.

"I'm gearing up to battle The Beast, remember, so I've been reading a lot. Should have done that a long time ago," articulated Olivia.

"And, so, what happens next?" broke in Rita with a blank look on her face.

"My guess is that he will propose that we talk to Carmelina so that she does not report the rape to the authorities, and, in return, he will transfer the company into an employee trust," continued Olivia. "It is important that he make the suggestion himself, so that, in the future, he will not be able to accuse us of blackmail."

"You are all full of shit!" growled Rosalba. "We are using Carmelina here like a pawn to get this or that. But she is a pregnant girl, and we cannot just treat her as if all her rights are negotiable. We are overstepping our liberties as her friends. Damn!"

After a few moments to let the expletives sink in, Sonia added, "Rosalba, you are right, but so is Olivia. What benefit does the girl get if Karl Williams is sent to prison for five years? That's an empty victory, if we can even call it that. Now, if Carmelina were to get, say, 25% of the company shares in the trust, and the remaining 75% were to be distributed evenly among the other 65-or-so employees, that would be a real benefit to her and her baby, wouldn't you say?"

"That's a great idea," opined Rita.

"Of course, our job would be to prod Williams into making the suggestion that he would place the company in a trust, on the condition that Carmelina not report the rape. We would inform Carmelina and her parents of Williams' suggestion and let them weigh the relative merits of reporting and not report-ing. It would be their decision, not ours. Would that be fair to all?" questioned Sonia, looking all the women in the eye. Nobody objected to the plan.

It was already late afternoon, and everyone was tired out from the intense discussion. One by one, they left, each with a little bundle of Matt's special tamales. Olivia and Gabriela got to their apartment by early evening, exhausted but more calm than they had been that morning. After putting Gabriela to bed, Olivia continued with her psychology readings. She knew that DSS would be calling again soon with another volley of demands to strengthen their case against her. But at the back of her mind was one more unsettled matter that tore up her insides. She needed to confront her grandfather who was also her father.

CHAPTER 12

In the morning, Olivia called her friend Rosalba and asked her if she could watch Gabriela. She readily agreed and came over within an hour. Rosalba had babysat Gabriela before, and Olivia had noticed that Gabriela really liked her. Before Olivia went off on her mission, she phoned Jason and told him she would like to see him sometime that afternoon to discuss all the new developments, and he responded that he definitely would like to see her that day. He would wait for her phone call at his home.

On the bus to East Houston to see her grandparents, Tomas and Florencia Cervantes, Olivia had time to think about the matter. Her mind had been preoccupied with so many other crises that she had relegated this issue to the back burner of her soul. *Should I hate the bastard who did this to my mother? But he didn't do it to me — he did it to her. That's her battle, isn't it? Yet, she, in turn, betrayed me. How should I open this subject? Should I hit him with the claw hammer I just bought in case I need to defend myself? And how should I feel about my grandmother Florencia, who kept quiet about it? Did she even attempt to protect her two daughters?* These were her thoughts as the bus sped to Red Bluff Road in the Pasadena section of East Houston.

There were lots of Hispanic folks in that neighborhood. Tomas kept the front lawn nicely trimmed, while Florencia took care of the inside of the house. There were three modest bedrooms — but two of them had horror stories to tell. The ugly green wallpaper remembered the muffled screams of terror in the middle of the night.

The bus arrived at the bus stop near the old house. Olivia walked the extra twenty yards to the house and rang the bell. She had no idea how this would turn out.

Tomas answered the door. "Olivia, it's so nice to see you again," he said as he hugged her — maybe not in the right way, as it did not feel like a grandfatherly hug to her.

He was now 70, beefy, bald, about Olivia's height, with wandering eyes. He took her by the hand and led her into the kitchen. "Hey, Flo — look. We have Olivia here. She came to visit."

Florencia came in through the back door — she had been tending to the clothesline. "Hello, Olivia. You are looking very nice. Where is the little one?" she asked, with a flat expression on her face.

"Oh, she couldn't make it, grandma. Feeling a little under the weather, so I got a babysitter."

Florencia was 68, but her permanently depressed face made her look like she was 85, and her skeletal body caused her clothes to just hang on her, as they would on a hanger — no shape at all. Her eyes were sunk deep into their sockets, her skin covered with dozens of age spots. Olivia felt it was very unpleasant just to look at her.

"Come, sit," offered Tomas as he pulled a chair from the small kitchen table.

"I will get the coffee started. We have some fresh *cuernitos* from Chucho's Bakery down the block," stammered Florencia, revealing a little of her neurological impediments.

It really was a very small kitchen, painted white, with some pink trim. The counters had a linoleum top which had been severely scored from cutting fruits or vegetables on it directly, without using a cutting board. Well, it was about 30 years old, besides. The sink had some rust on the bottom, and its two faucets looked ancient. Not a whole lot of cabinets — but their wood stain finish was too dark. It made them look almost black, so it was good that there weren't too many of them. But the kitchen was clean, and it smelled good.

They chatted aimlessly in the kitchen for about 30 minutes, until all the *cuernitos* were gone. Then they got their second cup of coffee. Florencia opted for a more comfortable seat, so she moved with her coffee cup to the living room, just a few steps away. Olivia had run out of neutral subjects to talk about, so she knew it was time to do what she had gone there for, but she didn't know exactly how to open that Pandora's box — this one with just venomous snakes in it.

"Grandpa, you know I am 28, so I'm at that age when we all start getting more curious about our histories. How did you find out in 1982 that my mamma had gotten killed on that highway in front of the motel?"

"Just like everybody else, I suppose. The police reported it."

"And how was she, my mamma, when she was growing up? Did she give you much trouble?"

"Not really. Kinda quiet. Spent a lot of time in her room. We all were devastated when we heard she had been killed on that highway — right, Flo?"

"We sure were," answered Florencia, unconvincingly, from the living room.

"But did the police come here to inform you, or did you just hear the police report on the news?"

"We must have heard it on the news. I can't recall that very clearly." He squirmed a little in his seat and answered without looking Olivia in the eye.

"And you, Grandma — how did you hear about it?"

"Your grandfather told me."

"Who went to her funeral?"

There was a bit of a silence as Tomas and Florencia both hoped that the other would tackle that question, but the silence went on for a couple of uncomfortable seconds too long. Tomas then spoke. "We all did. I guess you were too little and too scared to go."

"What cemetery is she buried at?"

Tomas started scratching his head in a vain attempt to project that he was thinking hard about it. His heart rate increased, and there was a hint of cold sweat on his forehead.

Olivia deliberately let a minute go by, permitting Tomas to continue with his pitiful ruse. The silence increased the pressure on his soul, she felt.

"The reason I ask is because, now, I am ready to go visit her grave. What cemetery is she buried at?"

"Olivia, it's been too long. I guess we've forgotten," offered Tomas.

"I can understand that. But, in the beginning, you knew, so, you must have visited her grave. Have you and grandma visited her often?"

Tomas was trying desperately to appear calm and collected, even sad, as he frantically constructed answers out of thin air, hoping that Olivia would just tire of not getting anywhere with her questions. But Olivia was one step ahead, for she, too, was trying desperately to appear calm and collected when her insides were already boiling because she sensed that they were both shamelessly lying to her. She planned to keep asking, because, sooner or later, Tomas would crack from having to repeatedly tackle the impossible task of inventing innocent answers for questions that would surely incriminate him in the rape of his two minor daughters.

"Yes, in the beginning, we visited often and took flowers. We even had a special mass for her at St. Patrick's Church. Now we are too old to be doing that."

"So, if I go to St. Patrick's Church, I can ask them at what cemetery they had the funeral, right? All churches keep records of that sort of thing."

All of a sudden, the kitchen started feeling rather hot and small for Tomas, who pushed back on his chair to increase the distance to Olivia's face and her now-piercing eyes. Olivia sensed this and leaned forward a bit to compensate.

"Olivia, dear — why ask these questions now? Just let your mother rest in peace," pleaded Tomas, feigning a caring attitude. He started to sense that Olivia was fishing for other, more damning information, but maybe it was just his paranoia. He wasn't sure.

"Grandpa, the other day, I visited Aunt Jenny, and she told me something about you that upset me very, very much. Shall I tell you what it was?"

Tomas's blood must have gone ice cold when those words reached his heart, for he well knew what he had done to his daughter Jenny when she was but a small child. Olivia could see that there was practically no blood left in his face — he was as white as powdered sugar. And, just as before, she waited and waited patiently and silently for his answer.

"I am surprised that you would pay any attention to her. Everybody knows that she is a split personality and that she talks to spirits and ghosts. She makes up some pretty wild stories, too."

"But grandpa — you are a smart man. Do you have any idea whatsoever why she might be suffering from multiple personalities? The root of these things is always in traumatic childhood experiences. That was her room, over there, on the right," specified Olivia as she pointed to little Jenny's room, hoping to bring into focus whatever had happened there, many years ago.

"You are asking me to do a psychological analysis of a demented person. How would I do that? We can't believe anything she says — she's a basket case."

"Isn't it sad that you refer to your daughter Jenny as a 'basket case'? Did you ever even love her?" she asked, with incredulity in her eyes.

"It's ridiculous that you ask me if I loved Jenny."

"When she's feeling calm, she remembers many details, grandpa. I am sure that the most horrid are stored in other parts of her soul — the personalities you talk about. Do you want to hear the awful thing she told me about you?"

They had been wondering, but now Tomas and Florencia knew for sure that this was no casual visit from Olivia. Both showed the look of death on their faces.

"I am beginning to feel that you came here just to insult us. I am your grandfather. I demand more respect than this," he stormed, with a growing hostility in his predator eyes.

Tomas knew that Olivia was skillfully painting them into a corner with every false response they gave her. They couldn't keep up the lie much longer.

"Okay, I won't tell you just yet what Jenny told me, but one thing I know for sure is that loving parents will never, ever, ever forget where they buried their child. Never, ever!!! Yet you are claiming you forgot. Either you are lying that you forgot, or you are lying that you buried her. Which is it, Tomas?" asked Olivia in a more aggressive tone.

For the first time in her life, Olivia had called her grandfather by his first name. Tomas knew that things were deteriorating rapidly, and the mounting perspiration on his brow showed it. "And you, grandma, do you know where mamma is buried?"

Florencia did not reply, and neither did her face acknowledge the question. But her eyes betrayed her inner workings — there was something percolating inside her.

"Look, Olivia dear. We don't know where you are going with this line of questioning, but you should show more respect to your elders. We detest your insinuations. Perhaps it's time for you to leave," scolded Tomas.

Never had Olivia's grandparents ever asked her to leave their house. Of course, never had Olivia had the courage to confront them about her past, either. Things were breaking down very quickly. They were lying to her, to her face, and, now, he wanted to get rid of her, to keep the ugly truths secret forever. Her indignant rage forced her to push back, with a level of determination she didn't know she had.

"Tomas, do you really think that you can get me to leave your house without my killing you first?" asked Olivia with a scowl on her face. Her cards were now on the table — there was no turning back. With those words, the illusory nature of her relationship to her grandparents was destroyed, and it lay in ruins in Olivia's anguished heart.

Her words sent a deep chill down to his gut, for never, ever, had he been threatened in this manner. And by a puny woman at that! Olivia, too, got scared that she had produced those words so spontaneously. She asked herself if she was serious, if she would actually do it. Maybe subconsciously? Well, why had she bought that claw hammer? Definitely lethal if it struck someone's skull.

The fuming coward weighed his choices carefully and opted to backtrack a bit. He said, "Well, at least show some respect."

"You mean just like you showed mamma when she was fourteen?"

He now knew that Olivia knew about Frida and the real nature of her pregnancy at that age. But maybe not. He was hoping that the situation was not as critical as he perceived it to be. Maybe he was just getting paranoid again. *Yes, that's it! She's just bluffing!* But just the same, he did not ask her what she meant by that remark.

""My last statement was quite ambiguous, Tomas. Why aren't you asking me what I meant by it?"

"What for? You are talking about simple respect. Anybody can see that."

"Tomas, did you respect your daughter Frida?" Olivia moved her gaze over to Florencia, who by now had the beginnings of tears in her eyes. Tomas, meanwhile, was oozing cold sweat, like a tall glass of ice water.

"Of course, I did. I had full respect for our two daughters. How dare you question my love for Frida and Jenny!"

From the living room, Florencia finally spoke up, in a weak voice. "Tomas, why don't you just go ahead and tell Olivia how you savagely raped both of your daughters?"

"Shut the fuck up, you old woman!" shouted Tomas.

Then everything went quiet. The only sound in that kitchen was the faint raspy mechanism of an old Haste wristwatch from Mexico, precariously hanging from the towel rack.

Olivia wanted to explode with full, unbridled rage at Tomas but was trying hard to contain her reaction — the only evidence of the enormous emotive pressure inside her was the rabid glare from her normally beautiful eyes. Tomas was expressionless as he looked at the surface of the table, and he was now dripping sweat. He definitely did not want to look at Olivia's eyes — he was no match for the rage radiating from them. But maybe he too was ready to let out his rage at being uncovered. It was his secret, they were his daughters, he was in charge, he could do anything he pleased to them — how dare anyone complain about it? *How dare anyone question his authority?* He just got madder and madder.

Florencia shuffled slowly toward the kitchen, pulled out a chair, and joined Olivia and Tomas at the table. The cracked dam was about to break.

She gave Olivia a very sad, hopeless look and spoke. "Your poor mother Frida was 13 when he raped her the first time. At 14, she was pregnant, and, at 15, she gave birth to you. Your grandfather, here, is also your father. That must have destroyed her soul. He continued with the assaults, and Frida gave birth again, this time to your brother Benito, when she was 20 — you were 5 years old. Your Aunt Jenny suffered through the same sexual attacks, but she never got pregnant, to my knowledge. He got started with her when we were still living in that hut in Monterrey, Mexico — she was barely 8 years old. Maybe that is why, tragically, she is now disturbed. That is the whole story, Olivia."

The story could not have been clearer. Olivia wanted Florencia to give her more damning details quickly, for she feared that Tomas was ready to explode, and he would probably force Florencia into silence, if not actually hit her. "And my mother at the motel?"

"She did not die on that highway, or anywhere else, at that time. From the newspapers, we all knew that she had abandoned you and Benito at the motel and that she had taken the bus to Dallas. Jenny made up the lie about her having been killed — she wanted to spare you the pain of the truth, especially because she didn't think that your mother would ever come back. Jenny knew the painful truths about your mother's pregnancies. She could understand why Frida would just want to flee from her past."

"So Jenny lied because she was trying to protect Benito and me?"

"Yes. When Tomas heard about how Jenny was handling Frida's disappearance, he said that the lie would serve us well because we would not have to deal with Frida's increasing hostility toward us for the assaults. With Frida declared 'dead' by the family, there would be no need to go look for her in Dallas — that could only mean continued trouble. So Tomas and I, regrettably, promulgated the lie about Frida's demise. There is no grave. She might still be alive. Please forgive me for not having spoken up earlier. I am as guilty as this repugnant animal sitting with us at the table."

"If I had known at age 9 or later that my mother was, indeed, not dead, I would have asked any official agency to help me find her, in Dallas or anywhere in the world. The lie, in a way, has kept me from looking for my mother for 19 years! Your actions were vile, unconscionable!"

"Yes, it was a tragic and self-serving decision."

Olivia chose her next words carefully. "You realize that this makes me want to kill you both?" Olivia started to tremble with barely containable rage. But she forged on to get the most out of Florencia's willingness to talk, in spite of Tomas giving Florencia hateful stares.

Almost in a whisper, Olivia directed her next question at Florencia. "And why did you keep the rapes a secret for years? Why did you not protect mamma and Jenny?"

"I was afraid. In Mexico, he threatened to cut out my tongue with wire cutters. After we moved here in 1971, he would threaten to call the immigration authorities to send me back to Mexico. I had nowhere else to go to. Besides him, I had no family. I was deathly afraid."

Tomas's dark shirt was drenched with panic sweat by now; he had held out as long as he could, but the vile truth was out. He reacted with volcanic rage.

"Listen, you tricky little bitch! You are a whore just like your mother, Frida The Slut! You can't come into my house and make these accusations. Do you want me to throw you out? Is that it? Is that it, little bitch?" screeched Tomas as he got up from his chair and assumed a threatening posture. But, at the same time, Olivia sprang from her chair like a ferocious tiger protecting her cubs, with the claw hammer she had hidden in her purse, just in case. In less than a split second she had the hammer high up in the air, ready to strike. Never in her entire life had she been driven to the point of aggression, but she was tired at being taken advantage of, and she was determined to defend her position, no matter what.

"Shut the fuck up, you filthy rapist, before I bury this steel claw into your miserable skull! I am not finished — so sit the fuck down!"

"Well, fuck you, bastard bitch! How dare you talk to me that way! I am your elder, so fuck you, and fuck your whore mother, too!"

It was clear to Olivia that Tomas was not going to back down easily. She already had her claw hammer up in the air, with a firm grip on it, so with all her strength she slammed it down on the hand that he still had on the table. His bones made an awful crunching sound, and then he let out an agonizing scream. "Aaayyyeeeeeee!!!" All his aggressive macho posturing quickly evaporated, and he turned into a clump of beefy lard, holding his broken, bloody hand and grimacing from the intense pain of all the shattered bones. Florencia hardly expressed any emotion at the scene.

"Put this dish cloth around your filthy hand. Sit down and shut up, unless you want me to go for your other hand, you perverted fuck." He reluctantly complied.

Olivia still was breathing heavily from the altercation. She really was itching to hit her mother's rapist on the head with the claw side of the hammer, but she was trying hard to restrain her emotions. Instead she violently smacked the table five times with the hammer to release her anger. It took a few minutes for her to feel a bit less furious. The previously beautiful table now had three major cracks, and the two coffee cups had bounced off the table onto the wooden floor.

In heavy-breathing spurts, she continued as well as she could, still with the hammer firmly in her hand. "Now, grandma — let's go back to what you said about him threatening to call the immigration authorities or cutting your tongue out. Didn't it seem to you that you were essentially making a deal with the devil? You made the decision to keep quiet about the rapes of your own daughters! That is inconceivable!"

"Well, it sounds craven and heartless now, I know. In Mexico, he was a part-time butcher, so I saw how, without any feeling, he would kill beef cows and slice them up — horrible, bloody scenes that he forced me to watch. I was afraid he would do that to me — had nightmares about it. And, here in Houston, I was petrified of being sent back to Mexico and never seeing my daughters again, so my protests against what he was doing gradually just died out. It was a very cowardly thing for me to do. I am sorry. I should have protected Frida and Jenny. That is why my life and my self-respect ended pretty much when I realized I had slowly made the decision not to say anything. I just withdrew to my bedroom and pretended not to hear their muffled screams of agony. I know my soul will go to hell for this. I know now I cannot blame God for giving me this sadistic, brutal husband, and I cannot justifiably ask for forgiveness. I ruined the lives of my two innocent daughters."

Turning to Tomas, Olivia growled. "And you, you piece of dog shit, what do you have to say about all this?"

He was still in a lot of pain, looking down at the kitchen floor. His shattered hand was not covered well, so it was dripping blood.

"I asked you a question, you despicable parasite!"

"What the fuck do you want me to say? You now know it all. What Flo said about my threatening her is correct, except that, when I was doing that, it didn't seem wrong at that time. It felt normal. Others were doing it, too."

"And, now, how do you feel about it?"

"Now it's too late; there are so many lies, too. Besides, if I hadn't fucked Frida, you would not have been born. So, in a very real way, you owe me, bitch! *You owe me your life, you cheap whore!*"

"You unrepentant motherfucker!" She got up from her chair again, and while Tomas quickly covered his face in defensive anticipation, she turned the hammer, claw side down, and she impacted his knee with the full force of all her rage. As the entire length of the sharp claw penetrated his knee, Tomas let out another horrible scream. *"Aaaaayyyyyeeee!!!"* She yanked the hammer out and wiped it on his pants. With hammer in hand, she waited for his groans to die out. "Are you finished moaning, you bastard?"

She needed time to calm down too, and, after about ten minutes, she proceeded softly. "So, what shall I do to you concerning what you did to my mother and to Aunt Jenny? The police will want to do a DNA test. Legal records will show that my mother gave birth to me when she was 15, a minor. Florencia and Jenny will testify that you first raped your two daughters when they were very young — Jenny was 8, and mamma was 13. I think you will be put away for at least thirty years. At your age, Tomas, that is equivalent to a death sentence. Too bad you'll just die and rot before the thirty years are up, you filthy sewer rat."

"Okay, little bitch — you win. I'm done. Now get the fuck out of my house. There's something important I have to take care of."

Yes, Olivia felt that there really wasn't anything else to cover in her mother's childhood house of terror. She had another short conversation with Florencia and then asked her if she felt alright, given that Tomas's heinous deeds had been exposed and he might become unpredictable. Florencia thought about it for a while and responded, "Whichever way it goes, I will be able to rest better." It was somewhat cryptic, but Olivia hazarded a guess. She, too, thought that something unpleasant was bound to happen and that there would be one or two cadavers in this house soon. She made peace with either possibility, for they both had done irreparable damage to their two young daughters and to Olivia — first by giving her a shameful paternal lineage and, second, by causing profound disarray in Frida's heart, which led to Olivia and Benito being left without a mother at a tender age.

As she was going out the door, Olivia stopped, turned her head, and said, "Goodbye, Florencia. You won't be seeing me again. Thank you for finally telling me the truth. I know you suffered, too. We all did. I will try to locate mamma, and, if I find her, I will tell her that you deeply regret your failure to protect her. I believe she would want to hear that."

"Yes, please do. And tell her to never forgive me for what I have done. I caused her far too much damage and pain; my heart is really beyond redemption. I just need to die."

CHAPTER 13

Olivia was still trembling when she got on the bus, as she was absolutely terrified at the realization that she had come so close to actually killing another person, her perverted and degenerate grandfather, Tomas. In fact, she was even feeling guilty that she had struck him twice with that hammer. So, to make herself feel better, she reminded herself that she had been dealing with a very evil person who had caused many people significant harm. And how could he ever have said that Olivia owed him her life, the life that was born because of his violation of Frida? Olivia just kept reviewing everything to pacify her guilt about how she had reacted.

It was just past one o'clock when she had to change buses, so, at the terminal, she called Jason to reconfirm their lunch appointment at his house. She also called Rosalba to see how Gabriela was doing. Everything was in order. She disposed of the bloody hammer in a trashcan and then sat on a bench reading the psychology book she had with her until the next bus arrived, although she was too agitated to concentrate on the material. That bus ride took about thirty minutes and took her to the corner of Kuykendahl Road and Interstate 45 in thirty minutes. She walked two blocks to his house and was about to ring the doorbell when the door opened. He had been eagerly awaiting her arrival. "Olivia, nice to see you again." He gave her a quick hug and the customary air kiss.

Jason lived in North Houston in a very nice Colonial four-bedroom house. Even though he was single, he had bought a large house just in case he happened to get married in a few years.

He asked her to step inside. Immediately she was in awe at the beauty of the foyer area and the sparkling chandelier that adorned it. An elegant arched staircase with a cherry wood handrail and bannister led up to the second floor, where all the bedrooms were located. There on the first floor was a very large, beautifully carpeted living room with oversized picture windows, easy chairs, and sofas — it could easily entertain about twenty people.

"Jason, this is not a house — it's a palace! It's gorgeous."

"Well, thanks, Olivia. I like a large house because I spend a lot of time writing here, and I tend to get bored with the same room, so I switch around every few days. Come to the kitchen. I'll start the spaghetti."

The kitchen itself was about the size of Olivia's entire apartment. It was fully equipped with just about every electrical appliance on the market and had about a dozen pots and pans hanging from a lighted pot rack secured by wrought-iron bars from the ceiling. "I've already made the meatballs, but, if you wish, you can just have the tomato sauce with mushrooms on your spaghetti."

"I had a rough morning, so let's go for the big sauce with meatballs," she said.

He served her a glass of red wine while the spaghetti cooked.

"Would you care to tell me how it went with your visit to your grandparents this morning?"

"I think that, within 48 hours, we are going to hear about a murder-suicide at their home."

"Olivia, what in the world makes you say such a thing?"

Little by little, piece by piece, Olivia revealed to Jason the horrific details of her history. She also told him how she had struck Tomas on the hand and leg with the hammer.

Jason had never thought that Olivia was capable of hurting anyone, so he knew that the situation had to have been rather explosive.

"So, now that Don Tomas's secrets are out in the open, do you really feel that he will kill your grandmother and then himself?"

Lunch was ready. They sat at a more intimate breakfast table to eat.

"Don Tomas is a ruthless and proud man. I think that he knows that Florencia and I have no more respect for him. More importantly, we don't fear him. It's almost like the end of his kingdom."

"But you also told him that the police would become involved because of his raping his two daughters, right?"

"Yes, I said that DNA tests were infallible and that court records would show that my mother Frida was 14 when he got her pregnant. He's expecting that it would get him a thirty-year sentence."

"That would be the end of the world for him."

"Right. That's why I feel that he might commit suicide. I'm not real sure if he would kill Florencia, although I suspect she might coax him into doing it. Yes, it would be a murder-suicide. And it might occur sooner, rather than later."

"But, Olivia, I feel this might have a very negative impact on your current problems with DSS."

Olivia did not answer right away and became pensive.

Jason continued. "Normally, they would have no reason to get involved with grandparents, but, in your case, I think they'll dig until they find something to use against you."

"I thought that, as long as I was a good parent, they could not do anything."

"Well, that is the PR myth they like to promote, but I've heard through my contacts how they do not like anyone questioning the way they work, and you said that you blew up at that doctor who did the weird exam on Gabriela."

"Yes, that creep. I was not about to leave her alone with him, Jason. He had a strange-looking instrument with him when she was on the examination table — a rod with a sharp hook at the end. Have you ever heard of anything like that?"

"Not for exams on five-year-old girls, but I've heard that sometimes doctors use a hard plastic rod with a small hook at the end to release the amniotic water during a delivery."

"So, Jason, what do you think will happen to Gabriela and me in this DSS case? I really am worried."

"It doesn't look good — for several reasons. I've already told you that the case worker, Greta Haroldson, is known for her bulldog tactics against families. You said yourself that she was really nasty toward you during her visit to your apartment. Then we have to worry about what else was said by the person who reported you to the agency. Maybe, out of some kind of vengeance, this person said other things that have not been revealed to you yet. We also have your strong defensive reaction toward that doctor. Finally, there is the problem of your painful history — lots of inappropriate stuff that DSS will unjustly use to indicate that Gabriela should not stay in your custody."

"Doesn't it seem that my situation is hopeless?"

"No, Olivia — it's not hopeless. It'll be a hard fight, but it's not hopeless. Besides, you have me on your side."

Just knowing that Jason would stand with her against The Beast was enough to help her see a glimmer of hope.

"I just hate what I've become."

"What do you mean?"

"It just seems that, since I learned that my mother did not actually die in front of that motel, I've become more aggressive — rageful, even. I used to be more peaceful."

"From what I know about you, I would not call it "peaceful." I would say you were passive, even depressive."

She thought about it for a moment. "But, depressed about what?"

"Depressed about your having been left without a mother at that tender age. I think Jenny did the best she could with you, but she's not the mothering type."

"But I did not feel depressed, or, rather, I did not think I was depressed."

"Maybe you had adjusted to that way of life. It was normal for you to feel that way. Maybe you just didn't notice the depression anymore, but I would bet that you certainly could not say you were happy, or that, several times a year, you felt pure joy in your heart during certain activities."

A certain solemnity came over Olivia, and the spaghetti started tasting rather bland. The word "joy" stuck in her heart. His words made sense. But wasn't it "joy" when she sat in front of the television to watch her soap operas? Wasn't she experiencing joy in life when she laughed with her friends at work? And wasn't she absolutely joyful when the hated Bull Garcia finally got off her and left?

"But, Jason, I have felt joyful many times in my life." She told him of all the examples swirling in her head, sure that he would see that she knew about joy.

"Well, let's see. When you are watching your soap operas, you are being entertained — you experience relaxation, comfort, and enjoyment. That is not joy. When you are laughing with your friends, you are having fun and the comfort of socializing with similar others. When that monster Bull Garcia finally leaves your apartment, you experience welcome relief from a very toxic situation. But that is not joy."

"Then I guess I am all confused." By this time, Olivia was barely nibbling at her food, and Jason had noticed. So he offered, "Olivia, you don't seem that hungry. Do you want to switch over to coffee and some Maria Cookies?" She readily agreed.

They were both sitting on the couch, in front of which was a beautiful walnut coffee table. Olivia had the habit of breaking up her Maria Cookies and dropping them into the hot coffee for a few seconds. She would then scoop them up with a spoon.

"I guess you are saying that I really do not know what joy is — right?"

"You've been through a lot, and now you are tackling some very difficult situations, one of which is finding your mother, who might still be alive."

"And what does it mean when a person does not know what joy is?" Olivia started feeling a bit defensive since she thought that maybe Jason was implying that he had a better way of life.

"In your case, it is a more unfortunate situation because you have a young daughter — parents, as a general rule, pass on their unhappiness to their children. But that can be remedied."

"Okay, so tell me about your definition of joy, since, obviously, I have no clue." She was now busy slurping up the wet cookies from her large spoon.

"Not sure if there is a standard definition, but I have friends who are joyful, and I myself can say that I have experienced joy on many occasions."

"So, spit it out, Einstein."

"The best example is a friend of mine who's the conductor of the Houston Symphony. He's not a religious man — never has been. But he tells me that, when he is conducting one of his favorite symphonies, Beethoven's Choral Ninth, and the orchestra is in full brass forte with chorus, he gets an incredible, uplifting feeling that goes beyond extreme happiness, beyond anything mortal here on earth. If there is a heaven, he says, he is there, in heaven, while on the podium conducting the strings, the brass, the percussion. He is permitted momentary entrance as the heavenly curtains open to reveal the face of God, creating a mixture of infinite awe, joy, and gratitude to be fully alive as a human being. It is a moment of limitless splendor, vitality, and life. Nothing else on earth even comes close to that incredible time in heaven, touching the face of God."

Olivia knew. She knew instantly that she had never experienced this thing called "joy," even though, all her life, she thought she had. How could she not have known?

"Jason, you are right. Those curtains have never opened for me — I have never touched the face of God — I never knew that it was even possible." Small streams of tears flowed down her cheeks; Jason held her hand.

There was silence on the couch as they both continued to sip their coffees. Jason poured another cup for each.

"That's alright, Olivia — your mother never taught you how to nourish your soul. No fault of hers — she was too depressed herself. Her mother Florencia did not teach her, either." He handed her a napkin for her tears and gave her a quick hug as he got up to clean the table and dishes. It felt like her arms did not want to release him.

As they were doing the dishes together, Olivia lamented, "I think I liked my old self better. I feel bad that I have to scream at people."

"It is actually a very good sign of personal growth. Before you stood up, people would walk all over you, and you let them. For self-respect, you have to defend your dignity and that of your daughter. If you have to scream, then do it. That is the only road to recovery from sadness."

CHAPTER 14

The following day, Olivia was at work when the floor manager summoned her over to his office — there was an emergency call for her. It was Aunt Jenny.

"Olivia, I have very bad news, I think. Police found grandpa and grandma dead in their house. They say they were both shot."

It was not exactly a surprise for Olivia — she just didn't know when it would happen. "Was it a robbery or what?"

"One of them shot the other, and the one who was left alive then committed suicide. I have no idea who shot whom. Do you know?"

"Couldn't even guess. Are you sad about it?"

"No, it doesn't affect me one way or the other. I hope their spirits don't come to haunt me!"

"Oh, no, Aunt Jenny — don't worry about that. If they're dead, they're dead for good. So, what now?"

"There was a police social worker who will help me do the funeral arrangements, but I think it's best to cremate them and skip the funeral."

"Hopefully, there will be no problem in liquidating their meager assets so you can have a little money to pay off your house."

"Well, I will keep you informed. I hope they don't suddenly wake up."

Even though Olivia still had a lot of anger against them, especially at Tomas, she nonetheless felt a sort of loss about their deaths. However bad they had been in reality, they had been good as fake-good people toward her. Their false loving faces had still made an impression on her, since her heart took them at face value. It was this philosophical and emotional conflict that troubled Olivia, for she knew that, in spite of it all, a portion of her history had died along with them. They were evil, but it left a hole in her heart, regardless.

The following two weeks were uneventful. Karl Williams did not bother her at work, although he was still badgering the other employees. If he had been the one who unleashed DSS against her, nobody knew, but maybe he was satisfied with the damage that his move would cause Olivia and Gabriela.

Carmelina was getting bigger, and the women on the soldering line were getting closer to implementing their plan against the ogre — it was a matter of maybe two weeks, they said.

As always, Olivia continued to help Mrs. Brunswick with her essentials, asking her questions more directly associated with her upcoming battle against DSS. Like the others, Mrs. Brunswick advised Olivia to keep on reading on social policy, psychology, and the politics of the legal system. In particular, she was very cynical about judges — she considered them pompous egomaniacs whose rulings were little more than just opinions or political decisions driven by forces the aggrieved would never get to see. Definitely, Olivia was learning a lot from this English lady.

And the monster Bull Garcia kept avoiding Olivia. He, too, was suspect as the one responsible for creating the DSS problem. Olivia would have to be content with just knowing that he was not knocking at her door at night; that was a huge relief.

But on the third week, Olivia received a call from Greta Haroldson's assistant, Susie Drake, and was ordered to attend an appointment with Greta the following day. Olivia arrived at DSS headquarters in downtown Houston at 2:30 P.M., as instructed.

Olivia's heart was pounding as she rode the elevator to the fourth floor. Was this a ruse? Was she going to be arrested? Was she going to be interrogated by Gestapo-type agents who were inclined to make her say the wrong things that would later be used in court? Was she going to be videotaped secretly? She was walking into a hyena lair, and she knew it.

The door was open to suite 408, a waiting room with Susie Drake at the desk. She was about 21 but already had that burned-out, cynical look on her face. "You must be Olivia Cervantes, the suspect in the sexual-abuse case of a five-year-old, right?" The other three people waiting there quickly turned toward Olivia and gave her hateful looks. *How could such an innocent-looking woman be a depraved monster preying on five-year-old children?* they must have thought.

"Well, I am Olivia Cervantes," she said meekly, having been caught off guard by the unexpected salvo.

"Take a seat."

The waiting room was dreadful. It felt almost like Death Row, just waiting to be executed by those in power. It was dull yellow with animal paintings, but not even the animals looked happy. The five cushiony seats looked like they had been there for at least ten years, lending the area an aura of hopelessness. That is how Olivia felt.

About ten minutes later, Susie Drake called out, "Mr. Hinojosa, Ms. Haroldson will see you now." There was a door in the back of the suite with her name in big, bold letters. He went in.

Olivia was perplexed, since this man was wearing a business suit and had a briefcase. The other two people waiting there looked like anxious parents, but he was clearly in a different category.

"Ms. Haroldson?"

"Dr. Manuel Hinojosa, right?" They shook hands.

"I understand you wanted to see me for a possible outside consultancy for DSS."

"Sit down, please."

He was a clinical psychologist, about 35, and eager to build his consulting business. Greta Haroldson had researched his background and learned that he was single, had no kids, was relatively young, and was yearning to earn more money. She had given him a call.

"As I mentioned to you over the phone, we are in need of an extra clinical psychologist with your expertise to serve on an as-needed basis to do forensic psychological evaluations on parents and kids. These will be used in court in deciding custody and treatment issues. We can't seem to keep up with the number of kids that have to be permanently removed from their homes. I understand that you've done quite a few evaluations, but these have been for psychotherapeutic purposes — am I correct?" Greta was looking at him with steely eyes and an almost menacing look, as if to establish some sort of hierarchical dominant order.

Dr. Hinojosa, feeling the radiation from Haroldson's eyes, squirmed a bit on his seat and replied, "Yes, I've done several hundred evaluations of children and adults."

Greta got up from her seat behind the desk, as always, dressed to kill. She was wearing a tailored-collar pink blouse with long sleeves, a white midi pencil skirt, and neutral beige pumps. Her hair was in a French bun, as always, and her radiant pink lips matched her blouse perfectly. She looked more like one of the glamorous women who handle perfumes for Bloomingdale's than a serious social worker. Without taking her eyes off her prey, she walked behind him and said, "I'm just getting some papers; you can keep looking forward if you don't mind." This just caused him to become more uneasy, but he did not complain.

"What we are looking for, Dr. Hinojosa, is someone who understands our mission and is able to work with us toward that end. In return, you will get more evaluation requests than you can possibly handle, with all the remuneration that will go with that, of course. You will prosper very quickly. Do you know what I mean when I say 'our mission'?"

"Yes, of course. Your mission is to provide the best possible service and care for all children and their families."

She went completely behind him and returned to her desk from the other side. "It's more complicated than that, doctor. When we get a case, we — and only we — determine if a kid needs to be removed from its parents. A conflicting psychological evaluation would be embarrassing for us in court and would definitely be counter-productive to our plans for that particular family and the kid. Can you read between the lines, doctor, or are you that fucking naive?" Haroldson gave Dr. Hinojosa a glaring, hateful look as she raised her voice and spit out those words.

Being used to good manners and cordiality, the doctor was taken aback by Greta's commanding hostility, yet he was very eager for the great professional opportunity to perform more than a hundred evaluations per month and for the considerable amounts of money that would entail. "I get what it is you are trying to tell me. You want me to look especially hard at each evaluation for data that will confirm the looming decision by DSS to remove a child from its home. Is that the gist of it?"

"You know, Dr. Hinojosa, at DSS, we have a small army of cooperating psychologists, psychiatrists, physicians, physical therapists, and even judges who know about our important mission and who will provide evaluations, recommendations, and decisions that are exactly what we want. If you ever, ever, perform an evaluation that concludes that a parent or a child does not exhibit a certain pathology that DSS says they do exhibit, you will never again be asked to perform evaluations for us. Actually, you would be very foolish to bite the hand that feeds you, wouldn't you?"

"Yes, yes — you have a point. I can see that you are very dedicated to the mission of protecting children, definitely." Even though he agreed with her verbally, he was almost in a daze as to her brazen directive to alter his evaluations to suit whatever DSS wanted for a particular case. But, like all the others who through the years had been in that seat before him, he knew he would oblige DSS and see his practice balloon in size. It was an irresistible offer. *Besides,* he thought, *it is all for a good cause.*

"Good. In the beginning, you will need to contact me before you write your final report on a case, but, with time, you will know what we want from the language we use in the file that we refer to you. So thank you for coming — and get out, as I have better things to do."

As the psychologist got up from his chair, Greta Haroldson spoke some final words. "Just one final point: Everything we at DSS tell you is absolutely confidential. If we ever discover you have uttered one word of this conversation with anyone, we will make sure your professional career is forever destroyed and your license revoked. Goodbye, doctor. Close the door behind you."

He walked out, still in a foggy state of mind because of the manner in which Haroldson had just treated him. Even though these new evaluation contracts would bring him lucrative business, he knew he had just sold his dignity, his professionalism, and his soul to the devil. Seems that almost everyone who dealt with Greta Haroldson felt diminished as a human being. Well, everyone except her immediate boss, Antonio Guerra, a 51-year-old bureaucrat at heart.

No sooner had Dr. Hinojosa closed the door when Greta went out the other door in her office — it led to a short hallway, directly to Director Guerra's office. She knocked.

"Yes?"

"It's me, Greta."

"Go ahead."

Antonio Guerra had made DSS his career — his life, really. But he was a bureaucrat who looked at budgets, foster-home placement goals, and the overall political scene in which DSS provided services. One thing he did not like was the down-and-dirty details of the business, which is what he called it. For that, he knew he could depend on his protégé, Greta Haroldson. All the department social workers knew what they had to do to meet DSS goals and objectives, but Greta was exemplary in that she had a seemingly innate, rabid disposition to force people to do what DSS wanted. Antonio Guerra often privately mused at the apparent contradiction of her having a hyena personality in a profession that required compassion and the ethics to do what was right for each particular child.

She opened the door, went in, and closed it behind her. He was at his desk. "Tony, guess what? I just firmed up another psychology consultant position. He's that Dr. Manuel Hinojosa I told you about. From the spooked-deer look in his eyes I could tell that he's going to do exactly what we tell him — just perfect. Are you pleased?"

"Well, Greta, that is really fine. I knew I could depend on you to increase our pool of available and cooperative psychologists."

In a sultry tone, she added, "Tony, you know me. I always do what you ask me to do. Always."

"Yes, you do. You are reliable."

"Just 'reliable,' Tony? Is that all I am to you?"

"Now, Greta, don't give me that look. Besides, I meant to tell you to please tone down a bit your manner of dress."

Without the slightest embarrassment, she asked, "Why, Tony? Does it make your tool hard?" She just could not take her eyes off him.

"Look, I've told you before that I am a happily married man and have no desire to do anything against my wife, so you are wasting your time. There are younger men out there who would be worthy of your attention."

"Don't kid yourself, Tony. I've noticed how you stare at my bountiful cleavage, especially when I purposefully drop case files near you so I can bend over to get them." She had that look of anticipation, waiting for his reaction to her enticing comment.

"I'm very busy right now. Is there any more news on other consultancy positions?"

She sat in the seat in front of his desk, the one that many a panicked parent had sat in to learn of the fate of his or her children. But she did not cross or close her long and slender legs. It was inevitable that Antonio Guerra's natural animal instincts would perform their biological function, so they guided his eyes, almost against his will and better judgment, and he caught a very enticing and clear glimpse of her smooth white thighs and her lacy black panties. Her eyes were still fixed on his, so she relished, with the excitement of victory, the brief moment when he was staring between her legs with the ardor of an interested and salivating dog but tempered by the anxiety of a married man whose conscience was already punishing him. It was a wordless three seconds that defined the arena where Greta's uncompromising passion would do battle against Antonio Guerra's increasingly feeble attempts to remain faithful to his wife.

Trying to recover from what he knew was a strategic victory for Greta, Antonio quickly turned his gaze toward some irrelevant files on his desk and wiped the sweat beads on his forehead and nose. But she was not going to let go easily. "What's the matter, Tony? Did you see something you like?"

"No, it's that I just remembered that I have a meeting at the Galleria offices of an attorney, so I've got to run. Thanks again for the excellent job of recruiting another sociologist for DSS."

Greta stayed there for about two minutes after he left, replaying in her mind what had just transpired. She had been working on him wisely and slowly for a considerable length of time, and she could sense that her moves were making it increasingly hard for Antonio to continue to resist her body.

It was just a matter of time, she knew, and then he would be all hers. Greta Haroldson always got what she wanted.

She walked back to her office and ordered Susie Drake over the intercom to send in Olivia, who had been getting more and more nervous about the nature of the appointment. She just knew that Greta hated her. Olivia entered the office and closed the door.

"Sit down."

The results of the physical exam on Gabriela were not in, but given the long-standing special arrangement Greta had with the doctor, she knew that the doctor would make them be whatever she wanted — whatever strengthened DSS's position. Because of his reliability, he often just presented his results in court; then afterwards, as a courtesy, he would provide a copy to Greta. To catch Olivia off guard, she bluffed when she said, "I can see in your file that Dr. Krodovic has performed the physical exam on the kid, and I am very much concerned about the results. This certainly calls for a complete and exhaustive investigation of your parenting skills and your background." Greta had a deadly smirk on her face.

"'Concerned'? But, what happened? What did he find? My daughter has never suffered any abuse of any kind!"

"The results are confidential. You are not allowed to see anything until the custody trial."

"'Confidential? This is my daughter. I am her mother. I am entitled to know what the doctor found!"

Greta did not like anyone to challenge her on anything, so she responded with unprofessional fury. "You are entitled to nothing! People like you should not even be allowed to have children. If it were up to me, I would have all of you aliens sterilized within one hour of setting foot on American soil. Not only are you despicable parents, but you also come here to steal our men and contaminate our gene pool!"

Ever since she had found out the truth concerning her mother, Olivia had grown perceptive and keen about personal insults and slights. This was one of them, but she was not about to tell Greta what she really thought about her — that she was a real bitch.

"And what is this about a custody trial?"

"It's starting to look like you are not fit to be a parent to the kid, but there is one thing that perhaps can prove otherwise."

"I'll do whatever you ask of me."

"I have scheduled you and the kid for psychological evaluations. Standard questions. Takes a few hours. He will send us the results, and then we'll see."

"Okay, I will cooperate in full. But I will appreciate it if you stop calling my daughter 'the kid' and call her by her name — 'Gabriela.'"

Greta's demeanor changed from bad to seething worse, as she bared her teeth and opened her eyes to almost twice their size, radiating pure hell and arrogant hatred. "You two-bit Mexican invader! You are telling me what to call your little neighborhood whore? I'll call her what I damn well please, and you can't do shit about it. We're done. Get the appointment slip on your way out. Don't dare miss the evaluation for you and your low-class mongrel."

On her way out the door, Olivia could no longer contain her ire, so she turned to Greta and said, "Women like you, Ms. Haroldson, will always have a barren womb, for God would never send an innocent child into the hell you would surely provide." Olivia closed the door before Greta could devise a response. But it stung, because it felt almost like Olivia had cast a curse on Greta Haroldson and her parched womb. The lack of opportunity to respond fueled the natural hostility that Greta felt toward Olivia and her daughter — toward most people, really, but especially toward those with children — and converted it into an unmitigated and passionate hatred toward mother and daughter. Greta was determined to inflict maximum pain and destruction on those two.

CHAPTER 15

Olivia had already put Gabriela to bed. She settled into her couch, together with some books and magazines that covered several topics in psychology, child rearing, and family relations, but her mind just was not in it. In this peaceful moment when she was not fighting her enemies, her pent-up emotions soon stole her tranquility and poked her heart to make their presence known. It still bothered her immensely that her mother had abandoned her and Benito. Mamma did so, she thought, because Olivia was not worth anything.

Yes, that's right, I am basically a worthless person. I could not give my daughter a father. He deserted me because he, too, knew I was just a piece of trash. I have a stupid, menial job soldering the same boring circuits all day long and breathing toxic metal fumes. And that horrid Bull Garcia raped me so many times with little or no resistance on my part. Maybe it wasn't even rape. Maybe it was masochistic submission, like it said in that magazine article. Maybe I just deserve to be taken and used by any man who wants me and then throws me in the trash afterwards, his animal desires satisfied. Yes, that's right — just throw me in the trash. Just throw me in the trash! Use me all you want, and then throw me in the damned trash!

They were all-consuming — her thoughts and feelings that she was an undisputed failure. And the shame, the shame, the toxic, repugnant shame of her grandfather also being her father. She had been told long ago that a young man identified as being her father had deserted mamma upon learning of her pregnancy. But that had been a lie, a damnable lie, a despicable lie constructed by those whose only concern was to protect their own interests, for her real father had been there all along, living in the same house with them! In the same house with them! He touched Olivia, he kissed her, he even placed her on his lap. She thought it was grandpa, but that was her father, and he was still raping his own daughter — Olivia's mother Frida — by night.

The shame, that awful shame — the only way to get rid of it was to destroy the place where it resided, uninvited. Yes, in her heart. She needed to be dead to end the shame.

These thoughts were coming fast and furious to Olivia, demanding to be acknowledged, not ignored or repressed, and creating revolting emotional reactions in her stomach, in her soul, in her trembling arms. Olivia even wanted to vomit as she thought of how it must have been when she was a toddler, in her crib, and her mamma was in the adjoining bedroom, being savagely raped once more by her own father, Tomas. Little Olivia had been in her crib, totally oblivious to the brutal attacks on her mother, repeated assaults that would eventually result in a second impregnation. Poor Benito — he, too, was born damned through no fault of his own.

Yet it could be that she had not been totally oblivious to the attacks, even at that young age. Olivia remembered her recent visit to her grandmother Florencia, who said that when the attacks were happening, she could hear them very well in her own bedroom but pretended not to. Maybe little Olivia did hear her mother's muffled screams and was scared, mortified really — *What was happening to mamma in the other room?* Now Olivia could not remember ever hearing mamma's screams during those old days when she must have been in her crib, so had she repressed those terrible memories? Were vestiges of these anxious memories now working behind the scenes in her subconscious, manipulating her insecure personality like an unseen hand inside her soul?

These were uncomfortable thoughts that she was having. She again started thinking about how other women, like Sonia, had decent husbands, families, homes. But Olivia had nothing. If it weren't for Gabriela, she thought, she already would have committed suicide. *Yes, suicide, suicide, suicide — throw me in the trash.* The words just kept whirling in her mind. The newspapers would carry the story of her demise:

**BODY OF WORTHLESS WOMAN FOUND IN RIVER
CADAVER TAKEN TO CITY DUMP**

Yes, the city garbage dump would be a fitting end to her miserable life.

The shock of finding out that mamma was probably still alive had already worn off and had been replaced by a moral imperative to find her to confront the abandonment issue with her, if nothing else. And, worse, she still felt very conflicted about her mother being alive. If she found her, would she want to resume some type of relationship with her, if not as mother-daughter, then as what? *If your mother abandons you, would she still be your mother, or would she be your ex-mother? After so many years, does it make a difference if she comes back on her own or if you go find her?*

Too many moral questions, and no answers, she thought.

Emotionally worn out, Olivia fell asleep on the couch, her eyes puffy from all the silent tears. Her books and magazines just slid off her lap onto the floor.

CHAPTER 16

$\mathcal{S}$ome days later, her phone rang at home — it was Jason. "Olivia, I have very good news for you!"

"Well, let's see. You have managed to eradicate DSS from the face of the planet?"

"You know I would if I could, but this is still good. For the last two weeks, I have had some of my Dallas colleagues following up on more recent addresses for Frida, your mother, and they have located the most recent. We found her!"

Olivia was stunned, or scared, because her excuse for not going to Dallas had been that she had no current address for mamma. Not that she did not want to confront her, but she just had unusual anxiety and fear about it. Still, she knew it had to be done — she had to talk to her ex-mother.

"Jason, that is wonderful! Is she in a hotel or a house?"

"My friends say it's a small, one-room house. She has moved several times, all within a small area, and has finally settled on a house about 10 blocks from her first address there — after the hotel, that is. Now she's at 3410 Rancho Street. You want to go?"

Olivia hesitated. This was it. She had to get this done. "How about tomorrow — Friday?"

Over the phone, it sounded like Jason was turning some pages, probably checking his schedule for tomorrow. "Okay, let's do it."

That evening, Olivia made arrangements for Sonia to take Gabriela for Friday, and maybe Saturday, depending on how things went in Dallas. Jason picked Olivia up at 8 o'clock on Friday morning, and soon they were on Interstate 45-North to Dallas.

"Are you scared or nervous about seeing your mother again?"

"I think of her as my ex-mother, Jason, and, yes, I am nervous."

"I've been a reporter for many years, and I read a hell of a lot, but I've never come across that concept — 'ex-mother.'"

"Neither have I, but, after thinking about Frida for many hours, I came to the conclusion that there are other relationships that we deliberately dissolve, like marriages for instance. Then we have ex-wives and ex-husbands. Well, Frida walked away from her responsibilities as a mother and abandoned my brother Benito and me. We could have been killed, alone in that motel, and she just left us. I cannot think of a more definitive act by a woman who wants to sever all ties to her offspring."

"I always thought that 'Once a mother, always a mother.'"

"That is generally true, but we do not have a typical case here — right?"

"Yes, Olivia — I see your point. But, if you don't see her as your mother, then what is she to you right now?"

"My ex-mother. Her decision to wantonly abandon us clearly showed she no longer wanted that relationship as mother to us."

"I am having a hard time understanding the concept of 'ex-mother.'"

"That is because you have never been abandoned, Jason. It was almost like the end of the world for me. I began a new life as a motherless child. My old 'me' died at that motel in 1982. My old 'me' is gone forever."

"You are right, Olivia, I cannot possibly understand what you have been through. So what do you hope to accomplish by visiting and talking to your mother — I mean your 'ex-mother'?"

"I have been thinking about that ever since I learned that she had not died that day in front of the motel. Initially, I was happy to hear the news that she had not died, but the crude reality hit me soon afterwards."

"And what did that entail?"

"It was a shock to realize that, if she had not died, then it meant she had abandoned my brother Benito and me. I felt rage toward her!"

"So, when you see her, you will rage against her to her face?"

"You certainly don't expect me to kiss her, right?"

"Is there any value in trying to understand your ex-mother's motives as to why she abandoned you and Benito?"

"Well, when I found out through my Aunt Jenny that my grandfather had raped her and gotten her pregnant, I felt cornered."

"'Cornered'? What does that mean?"

"Knowing that my mother had given birth to me and to Benito as products of a series of rapes by her own father forced me to see that she had been living in hell and shame, through no fault of her own."

"Olivia, you said 'mother' and not 'ex-mother.'"

"You know I meant to say 'ex-mother.' Okay, to make things easy for you, let's just stick to the term 'mother,' even though you know I mean that she's my 'ex-mother.'"

"Does knowing about your mother's personal situation at the time make it harder for you to feel justified in your anger or rage?"

"Damn it — it does! As an adult, I feel I have to take into account her suffering and how it must have impacted her life, her decisions."

"You seem to imply that knowing about her pain makes it unfair for you."

"Well, am I not justified in feeling rage for the pain she caused Benito and me?"

"You just said that, as an adult, you have to take her intolerable pain into account."

"If I try to understand her, do I just let my soul corrode with rage? If I try to understand her, then who will understand me? Who is on my side, Jason? Who will bend to make my needs and feelings their primary concern? Who will agree with me that I am justified in feeling abandoned, indignant, and spiritually violated?"

"It seems to me, Olivia, that, in a relationship, the two persons try to understand each other's needs and motives, and that each will try to accommodate the other to the extent that their psychological structures permit."

"Does your dictum apply to mothers and their young children, Jason?" Olivia shot back, with an edge of hostility.

He had painted himself into a corner, for, clearly, children do not have a large capacity to accommodate parents' pathologies. "No, I guess not. You got me."

"I read in one of my library books that children deserve to be loved and treated morally, irrespective of their parents' shortcomings. A child should not be required to understand why a mother or father fails. In the eyes of a child, there are no excuses for moral failures in parenting. Clearly, Frida, The Mother From Hell, failed us!"

"Maybe that is the key to your conflicted situation, Olivia."

"I don't follow you."

"I'm beginning to feel that maybe your conflict is coming from your divided self."

"Careful, Jason. Are you saying now that I am some sort of weirdo with multiple personalities due to my traumas?"

"No — of course, not. Well, not in a psychiatric sense, but in a normal sense — like all of us."

"You lost me again."

"It's simple. Somebody on the outside — like me, for example — can easily see that Frida failed in her moral responsibilities as a mother, but yet this outside person does not feel angry with her. You, on the other hand, have lived through it, so various parts of your personality have become involved, and they seem to function independently of one another."

"Psycho-mumbo-jumbo, Jason. What does it all mean?"

"The little girl inside you is depressed and angry."

"I never thought of it in that manner, but it does make some sense."

As they drove along, Olivia was silently thinking of all the things she would be telling Frida the moment she opened her door. The anger, the rage, the hurt, the animosity, the pain of a life without a mother — they were all building and percolating inside her, ready to explode at the sight of Frida's face. How dare she leave two defenseless children in a seedy motel, alone, forever! No telling what Olivia would do, but she knew that, this time, she would not take a claw hammer with her. She was afraid she would use it in a most terrifying way.

They were on the outskirts of Dallas at around 12 noon, so they decided to stop at a restaurant. Her stomach was all acid, so she was not about to eat anything, but the stop gave her a bit more time to prepare herself. Jason gave her a few more words of encouragement and support, and advised her to try to be civil with Frida in spite of what Frida had done. They left the restaurant and, with the aid of a map, headed for 3410 Rancho Street.

Soon they found the neighborhood — mostly Mexicans and other Latino groups. The only good thing was that it was a residential area — there were no businesses nearby. But the houses looked like they had been built in the 1940s, when there had been a great influx of Mexican seasonal workers into the area, all part of the U.S.-Mexico Bracero Program. Houses stood on short stilts and were built with sorry-looking wooden slats that didn't quite fit flush with each other, leaving slits through which light and mosquitoes could enter.

They turned right onto Rancho Street, on the 2900 block. Very poor homes, but they all seemed to have cars parked on the street right in front. Of course, they were not like the gringo cars one would find in the Georgetown section of Washington, DC. One could see macho Mexican teens repairing their vehicles and many small kids running all over the place.

One minute later, Olivia and Jason arrived at 3410, a very small white house set back from the street about 30 feet. It had a small, grassy yard in front and some bugambilia shrubs right next to the house. It looked like it had not been painted in twenty years.

Olivia got out of the car, and Jason reminded her, "Remember, after you finish, take a cab to the hotel. I'll be in the restaurant, bar, or lobby area. I'll stay here for one minute to make sure that someone answers the door."

"Thanks, Jason — I appreciate your help." She squeezed his hand as she got out.

Olivia took a very deep breath and walked slowly toward the door, still rehearsing the very first few cutting words she would say to the mother who had abandoned her nineteen years earlier. She knocked on the green door with the peeling paint. As she waited, she tried to slow down her breathing, for it was much too fast. Maybe there was no one home — there was no prompt answer and no noise inside. So she knocked somewhat louder the second time. She heard some latches rattle from the inside, so she knew the time had come to face her destiny. The door slowly opened, Olivia held her breath, her lips ready to spew venom.

There stood in front of her a woman who appeared to be in her sixties. About Olivia's height, but very thin, grey-haired, protruding cheekbones from the emaciated and wrinkly face. She was wearing a yellow, worn-out, knee-length dress and brown, flat shoes. Olivia's immediate reaction was that this woman could not possibly be her mother, since, by her calculation, Frida would be about 43 years old. But it was the woman's spontaneous expression of horror that sent chills down Olivia's entire body. She just had to confirm what her heart already knew.

She asked meekly, "Frida?"

The woman's lips made some trembling movements as if trying to answer, but her sunken eyes, glued to Olivia's, spoke better; it had been almost twenty years since Olivia had looked into her mother's eyes. Olivia's soul spoke to her heart: it was definitely Frida.

With a quivering upper lip and a single tear, the old woman answered in a weak voice.

"Olivia?"

They were frozen in time, almost if, in an instant, they had been taken back to 1982 to that infamous motel in Houston, Frida as a suffering young mother, Olivia as an innocent child nowhere near ready to let go of the bonds to her mother. Neither of them knew just what the next step would be, as they were both staring at each other's faces as if looking for some etched signal on how to proceed. But Olivia had not counted on what happened next, for quite spontaneously, without any conscious forethought, it was her heart that made the decisive move.

"Mamma!" she screamed, as she went forward into the open arms of her mother.

"Oh, my baby, my baby — I am so sorry. I am so sorry."

The two women continued to hug each other for a long minute, releasing momentarily only to look at each other's face again and again — Olivia full of tears, Frida with a sad face and one or two tears. Olivia could feel that Frida was glad to see her, but it just did not show on Frida's permanently sad face.

"Olivia, you have blossomed into a beautiful woman," said Frida as she looked intensely into Olivia's eyes.

"Thank you, Frida."

"Come — let's sit down over here. Coffee?"

"Sure," answered Olivia as she sat down at the kitchen table.

As Frida was wordlessly preparing the coffee, Olivia took the opportunity to look at her surroundings. The house consisted of one room that served as living room, work area, kitchen, and bedroom, with the bathroom being separate. There was no inside finishing on the walls, as one could see the exterior slats, vertical studs, and horizontal fireblock studs, together with the outside light that came through the slits between the slats. There were just a few pieces of furniture, all pretty much worn down, except for the ironing board and iron, which appeared to be new. Next to the ironing board was a garment rack with wheels on which were hanging a variety of ironed clothing of varying sizes and styles, perhaps indicating that Frida ironed for a living. The kitchen area was one corner of this one-room arrangement, and it looked cozy and warm, with typical Mexican flower decorations on the wall and fridge.

Not only was Olivia observing the particulars of the inside of Frida's house, but she was also thinking about, and bothered by, her sudden positive reaction toward Frida upon seeing her. She was afraid that it had ruined her plan to unleash her very real rage against her. So she started concentrating on all the hurts inside her instead of the positives in having finally located her.

"Olivia, how did you find me?"

"I have a friend who is a newspaper reporter who asked his colleagues here in Dallas for help. I believe they looked at water and electricity bills."

Frida served the coffee and some Mexican *revolcada conchas* and joined Olivia at the table. It was the longest minute as they drank and ate without a word.

"Are you married? Do you have children?" Frida asked, without looking at Olivia.

"No, not married. Have had several relationships, but they haven't worked out for me. I do have one daughter, Gabriela. She's five and doing well."

And then more silence, as if they both knew there was something very important to put on the table, but neither knew just how to open the discussion. Olivia continued to consciously suppress her positive feelings in the hope of bringing her anger to the forefront, but she was more conflicted than she had ever been about her mother.

"You don't look well, Frida. How's your health?" asked Olivia as she reached over and patted Frida's bony lower arm. Frida responded warmly but still seemed to have a bit of a problem looking again into Olivia's eyes.

"Nothing major. The government doctors have been telling me for a long time to eat more, but I can't seem to. Just not hungry. I've been taking anti-depressants for years — maybe that's the problem. But you — you look radiant and beautiful, Olivia."

Olivia knew she had to get down to the business she had gone there for.

"Look, Frida, finding you and hugging you is fine and all that, but there is a part of me that was mortally wounded by your having abandoned us at that motel. I guess I want to hear what you have to say about that."

Frida looked more intensely at the table, now full of crumbs, and conceded, "Yes, that has been the nightmare that never ends."

Olivia waited silently for more specifics; she had already tilted the scale toward her true mission of expressing anger and rage.

"I realized afterwards that I had left a nightmare and entered another one, but it was too late to go backwards," added Frida.

"I hope you realize that you are referring to your feelings and ignoring ours," goaded Olivia, with growing hostility.

"Yes, you are right — my feelings. There's no doubt that, in leaving, I failed you and Benito. Selfishly, I have asked God to take my worthless life to end my suffering, not even considering that, in trying to diminish my pain by going away, I inflicted worse damage upon you both."

"So, what pain are you referring to?"

"It has been many years, so I suspect that some friend or relative might have mentioned to you the awful things that happened when my sister Jenny and I were living at home with our parents."

"I learned about it only recently. Your father Tomas was raping you and Jenny. Is that correct?"

Frida covered her face with both hands; she wasn't crying — she just didn't want Olivia to see her toxic shame. Olivia gave her a few moments.

"I used to cry about that every night, as a young girl, as your mother, and then when I moved here. Did anyone tell you about the result of those rapes?"

"Yes, I think I know all the details. Our grandfather is also our father."

Frida started to tremble. "Oh, my God — you know! You know! What a disgraceful life, what a shameful existence! What an unforgivable sin! A sin!" she screamed.

"The truth is, Frida, that it was his sin, not yours. You were the young, innocent victim. But he has paid for his attacks upon you."

"How, Olivia — how did that monster pay for what he did?"

"He first shot Florencia dead, and then he put a bullet into his own, worthless brain."

This time, Frida looked intensely and incredulously at Olivia, perhaps unable to assess if it was better to have evil parents alive or evil parents dead. Frida asked, "But why would he do such a thing? He was always so self-assured, confident."

"Aunt Jenny told me about the rapes recently, so I went to his house and confronted him face-to-face. Grandma admitted that she knew of the rapes but was too afraid to intervene. Having me there confronting your father Tomas must have given her some courage, for she told the whole story and urged him to admit it. I cursed him repeatedly, so he finally did, the scumbag! That was about one month ago."

"I've hated my father for the longest time, but, now that he's dead, I'm not so sure how I feel. He was my father."

"Don't forget — he was my father, too, and I am glad he's now in hell, where he belongs."

There was another lull in the conversation as Frida seemed to be in deep thought about what Olivia had just said.

Olivia interrupted, "I thought you should also know that, at the end of that conversation, your mother Florencia said that, if I ever found you I should mention to you that she was regretful and profoundly sorry about her not defending you during those attacks."

"And I always thought she just didn't care — that my mother just never loved me," Frida muttered.

"She also said that, because of the immense pain you had suffered, you should never forgive her — that her failure as your mother was unforgivable. After her confession, in fact, she said she was ready to die. It didn't sound to me like she didn't care about what had happened to you."

Frida listened with quivering lips to Olivia's words, and, after a few moments, she inquired, in halting words, "Olivia, why didn't you bring Benito with you? I would have liked to have seen him even once before I die."

"When you told us, Frida, that you were quickly coming back to our room at that motel, we believed you. Remember that Benito was only four years old, and I was nine. He looked out the window, asking many times, 'Where is mamma? Where is mamma?' We waited for hours. His little face lit up every time someone walked by our door — he never gave up thinking it was you. It still breaks my heart when I think of it. The thought brings the image of his little face forever looking and waiting for you. Finally, we both collapsed from hunger and exhaustion. The police later took us to live with Aunt Jenny, but Benito continued to believe for a long time that you just had gotten lost and that, at any time, you would show up. After school, he would spend long hours sitting by the window, waiting for you. Tragically, he died in a swimming accident when he was ten years old. Your young son died waiting for his mother to show up, but she never did. She had run away to Dallas. That was my little brother's tragic life. How does that make you feel, Frida?" asked Olivia, with a hostile and cynical smirk.

It took Frida the better part of two minutes to answer, her expressionless face made human by some muscular quivers that were beginning to show up. She whispered, "I have been able to tolerate my grave failure by burying it very deep in my heart and not thinking about it. I know I did wrong. I am sorry about my Benito."

"I suffered, too. All the kids in school had mothers who came to their programs. I had no one. We had special assignments for Mother's Day, year after year, and I had no one to write a letter to. When I got my first period, I was terrified — I didn't know what to do." Olivia's face was now covered in long streams of tears. She continued, "All the kids had their families present at high school graduation, but I was like a lonely street dog. I desperately needed to talk to a mother about boyfriends and such, but I had no one. It made me feel like an inferior human being not worth having its own mother. I was only slightly better than a motherless maggot. And I am raising my daughter Gabriela without a grandmother!"

Frida, now looking only at the floor, turned her face away from Olivia. "Do you think I ran away because I was a bad person?"

"Does it fucking matter, Frida? Are you now trying to come up with some justification?"

Almost whispering, Frida answered, "If, by that, you mean an excuse, then, no — there is no excuse for what I did. You are justified in feeling that I am worth less than dog excrement — I feel that way about myself, too. Can't blame you. I failed. But if you don't want to hear my story, then where do we go from here? You talk, and I listen?"

Olivia immediately knew that Frida had a valid point, so she held her tongue momentarily. Exactly what did Olivia expect from Frida on that visit?

Effusive begging for forgiveness? Groveling on the floor so that God wouldn't send her to hell? Admitting that leaving had been a horrible mistake?

Since Olivia was still contemplating the impasse, Frida offered, "Look, Olivia, just tell me about how you feel, and I will listen. I won't interrupt you."

Rather than opening the door for Olivia, Frida's kind words served to stifle her, for it seemed rather inappropriate to bash Frida after that. But Olivia came with a mission, so she was not going to let kind words get in the way of getting her job done.

Going against her feelings of pity for Frida, Olivia continued. "I understand that you suffered immensely at the hands of your father Tomas, but, being a mother, for whatever reason, means responsibility, and there is no excuse for failing in that role. And you, Frida, you failed miserably, and you abandoned us — you left us as unwanted children. That was a dastardly thing to do! Oh, God, what a contemptible example of motherhood you were and still are!"

Frida was now looking at Olivia, with her head tipped slightly sideways, as if it were too heavy to hold up. "You are right. I did not make it as a mother."

"For many years, we thought you were dead, and it was only recently that Aunt Jenny told me the truth about you having left. At first I felt joyful, but, soon after that, it dawned on me that your being alive meant you had abandoned us."

"So, then your feelings changed?"

"When I heard that you had abandoned us, I felt like killing you, Frida. Killing you, killing you! Splitting your damned forehead open with a heavy butcher knife. Ripping you apart into many pieces and feeding your fucking body parts to rabid dogs. For what you did! You hear? You miserable bitch!"

"Had you done that, it would have served us both."

"What? You want me to really kill you?"

"Why act surprised, Olivia? I can see it in your eyes."

"So you don't even have the courage to kill yourself, and now you suggest that I should do it for you? Not only are you a repulsive example of motherhood, but you are also a contemptible human being. If I kill you, I remain behind as a murderer, probably in prison, and would leave my daughter Gabriela motherless. That would be okay with you, I suppose, since you have such a track record. I can see that motherhood is just not in your veins!"

"You still can't see that motherhood was brutally forced upon me?"

"So what? Once you're a mother, you have responsibilities for that life that came from within you!"

"Maybe in an ideal world, Olivia, but my soul was destroyed by those nightly savage attacks. I was thirteen! By the time you were born, I was just a cadaver that people had forgotten to bury."

"So you didn't have it in your heart to be a mother?"

"It was a nauseous and disgusting feeling to have my father on top of me." Frida's eyes were beginning to water more than before. "But it was abhorrent and repugnant to have him inside."

"I fucking ask you again, Frida! So you didn't have it in your heart to be a mother?"

"Olivia, you are so lucky never to have been raped."

That hit Olivia in her heart, for she knew exactly how it felt when Bull Garcia had forced himself upon her numerous times. She knew in her heart that, definitely, she would not want any babies from him, babies that would forever remind her of his filthy and repulsive organ inside her, babies that would carry the aura of sinfulness and damnation, through no fault of their own. That is why she had voluntarily put herself on contraceptive medications. But if she felt this way about a possible sinful baby from Bull Garcia, had Frida felt the same way about the *two* babies that her own father Tomas had sired inside her womb?

Those thoughts silently drove her to a very uncomfortable question. If Bull Garcia had made a baby inside her, would she have loved this child as much as she loved Gabriela? Olivia was terrified of how she would honestly answer her own question, but the question had already been born, and there was no way to send it back into the unknown, into the land of the unasked.

The question itself was supremely threatening, yet the more perturbing issue was that it compromised Olivia's self-declared moral superiority over her mother. Frida had rejected the children that had been violently forced upon her, but Olivia would never even *think* of doing that — right?

She still had a lot of fire and anger in her, enough to scream at Frida, enough to hit her, but maybe not enough to kill her or use a claw hammer against her. How dare a mother abandon her children! What kind of a miserable human being would do such a thing! Not even lowly sewer rats abandon their brood!

Yes, Olivia was still very angry, but she was slowly and reluctantly realizing that the legitimacy of seeing Frida as having acted irresponsibly out of her own free will — and thus being the justifiably proper target of Olivia's moral rage — was gradually evaporating before her eyes and that, if she wanted to be fair and moral toward Frida, as Jason had suggested, then she soon might find herself raging just against the wind, against the darkness, really against life itself. Maybe the real problem was not so much Frida, but the harsh and brutal realities of relationships and human weaknesses.

So the crack in her soul thus came to the surface. As a moral adult, she would have to understand her mother's suffering and her subsequently crippled ability to carry out her normal and required duties as a responsible mother. But that should not negate Olivia's very real rage about having been abandoned — right? As Olivia was coming to terms with the fact that her mother may have acted out of intense and unbearable desperation, she was also realizing that her anger was the abandonment rage of nine-year-old Olivia. And for children, abandonment rage and depression can never be explained away, even if the failed parents have the best reason in the world. Even, in fact, if the parents had been given orders to act that way by God Himself!

That was about the best Olivia could do to understand her conflicted and convoluted feelings toward her mother. Important too, was that she realized that it was almost impossible to understand one person's behavior without first accepting the fact that all people, at one time or another, will act in a stressful situation under the belief that they really had no choice at all to have acted differently. Only someone who disapproves of that action will likely believe that the other person had full will and freedom to have taken a different course, as Olivia had been believing about Frida for some time now.

Frida could see that Olivia was experiencing self-doubt, that her face had lost some of its justified hostility. "Just imagine, Olivia, to me, it did not happen just once, which is bad enough, but twice. He impregnated me again when you were four years old, and poor Benito was born out of sin, too."

"Why didn't you go to the police for help?"

"I was afraid that, if they took him away, my mother would be left without a husband. But besides that, I was also terrified of him. He threatened my mother and me many times."

"So, okay, Frida — I can understand the terrible things you went through. But does that mean then that you are justified in having left us, and, so, therefore, I am not justified in feeling angry about it?"

"No, all children have the right to expect love and security from their parents, and all parents have a moral duty to care for their children. But that's not how it happens in the real world, Olivia. Real parents have imperfections and weaknesses, some more than others, that will lead them to failure under family duress. But it should be called 'failure' nonetheless."

Failure! That word had been very salient in Olivia's mind recently, so when Frida mentioned it, Olivia's mind quickly recalled how just recently she had called her daughter a "pig" and had even confessed to Sonia that she was afraid she might hurt Gabriela. She painfully thought of how she had refused to let Gabriela into her bed to sleep and the unfortunate incident at Dr. Krodovic's office a few weeks later. Olivia knew that she loved Gabriela very much and would do anything to protect her. But, in retrospect, how could she have ignored her young daughter's urgent and agonizing pleas to prevent the sinister DSS doctor from lifting her gown and examining her? Gabriela's painful words quickly re-surfaced in Olivia's heart: "Mamma — no, mamma! Don't let him touch me!" But instead of protecting her, Olivia assisted the doctor and urged her daughter to submit to the trauma. Because the state had ordered it. How could she ever have done that to the daughter she so loved? These thoughts made Olivia feel regretful, inadequate, and even more confused.

Frida was starting to tire from the discussion, for she did not have that much energy to begin with. She got up to serve herself another cup of coffee and offered Olivia the same.

"So, what happened in the few days leading up to your decision to take Benito and me to the motel to leave us there?"

"For years, I had lived with the lie that your father was just a menial worker who had skipped town after learning I was pregnant. The only soul on earth I told the truth to was my sister Jenny. She understood — she was being raped, too. Meanwhile, the repulsive real father of Benito and you was still very much a part of my life — I lived with that animal Tomas in the same house!"

"But why couldn't you just move away?"

"Couldn't. I was afraid he would hunt me down and kill me. He had said as much."

"And what else?"

"I am sorry to say this, but every time I looked at you and Benito, I could not help but see his image. I even smelled his alcohol breath and his body odor, as when he was on top of me. Ghastly to say, but sometimes I even smelled his semen when I looked at you or Benito. It was a dreadful black cloud in my relationship to you and Benito."

Frida's last few comments immediately sent Olivia into the netherworld of vivid memories which invoked sensations on all the five senses, as she, too, had had similar experiences about her own rapes. She knew Frida had lived through intolerable suffering far too long.

"But, Frida, didn't you think that leaving Benito and me at a shady motel would endanger our lives?"

"The truth is, Olivia, I didn't care by that time. I couldn't care — or wasn't able to. Something had happened to my sense of responsibility, and I was just numb and halfway dead inside. I didn't even have enough spirit to kill myself, which is what I thought about all the time. But after I had been here in Dallas for about three months, I took a bus to White Rock Lake and threw myself into the deep waters. Since I can't swim, I was hoping to drown my life away. But some people saw what was happening and pulled me out. I guess God must want me alive to suffer, to suffer in atonement for having been such a terrible mother to you and Benito. Yes, I deserve to suffer — I don't know what other purpose I have in life."

Frida was now quietly dripping tears, tears she had been storing in her soul for more than twenty years. She'd had no one to share them with. Olivia gave it some serious quick thought; then she decided to do what she had promised herself she would never do: She reached out and held her mother's hand. Frida raised her head, looked at Olivia, and the floodgates of bitter tears burst open. As the crying turned to wailing, Olivia moved her chair closer to Frida and said, "Oh, mamma," as she wrapped her arms around her.

CHAPTER 17

Olivia arrived by taxi at the hotel that Jason had designated, and, after a quick call to Sonia to check up on Gabriela, they promptly began their trip back to Houston. It was already late Friday afternoon. Since she had reddish and puffy eyes, Jason did not venture to ask her any direct questions about the meeting with Frida, but he knew it had been intense. About an hour into the trip, near the town of Ennis, it was Olivia who first spoke.

"Jason, do you think it is a good idea to forgive people for having done something very wrong? You know, we all speak of forgiveness, but is it really a good idea?"

"I don't think there is one right answer for that question. There are so many variations of circumstances and personalities that it might be impossible to say that one answer will satisfy all."

"Yeah, I know, but let's stick just to my case, for example."

"You mean if you should forgive your mother?"

"What would you say?"

"Here's what I think. If Frida could do or say anything you wanted, would you then want to re-establish a relationship with her?"

"No question about it — yes!"

"And what is it that you would want her to do or say?"

"That she is very sorry for what she did and that she would like to re-start her relationship with me and Jenny."

"Didn't she apologize when you were at her house?"

"Yes, but she also said, 'Never forgive me for what I have done,' just as I was leaving."

"What do you make of it?"

131

"She is sorry. Didn't act out of malice. Knows it was wrong. She didn't start a new family. I guess she was saying that her failure is unforgivable."

"Is it?"

"But if I want to forgive her?"

"So, some things in life are immoral, but if you do them, you'll be forgiven by a kind-hearted person, and you can continue life as always?"

"I guess so," Olivia said meekly, obviously not sure of her answer.

"I propose, then, that we don't consider anything immoral, just 'uncomfortable' or 'not recommended,' or even 'just not advisable,' and, in that manner, as soon as we get over the discomfort of whatever someone did to us, we will be able to resume the relationship, if that is what we want."

"It sounds almost like you are saying that I should never forgive my mother."

"No, it sounds like I am saying there is a profound lesson here."

"Like we should always forgive?"

"Not quite."

"If I am a moral person, I should forgive?"

"Quite the contrary, Olivia. If you are a truly moral person, then you should never forgive grave moral transgressions, for, in forgiveness, you violate the truly repentant person's desire to set herself apart from those in her circle who have been morally wounded by her actions."

"Is that what my mother is doing?"

"She asked not to be forgiven."

"But do I have any say-so in this?"

"She knows she did wrong — she feels the intense hurt she caused in your soul and empathizes with your pain. Her subsequent and genuine repentance tells her she is not worthy of being in your heart. Her abandoning you at that motel in 1982, however highly justified, broke something very sacred in the mother-daughter bond."

"Jason, I don't get it. What am I supposed to do?"

"Seems to me that if you truly believe in, and uphold, the moral nature of the mother-daughter bond, then you are in a moral dilemma."

They were now entering Huntsville, on the northwestern outskirts of the Sam Houston National Forest. Traffic had been heavy because of the Dallas/Houston business commuters. Soon Jason and Olivia would be arriving in Houston — it was almost 10 o'clock, Friday night.

"But shouldn't it be up to me to forgive, damn it, and not up to her to accept or not accept forgiveness? I was the one who was hurt by her actions!"

"Haven't you considered that she morally hurt herself, too?"

Olivia was caught off guard by Jason's question. "Over the last few weeks, I've been reading a lot of stuff on psychology — and on legal tricks by the government, like the ones I am anticipating by DSS — but you know a hell of a lot more. How?"

"Olivia, remember that, for years, I have been writing newspaper stories about Houston's troubled families, so I've learned a few things."

"Alright — your thoughts on how my mother hurt herself."

"Seems to me that Frida acted out of desperation, out of intense pain and septic shame that overran and unfortunately repressed her sense of responsibility and morality to the point where she just did not care anymore about her children. In a way, she no longer could feel her morals inside her. So her being away from it all, in Dallas, diminished some of the original panic and crisis, thus allowing her sense of responsibility and moral beliefs to return to the surface of her soul, but it was too late — Frida had already damaged her relationship to her children. Her moral realization of what she had done multiplied her sense of worthlessness and her belief that she was an irredeemably deficient and unholy mother. What sane and righteous daughter would want to restore her relationship to this cursed mother from hell? I believe these are her most prominent thoughts and feelings now."

"You said a moment ago that you felt I was in a moral dilemma."

"If you believe that morals exist for a reason, that they should not be broken, that there are no excuses for acting immorally, and that relationships with people who act immorally are permanently altered, then perhaps you should not forgive your mother. Besides, she asked not to be forgiven. And, according to you, she is your 'ex-mother.'"

"And the other part of the dilemma?"

"But if you want to follow your heart and re-establish a relationship with Frida, then you need to be honest with yourself and just accept that, with you, love and attachment trump the need to uphold moral rules as far as Frida is concerned. In other words, you will accept Frida no matter what she does. Which is no different at all if you had no moral rules yourself, because the relationship would be based mostly on the bio-psychological instinct of attachment. Even mafia mothers and fathers love their sons in spite of these sons being vicious and brutal assassins."

She didn't like the comparison, but yet she had no easy and credible rebuttal. "Here you go again with your mumbo-jumbo psychology, or philosophy, or whatever you call it. Be simple — what do I do?"

"You won't like this, but I'll tell you for your own good, even if you hate me for it. That's too bad, because I was already becoming fond of you, Olivia."

"Me, too, Jason, but let's have it."

"Go ahead and try to re-establish a relationship with Frida, since that is what you want. But keep in mind: she feels she is no longer worthy of it because of how she failed. You are driven by a child's love for mother, she by more mature but devastating guilt over her moral dereliction. To be real and honest, you might have to call this new relationship one of 'ex-mother and ex-daughter,' terms you invented, since you cannot actually return to the relationship you both had up to 1982, no matter how hard you both may try. Besides, it wasn't that good for Frida anyway — that is why she left. What you decide will affect your relationship with Gabriela and her moral compass for the future, for her eyes and ears record everything you do."

CHAPTER 18

Very early on Monday, Olivia received a message from Susie Drake at DSS, informing her to show up the following day at 8 o'clock in the morning for the court-ordered psychological testing for her and for Gabriela at the offices of clinical psychologist Dr. Manuel Hinojosa. Olivia had previously been told by Greta Haroldson that this was coming, yet knowing that the actual testing was already scheduled made her jittery, for she feared the worst. And even though she asked Susie Drake for specifics, she received the bland response that Dr. Hinojosa would explain everything to her — that it would be as simple as answering some questions. Olivia had recently read some horror stories about how overzealous and covertly pathological case workers use the results of such tests to act out their own unresolved family issues against the parents and children they are supposed to help. Her recent painful experience with Dr. Krodovic made her decide to be ever more vigilant and on guard about the appointment with the clinical psychologist — chosen by DSS, of course.

At Williams Circuit Components, everything seemed to proceed normally, and, as usual, Olivia's group sat in a corner in the lunchroom, talking mostly about her visit to her newfound mother. None of the women had had that type of experience with their mothers, so they all were intensely curious and were asking Olivia who said what and why. Especially Glenda. She appeared quite offended, and then she opined, "But Olivia, I think what you did was wrong. We should never judge our mothers, especially as harshly as you did yours. In my opinion, my mother is sacred, the best mother anyone could ask for, so I will never judge her at any level. I honestly don't think she ever made any mistakes as a mother. Really!"

Rosalba, having *chorizo-con-huevo* tacos and *limonada* for lunch, joined in. "Glenda, how can you say your mother never made any mistakes! Forgive me for saying this, but your mother's four children have three different fathers, as everyone here knows — that is not setting a good example for you and certainly not for the children. On this planet, all mothers and fathers make mistakes, even if their children put them on a pedestal — for lack of insight, I would say."

Sonia had been listening, and it was time to come to Olivia's defense. "I feel Olivia did the right thing. She has to judge her mother if she wants to be a better mother than Frida ever was to her. If one is blind to one's mother's mistakes, then one will repeat them with one's children. Only people in denial say that their mother never made any mistakes in raising them. Seeing the mistakes means you are judging, that you now know better."

"Okay, cut it out — let's not ruin our lunchtime. Olivia, we gotta give you an update on the tentative plan with Carmelina," whispered Lizbet.

"Have you informed the bastard, as we had planned?" asked Olivia.

Judith offered to provide the details. "You weren't here of course, but, on Friday, Sonia, Rosalba, Lizbet, Carmelina, and I met with Mr. Williams at his office, and we pretty much said what we all had talked about. The man turned white when Carmelina stated in front of all of us that she was pregnant with his child, so we sort of knew that he knew he was the father."

"What'd he say about the plan?" queried Olivia.

"He denied he was the father and said we were trying to extort money from him. We went in circles for a while, and then I suggested that we terminate the meeting and that he should just think it over and let us know," explained Judith.

Olivia then directed her next question at Sonia. "So, where do you think we stand on this?"

"I think he's scared. He probably will not give up the whole company, but, what the heck, we'll give him several days to stew in panic. Then, we'll ask to speak with him again," responded Sonia.

"Let's hope he doesn't send any of his thugs to make Carmelina suddenly disappear," warned Lizbet.

CHAPTER 19

Right on time Tuesday morning, Olivia and Gabriela arrived for their appointment at the offices of clinical psychologist Dr. Manuel Hinojosa, newly ordained by Greta Haroldson at DSS, with the full blessing of her boss and lust interest, Antonio Guerra. His office was beautifully decorated, with lots of art reproductions on the walls, a very soft sofa and several easy chairs, and a whole wall filled with books. One corner was dedicated to toys and kid-sized chairs, as well as several anatomically correct dolls.

"Good morning, Olivia and Gabriela — please take a seat over here," he said, with a smile that Olivia characterized as suspicious and patently false. "I just want to tell you that I am here to serve you and not DSS, so I will be asking you some questions about your background. I will also be administering some standard psychological tests, very simple. One thing that is very important is that you be honest with your answers. Is that clear?"

Olivia did not trust him one bit, for she suspected he was no more than a professional hired gun, an assassin of some kind, prostituting his expertise and knowledge so that DSS could get its way. He did it for money and for the power high it brought him, she felt. Just another bastard professional like Krodovic, the pervert, feigning to serve their patients. But not wanting to appear resistant or uncooperative, she smiled at him and answered, "Of course, doctor — we all want to do the correct thing here."

Dr. Hinojosa situated Gabriela in the kid corner and placed a parlor partition so that he and Olivia could have a bit more privacy in the diagonally opposed corner. Gabriela didn't seem to mind.

After a few bland questions and more smiles to create the rapport he needed to surreptitiously disarm her defenses, he turned to the hard subject of family of origin — the blueprint that would reveal how Olivia's psyche had been formed.

"Olivia, how would you characterize your relationship to your mother, Frida?"

She knew instantly that the real test had begun. Should she answer each question honestly in the hope that the psychologist would see that she, Olivia, was a good mother? But could she trust this psychologist? Did he really support her efforts at being a good mother? She knew she had to quickly remember all the details of the various books and magazines she had read on the subject of love, caring, family relations, perversions, and human development. She knew that how she answered his questions would determine what he would report to DSS about her suitability to be a mother to Gabriela. She felt deep in her heart as if she were in front of a firing squad ready to terminate her life — and Gabriela's — if she did not answer their questions to their liking. In one calm and gargantuan silent effort, she forcefully concealed the almost unbearable panic that was overtaking her entire soul as she was sitting on that easy chair, in front of her smiling executioner. She had to answer, even if her words would mean the end of her relationship to her daughter.

"Well, we have not really been close. For economic reasons, I went to live with my Aunt Jenny." Olivia had read it was wise to keep her answers short when speaking to a potential adversary.

"And so you see your Aunt Jenny as a mother?"

"Yes — she has always been there for me."

"Have you ever harbored any ill feelings or anger — or even hate — toward your real mother?"

With each question, Olivia realized that she was getting deeper into a web of lies and half-truths. She feared that Dr. Hinojosa might have some DSS-supplied confidential information of her family situation that would expose her twisting of the truth. No doubt he would then write her up as a pathological liar — quite unfit to instill proper moral values in a young child. Or worse, as a delusional woman becoming increasingly psychotic, unable to tell fact from fiction. Definitely, this was a high-stakes psychological assessment, she thought, and whatever the risks of sugar-coating her responses, these were preferable to trusting him with Gabriela's future.

"In the past, I was somewhat angry at her for having sent me to live with my Aunt Jenny, but, as I got older, I realized that she had made a difficult decision for my own long-term good."

"And now? What kind of relationship do you have with Frida?"

Was that a standard, follow-up question, or was Dr. Hinojosa trying to corner Olivia? DSS knew where she worked, so had Greta Haroldson talked to some of her co-workers, threatening them with legal action if they did not tell the truth about Olivia's family? But Olivia's friends would have revealed that to Olivia, right? Well, maybe not, if Greta had threatened to call Immigration Services if they spoke to Olivia about a visit. Could Dr. Hinojosa, whose piercing eyes were now fixed on Olivia's, tell that her legs were trembling, that she was becoming very uncomfortable with the questions? Was what she was feeling normal, motherly concern, or was it a paranoid personality trait coming to the surface — something she had picked up from living so many years with Aunt Jenny, who painfully had learned never to trust men?

"Yeah, I talk to my mother. I remind her of my pain from the past, but I also hug her and hold her hand." Olivia looked at the psychologist's face, trying to detect if he was believing her answers fully. No luck — she couldn't decipher his bland look. No doubt he had been trained to present a simple, flat affect so as not to reveal what he was feeling or thinking. Maybe he was also a criminal interrogator or a profiler for some secret intelligence service, she conjectured.

"Okay, good so far. Now, Olivia, tell me, in your extended family, is there any history or any suspicion of violence or sexual abuse?" He leaned slightly toward her and looked squarely into her eyes as if to be maximally sensitive to any effort on her part to say anything but the truth. Olivia could not handle his blistering gaze, so she finally looked up to the ceiling as if searching her mind for any remembrance of someone in her family ever having said something even remotely related to sexual abuse.

Olivia just knew she had to say "No," for any other answer would open a vile can of worms that could seal her fate — and Gabriela's. She was beginning to feel hot under her clothes — could feel wetness in her armpits and her buttocks. How could she do battle against this man, who was a professional at psychological assessment, who could figure out what psychic forces were operating just under the radar? Barely holding herself together as well as she could, she opted for a defensive move and said, "You know, Dr. Hinojosa, as hard as I can try to remember, there was never any incident or any talk about sexual abuse."

"It's interesting you say that, Olivia, because your file shows you have admitted to acquiescing to forcible sex multiple times and claimed that you had no choice. Maybe you don't have a clear notion of just what sexual abuse is, and that is very disturbing, given that you are the mother and main caretaker of a five-year-old child. Would you care to explain this to me?"

With her face now completely covered with cold perspiration, Olivia's mind went back to the occasion when she had confessed to that dreaded Greta Haroldson about how Bull Garcia would force her to have sex in return for breaks he would give her concerning her rent. Now Dr. Hinojosa knew about it, and Olivia would have to explain it to him more convincingly so that he could understand the situation she had been in and perhaps be more charitable in his interpretation of it. Was that even possible? She didn't want to lose, but she felt she was desperately pushing back on a door on the other side of which were legions of frenzied demons trying to force their way in. It was a huge task just being on high alert and defending her position and an almost impossible one trying to appear calm while doing it. Olivia had reached her limit of endurance, and she thought it better to break down gradually instead of catastrophically.

"Dr. Hinojosa, you are a psychologist. You were trained to help people in psychological distress. Can I trust you with the details of my life?" ventured Olivia, this time with glistening eyes.

"Now, why would you even ask that question? Yes, I am here to help you and Gabriela. You can trust me. Think of me as your friend." His chisel-sharp gaze softened, but just a bit.

"I, I don't have money to pay you for your services. Does the government pay you?"

"I will get paid by DSS when I complete this assessment."

Olivia had read somewhere that the master is the one who pays the consultant. Still, she had no choice but to slowly let her wall crumble in front of Dr. Hinojosa. *He could well be a lizard in a business suit*, she thought.

With tears starting to stream down her cheeks, she admitted, "What you said is true. About being forced into sex. The manager of my apartment building, for some time, he would come to collect the rent at night. If I did not have all the money available, he would come on to me, saying he would take care of my problem."

"And what was your response?"

"Of course, I would reject him — didn't want anything to do with him. He disgusted me. But he would bring up the fact that the building owner would evict my daughter and me if I did not immediately pay the rent. We had nowhere else to go. I dreaded the idea of my daughter being out on the street."

"Would he forcefully drag you to bed and mercilessly rip off your clothes? Would he cover your mouth so you wouldn't scream?"

She hesitated, for he sounded so much like Greta. If Olivia were to be totally truthful, this revelation would be a major acknowledgment. She was fearful but proceeded with caution. Olivia bowed her head and seemed to whisper, "No, I would walk to the bed and reluctantly cooperate when he took my clothes off. There was no need to cover my mouth."

"So was this consensual sex? Rape? Serial seduction? Grudging performance of a duty? What would you call it, Olivia?"

"I would call it disgusting and degrading."

"But yet, you never called the police — did you?"

"What are you insinuating, Dr. Hinojosa?"

"Seems to me that you fell into a comfortable pattern with this guy. Are there other men in your life, now or in the past, with whom you have had this type of impromptu sex?"

His thinly veiled accusations made Olivia think of what Greta and Bull Garcia had called her — a whore. A woman who does it for money. Only Olivia did it for the rent. But, in a sense, it was just the same. Maybe it really didn't matter why — it was for reasons other than love.

He waited for her to answer, but she was inwardly lamenting about her history and about her self-respect, her definition as a woman, as a mother, as a person.

"Look, Dr. Hinojosa, you are not a woman or a mother, so I do not expect you to understand my situation and why I did the things I did with that horrible man. And you are comfortably middle class, not struggling class like me. I have to do desperate things to provide for my daughter, to keep my life going, to do the right thing. I don't do drugs, I don't steal, I don't pick up men and bring them home for sex. The only whoring I do is at work at the circuits company; I force myself to go to work at soldering even though I hate the job and have to endure numerous humiliations. But I do it — I do it for the money and for no other reason. I sell my soul at work just for the money. Have you ever done that, doctor?"

He had been listening intently to her story with an air of superiority, for he felt that, in contrast to her painful life, he had an exemplary and rich, intellectual life full of the right decisions and ideals. All good, except for her question at the end — that threatened to bring his personal life into the discussion. He would never allow that, of course, but she had inadvertently succeeded in making him quickly think back to the years he had been in the very rigorous clinical psychology graduate program at Yale University in New Haven.

Manuel Hinojosa had been in his senior year of high school there in Houston when he applied to several colleges and universities to study psychology. Only one college accepted him — Winslow College in San Antonio — so he enrolled there. While studying at Winslow, he had made up his mind that he wanted to go on to graduate school. He had gotten lucky in his senior year, when the visiting recruiters from Yale University promised him admission and a full clinical psychology fellowship to the Graduate School of Arts and Sciences.

He was jubilant of his acceptance at Yale, feeling that his sharp and erudite mind had finally bore fruit. Once there at Yale, he met with his principal clinical advisor, Dr. Iselin Vilhjalmsson, age 55, widely published in the field of schizophrenia and other psychotic disorders. Never married, it took her just about three weeks to proposition Manuel, then 22, during one of their regular meetings in her very large and private campus office.

"What's the matter, Manuel? Don't tell me you are the shy type," she cooed while they were both sitting on the large sofa in her office.

"No, it's not that. Well, you are my professor, and, well, I always thought we students should respect our teachers."

But his response had been a lie, for, in reality, Manuel had been feeling sick at the idea of making out with this very large Norwegian woman who looked ancient and wrinkly, and who had monstrous, sagging breasts. She leaned over and kissed him on the lips, but all it did for him was to accentuate her pungent body odor — a kind of cheesy smell normally associated with the parmesan type used on pizza.

On another occasion, feeling that Manuel was still not responding to her over-active libido toward very young men, she laid down the facts while the two were in her office.

"Come, sit closer." She maneuvered his stiff hand and set it on the part of her considerable thigh exposed by her slightly raised skirt. "Let me tell you, Manny, how this works. Maybe because you come from Texas you don't know the give and take of situations. Have you ever wondered how the hell an ignorant and culturally backward Chicano like you got admission and a fellowship into Yale, one of the best universities in the world?"

"I made an application, and I had good grades as an undergraduate," he proudly responded.

"See what I mean? You have no idea. Good grades? Even retards get good grades at Winslow College, your alma mater. In all the years that Winslow College has been in existence, never has Yale accepted anyone from there — no one but you."

Manuel was starting to feel resentful at the manner in which Dr. Vilhjalmsson was talking, but he still had no clue as to where the conversation was going.

"I am on the psychology selection committee — have been for years — and, when I saw your application for graduate school, I fell in love with your photo. Do you get what I am saying?" She placed her hand on his and then moved his hand higher up her exposed thigh.

"Are you saying that you did me some special favor?"

"Let me put it this way, Manny. I was the only one on the committee who voted in favor of admitting you to our graduate program. I told the rest of the members that we needed more minority representation in clinical psychology and that I would personally make sure you succeeded in all your work here."

"That was kind of you, and I appreciate your support. I do promise to work hard so that I do not disappoint you or the committee." He slowly started to withdraw his hand from between her thighs, but she grabbed it just in time and thrust it all the way up her skirt onto her moist crotch. He pulled harder and managed to free himself. Manuel then stood up, more nauseous than ever, and wiped his wet hand on his pants. "I don't know what you are trying to do, Dr. Vilhjalmsson, but I have a girlfriend, my age, who lives with me, and we are happy with each other."

"Don't overvalue yourself, dear. You are not even in my league. I'm not asking you to marry me. I just need that regular personal contact, if you know what I mean."

"Maybe it would be a good idea if I get another main advisor, just to avoid problems," suggested Manuel as he struggled to make his stomach settle down.

"No, that will not do. Committee members warned me not to try to pawn you off later on someone else if it didn't look like it would work out for you. I stuck my neck out for you, Manny. I think I deserve some understanding. You will eventually be graduating from one of the best universities on the planet. I have given you an enormously valuable gift, don't you think?"

He stood there, a good distance from where she was sitting on the sofa, thinking about his options. In his very private fantasies, yes, he had dreamed of making passionate love to a mature woman of 45, maybe even 55, but, as he looked at his advisor sitting provocatively on the sofa, he felt a revulsion — her obese body and her slightly mustachioed face seemed immensely repulsive to him. And her body odor — he knew he might just vomit all over her if he ever found himself between her legs.

"Sorry to say, but it seems that my only option is to finish the semester and then transfer to another school. I am really sorry."

"In case you were not aware, all students in the graduate clinical program are accepted only provisionally the first semester. The committee takes another vote at the end of that time. Many will be terminated and not allowed to continue. I am beginning to feel unappreciated for what I have done on your behalf. Maybe I shouldn't do any more favors for you."

Manuel could read between the lines — he knew that if he did not acquiesce to his advisor's desires, he would be terminated at the right time. Worse, he would not be able to get into another school after a big failure at Yale. His options were clear.

He would always remember the first time he permitted himself to be touched all over by his professor, and it was an excruciatingly difficult endeavor. Because his body was consumed by the secret revulsion he felt, he could not respond sexually and was not able to achieve an erection. But she was experienced in these matters and instructed him as to what she wanted him to do to her body, short of intercourse, and he was able to bring her to full orgasm by performing oral sex on her. It was only by mercilessly squeezing his testicles and pinching his forearms that he prevented himself from throwing up all over her pubic area.

As happy as she was with her volcanic orgasms during those first few meetings, she still let him know that she expected him to get hard on subsequent encounters, so he resorted to medications — mild street drugs — and cotton balls jammed deep into his nostrils so he wouldn't have to smell anything. Manuel knew he had to perform like an Olympian to keep his advisor happy on the couch. So, over the next four years of graduate school, he had full and disgusting sexual intercourse with Dr. Iselin Vilhjalmsson about 400 times — an average of about twice a week.

She was 60 when he graduated with his doctoral degree, and, on the day Hinojosa left New Haven, his advisor told him with tears in her eyes, "I'm going to miss you, Manny. You are the best thing that has ever happened to me. I wish you all the happiness in the world." He was just itching to get out of Connecticut as fast as possible on that day. Manuel never again spoke to his mentor.

Oh, yes — all those uncomfortable memories from his years at Yale came screaming at him upon hearing Olivia's question, "Have you ever done that, doctor?" Surely what he had done against his will at Yale was materially different from what Olivia did to hold back the eviction process month after month, right? He was educated, and his sexual sacrifices were for a very noble and moral cause, he thought. On the other hand, she was just an ignorant circuit-soldering tech living in a welfare building, and her sexual behavior with Bull Garcia was more indicative of a personality aberration than anything else. He was sure of it. Whatever thoughts he had, to secretly admit to himself that his agreeing to do disgusting things against his free will was similar in some way to what Olivia had reluctantly done, were quickly buried and repressed because of the emotional threat they represented to his ego and self-concept. Besides, as a professional, he was supposed to be above all the mundane and earthly psychological conflicts and self-doubts that consume lesser individuals.

Unknowingly, Olivia had cut him down to size. But he was guarded about his feelings and thoughts — a trait he had developed when having sex with Dr. Vilhjalmsson, so as not to offend her with his real feelings during the act. Yet Olivia would never know the true impact of her simple question.

To get back to his comfort zone, he moved on to his next question. "Okay — enough of that topic. Let's go to the next question. Olivia, have you ever had thoughts or feelings about hurting yourself or your daughter Gabriela?"

Olivia froze upon hearing that threatening question, because she knew the unsavory and incriminating correct answer. But, in an instant, she also knew she should not appear nervous or overly tense to him. Yes, she was now trying to be honest, because she no longer could handle the intense emotional effort required to appear calm while lying to the devil. Yet she also realized that she was practically in a life-and-death struggle with this man, who had the power to permanently destroy her relationship to her daughter. Her heart screamed silently for someone to help her, for she felt all alone and ill-equipped to defend herself and her relationship to Gabriela against this ravenous shark circling her as she desperately treaded water in the middle of a vast ocean. She would either be eaten alive, piece by piece, or she would first slowly drown, terrified while trying to keep the fiend at bay, and then she would be eaten nonetheless. Olivia was quickly being reduced to feeling like a helpless child, not knowing the way, unable to find her home. *What a blessing it would be just to have mamma hold my hand*, she thought.

As her soul was fast undergoing a meltdown inside her, she told herself that she did not have the luxury of feeling the gravity of her situation, for she had to act boldly, to meet the challenge. But was it true that she was a threat to herself or to Gabriela, as Dr. Hinojosa's question had implied? Olivia had even confessed to Sonia recently that she feared she would hurt Gabriela. What kind of "hurt" was she talking about? Insulting? Slap across the face? Pushing? Kicking? Burning with a cigarette or hot spoon? Hitting with a belt? Fist to the face? Various punches? Olivia even remembered newspaper stories of how some desperate mothers reach their breaking point and kill their children. Had Frida felt that deadly impulse back in 1982? Was that the reason she ran away — to save her children from her demons of desperation? And was Olivia referring to these ugly thoughts when she said she might hurt Gabriela? More accurately, were Olivia's life stressors pushing her to the breaking point?

Things were already bad enough on that chair of inquisition where she was sitting in the psychologist's office, and, as she asked herself those reasonable questions, the fog of panic, confusion, and abject loneliness in this crisis situation clouded her mind. She wasn't certain what she was capable of. She didn't know what was real, what was hysteria, what was delusion, and what would be a believable defensive answer to his question. Should she be honest with herself and admit that maybe DSS and the piranha behind the desk were right — she simply was not capable of being a good mother?

She turned her head to look at the other corner of the office, where Gabriela was playing behind the parlor partition; she realized that her daughter was totally unaware that, at that very moment, her future was being decided by how her mother answered the questions posed by the cocky DSS psychologist with a pad and pencil. Olivia did the best she could to pull herself together and finally answered the question.

"You, obviously, are not a parent, Dr. Hinojosa; otherwise you would know the answer to that silly question. All parents feel exasperated from time to time. Of course, I've felt like hurting myself, like when I think I deserve to pinch my arm for having made a stupid decision. As for Gabriela, yes, sometimes she gets cantankerous, and I feel like whacking her on the leg with a fly swatter, but mostly I just give her a penalty of not watching TV for that evening. It works fine. She's a good kid."

"You've never had suicidal thoughts or feelings?"

Of course, she did, but she was not about to admit it outright. "Well, when I was younger and we were extremely poor, I sometimes wished I'd never been born, but that's all. Does that qualify as a suicidal thought, doctor?"

After a few more questions about her feelings and her history, Dr. Hinojosa administered several standard paper-and-pencil psychological tests and sexual-aberration protocols to Olivia. Afterwards, he picked up the sheets, saying nothing at all.

"That pretty much sums it up for you. Now I will ask you to step outside the door while I perform some standard tests on Gabriela."

The hairs on the back of Olivia's neck practically stood up as memories of Dr. Krodovic's physical exam on Gabriela came gushing forth. Dr. Hinojosa was just another DSS doctor, and Olivia was not sure she could trust him with Gabriela. "Doctor, if you don't mind, I would like to stay here in the room; I promise I won't bother you at all."

"No, that is not possible. Standard practice calls for the parent to wait outside while I talk to the child."

"I understand, Dr. Hinojosa, but I am very protective of my daughter. I will sit over here, behind the parlor partition. She will not see me, and I will not say a word until you call for me."

Something told the doctor that Olivia was not going to acquiesce on this matter, so he reluctantly agreed to her proposition.

The psychological testing on Gabriela did not take long. She answered some verbal multiple-choice questions on what she would do in specific situations. The psychologist also asked her to draw pictures of her family and friends. And finally, using the anatomically correct dolls, he asked her if anyone had ever touched her in her private parts, and, after a little coaxing, she said "Yes." Behind the parlor partition, Olivia was feeling horrified, for she had never been aware of anything of the sort. Yet the psychologist was energized by Gabriela's response — in a sense, salivating, for he was already anticipating he would be writing a very interesting report for DSS and justifying the considerable fee he would be receiving.

As was standard procedure, the psychologist wanted to zero in on the details of what had happened, so, little by little, Gabriela revealed that it had happened only one time; it did not hurt she said, but she added that she had been very scared. It did not happen at home, and the man was not a family friend. When asked, she said she still was having nightmares about it.

"What did this man look like, Gabriela?"

"He had very big ears. His lips were very small. Like the lips on a snake."

"Anything else you remember?"

"He was wearing a long white pajama. But it looked dirty."

"Where was your mother when this happened?"

"She was there. She told me to let him touch me."

Dr. Hinojosa knew he had struck gold with this case — he was professionally ecstatic in having uncovered a sordid occurrence of a mother farming out her pre-school daughter for the sexual gratification of perverts. And for money, no doubt. DSS would love him when he delivered the news! His written report would seal the case against Olivia and vindicate DSS in wanting to remove Gabriela permanently, Surely, Dr. Hinojosa would bask in DSS glory!

But his quiet jubilation, masked as a genuine and ethical concern for the welfare of a young child, was short-lived. Olivia, who had been listening in quiet and increasing horror at her daughter's story, suddenly jumped out of seclusion from behind the parlor partition and cried out, "Oh, my God! It just dawned on me. She's talking about that damned Dr. Krodovic! DSS had ordered me to take her to see him for a physical exam, and he turned out to be a sick pervert!" Realizing that Gabriela was still much affected by the incident, Olivia knelt down in front of her and took her into her arms. "Sweetheart, I am so sorry I forced you to obey the doctor — I am so sorry. That will never happen again, ever, ever! I will always protect you." As Gabriela hugged her tightly, Olivia felt like taking her daughter and just running away — running very far away.

"Mamma, please take me away from here! His eyes scare me."

CHAPTER 20

Over the next few weeks, Olivia conversed with Jason over the phone several times, and they even went out for dinner, taking Gabriela along. For the first time in her life, Olivia felt she had met a decent man but lamented that she had too many crises distorting her personality — Jason surely had more attractive and stable women in his workplace. Why would he even seriously look at someone who was coming apart at the seams? But as Jason had said, he was already fond of her, yet she feared she was too much of a liability in his well-ordered and productive life.

One night, he invited her to a down-to-earth dinner at El Cuerno, an easy-going Mexican coffee shop on Quitman Street, and they sat at the corner table, next to the jukebox. And then came the waiter. They ordered delicious, greasy beef tacos on flour tortillas and two soft drinks. Maybe it was the company, maybe it was the grease, but Olivia said she loved them to no end. Jason, who was not even Hispanic, loved the combination of beef, lettuce, tomato, cilantro, jalapeño peppers, and raw onions. They had a great time.

Over coffee and chocolate *conchas*, Olivia popped the next-to-the-big question to Jason. "You know, Jason, that I have had terrible luck with men. Maybe I'm stupid, maybe it's because I've never really had a solid father figure, or maybe it has to do with chronic insecurity because my mother disappeared from my life when I was nine."

Jason interrupted her. "Olivia, don't do that! Don't start putting yourself down again. You are a good person. You are a beautiful woman. You are a valuable human being who happens to be struggling with a variety of family issues. If I were in your shoes, I'd be a nervous wreck, too."

"So, you are saying I am a nervous wreck, eh?"

"Oops! Yes, I guess that is what I implied. You caught me, detective. Seriously, we all become nervous wrecks when we are under stress, just like you are. This does not reflect on your character but on your human effort to try to make things work out. Anyway, we are going off on a tangent. You were saying?"

"I forgot what I was saying!"

"You were starting to say how wonderful I am!"

Olivia almost believed he was serious but caught on right away. And to punish him, she playfully kicked him under the greasy and wobbly table. And the tit-for-tat and laughs continued for a few more minutes. They then became quiet.

"I think I know where your train of thought was going a moment ago when you started talking about men, but it's not for me to continue, so go ahead," suggested Jason.

Olivia became very pensive. She hesitated. "Okay. I really enjoy our times together. I love the way you treat me and Gabriela. Maybe you feel I treat you well, too. What I am trying to say — the truth, Jason, is that I'm falling in love with you, and I feel very afraid that you'll break my heart. All my life, I have felt like a loveless street dog, always being shooed away…"

"Olivia, don't. Don't continue — please."

She felt immediately that Jason's interrupting her in mid-sentence meant she had committed a social blunder. *More mistakes*, she thought.

"Look, Olivia. Let's just say that our relationship is more than just a friendship. Let's give it time and see what happens, okay?"

She gave him a restricted smile, but, inside, she was as jubilant as a young girl who had just been given a beautiful new dress and a blue ribbon for her hair. Out of sheer joy, she stole the last little piece of chocolate *concha* from his plate and put it in her mouth before he had a chance to protest. He gave her a big smile and wiped the crumbs off her lips.

About three times over the next few weeks, Olivia visited Frida in Dallas, and, those times, she took Gabriela with her. Frida, though depressed, was elated in having Gabriela around. Olivia could see that Frida truly loved having the two of them visit her. They even started going out to restaurants for lunch.

When Olivia was not visiting Frida, she would write her long letters expressing her feelings. In one of these she wrote, in part:

There's a part of me that just wants to hug you and love you — just like a nine-year-old girl who needs her mother desperately. But another part of me, the adult part, I guess, recognizes that you left me at that motel when I was nine, with the intention that it be forever. If I just love you, I would be ignoring my sense of profound hurt and indignity at your wantonly irresponsible actions as a mother. But if I remain angry and hateful, I deprive my heart of loving you again as my mother. I guess these forces split me in two, and it is my hope to be only one Olivia when I'm around you, for it would not be healthy for you, for me, or for Gabriela, if I remained a divided self for long.

And Frida would always write back, apologetically addressing some of the points in Olivia's painful letters. There was nothing extraordinary about the apologies, although Olivia could sense they were heartfelt. But the letters gave Olivia the opportunity to express her feelings over and over, each time reducing the anger and the hurt that dominated her thoughts about her mother. At the same time, Olivia was fully aware that her poor mother had no one she could lash out at for the repeated rapes she had suffered at the hands of her own father, now dead by his own hand. Somewhere, deep inside her mother's soul, there must be a massive store of rage against him, Olivia thought — a passionate fury that had been restrained and encased all those years only because it had morphed into a ravaging depression in her heart. In contrast, Olivia did not only feel outright hate for her grandfather for being her father too, but she also felt generalized toxic shame, a profound humiliation and debasement on her definition as a person, as a human being, for she had come into existence as a product of one of the worst family sins known to civilization. Olivia was tempted to discuss this matter at length with Frida, but always refrained so as not to overburden her mother with an even heavier emotional load.

So the visits, the tears, the rages, the complaints, the hugs, and the letters — they were tools for real progress in their relationship. And Olivia was feeling good that Gabriela was using the term "grandma" quite frequently and in a loving manner.

But one day, back at home in Houston, the phone rang — it was Greta Haroldson. "Olivia, don't think that we have forgotten about your sordid child-abuse case."

This time, Olivia could not resist showing her disdain for this woman, so she said, "You are about as hard to get rid of as an infected pimple, Greta. What do you want?"

That ignited Greta's rage, for she felt that the low-life immigrant had stepped outside her bounds in insulting the glamorous and well-bred Greta. Not wanting to let Olivia know that the arrow had struck her, Greta said, bluntly, "Listen, immigrant, I was just calling to inform you that your hearing is scheduled for this Thursday at 9 A.M. in District Court. Don't bring the kid. We'll take care of that later."

Click.

Olivia was petrified; she thought that maybe she should not have insulted Greta, but then, appeasing her would have been like a field mouse begging for mercy from an attacking rattlesnake. Almost in a panic, she opted to call Jason.

"Jason, please help me. That horrible Greta Haroldson from DSS just called and told me that we have a hearing this Thursday. What are they going to do?"

"First of all, Olivia, calm down. It's a hearing, not a trial. DSS will present the results of that physician exam and the psychologist who did the testing. The judge will ask you if you disagree with anything. He will probably say that he will consider the matter and make his decision known in about one to two weeks.

"Do you know which judge will hear your case?"

"She said it would be Thomas Silleni."

"A real bastard. He's a cruel and despicable man who handles only DSS custody cases, but he's more suited to be a Death Row executioner. I don't understand why he's in charge of a judicial process that is supposed to help people. Pure politics, I would imagine. I imagine that DSS pulled some strings to get your case before him."

"So, why are these people so mean, Jason? If they truly intend to help families and children, they would be more loving, more understanding, don't you think?"

"It's hard to figure out their motives and why they cover them up with pretenses of concern and love for the children. They routinely break the law, and they lie to parents to intimidate them into not demanding that their rights, and the rights of the children, be respected. Judges are in on it, too."

"I have done nothing wrong in caring for Gabriela. Will this judge just dismiss the case?"

"On Thursday, just go there, be polite, and answer their questions. Let's see what happens."

Even though Jason was trying to help Olivia calm down, she still felt apprehensive, and, over the next two days, the only thing she thought about was the hearing. She discussed it with Mrs. Brunswick, and she gave Olivia her kindly moral support. But she needed more, so she went to see her old friend Don Chago, the shoe repairman. After giving him all the details, she asked him, "So what do you think, Don Chago?"

"My child, I've been living here in Houston for the longest time, so I've heard many bad stories about DSS. They make up their own mind, and they don't play fair. Be prepared to take action outside the normal course if the hyenas are unleashed and they come for your child. There will be no other way to save your relationship to your daughter."

CHAPTER 21

Thursday morning, 8:55 A.M., Harris County District Court in Houston, Courtroom 8. Olivia was all jitters sitting alone at a table near the judge's bench. She deliberately had not eaten breakfast so as to reduce the chances she would vomit in court from the intense anxiety. At another table was her nemesis, Greta Haroldson, dressed immaculately in a light lavender dress, high heels and all. Sitting with her was the suspected pervert Dr. Krodovic, psychologist Dr. Manuel Hinojosa, and two other men she did not recognize — probably attorneys for DSS. After the usual courtroom formalities, Judge Thomas Silleni opened the hearing at exactly 9:00 o'clock.

"This hearing is to consider a motion by the Texas Department of Social Services to permanently remove child Gabriela Cervantes from the home of Olivia Cervantes, her natural mother, secondary to a report of child abuse and neglect. DSS Social Work Specialist 1 Greta Haroldson, please explain the allegations," uttered the judge.

Greta stood up, adjusted her hair and dress a bit — she wanted to look perfect, of course — and began her report. "After we received a report of sexual abuse of a child at this office, I personally visited the home of Olivia Cervantes, and I identified myself. Immediately she was very hostile and uncooperative. The kitchen was in disarray, as if it had not been cleaned in several days, while the bathroom was disgusting. I asked Olivia Cervantes if that was the tub where she gave child Gabriela her baths, and she said 'Yes.' It was so filthy that it had green scum all over it — looked like it had not been cleaned in weeks. The main bedroom was okay, except for the bed that reeked of urine and semen. I asked Olivia Cervantes why her bed smelled like semen if she had no husband, and she reluctantly admitted that she brought men to her apartment for sex, and that they would leave promptly afterwards."

"That is a lie, judge — she is lying!" screamed Olivia while she gave Greta hateful looks.

"Miss Cervantes, sit down. You will have your chance to speak," ordered the judge. "Continue, Miss Haroldson."

"As I said, when she admitted she brought strange men to her apartment for sex, I asked her if she was at all concerned that she was placing the child at grave risk, and she said 'No.'"

"Did you speak to the child?" asked the judge.

"Yes, I did. She has her own bedroom. I quickly noticed that her mattress had urine stains, indicative of physical and sexual trauma. The poor child said to me that, at night, she oftentimes would hear her mommy making strange noises in the adjacent bedroom and that she was afraid that the visitor was hurting her. She could also hear and sense the banging on the shared wall. She was terrified. This has been going on for a length of time. That poor little girl is traumatized. And, Your Honor, that is not all. The helpless child told me that her mother likes to bathe her a lot. Her mother likes to repeatedly rub her private parts with a sponge, and she asks the child if she feels a tingle. Gabriela told me that, yes, she feels that tingle when her mother rubs her."

Olivia's world was fast crumbling around her as she listened in horror and disbelief to Greta's interpretation of what transpired during that wretched home visit. All the hyenas were encircling her — what could she possibly say to contradict this witch's testimony? Would the judge believe her? Or more troubling, was the judge even fair and impartial? Was he part of the crucifixion?

Alone — she felt all alone, facing the demons bent on devouring her and her daughter. How she wished she had a mother there with her to hold her hand and tell her to fight these bastards to the end. But no, Olivia had never had good luck with that — she was used to meeting the world all alone and failing at it. Her current relationship to Frida was still essentially in ruins or, at best, in a state of slow reconstruction. Besides, Frida didn't seem ready to even hold Olivia's hand as a show of moral support, for she was in a perpetual cycle of anxiety and depression herself. But yet, that Olivia wanted to have a mother hold her hand made her realize that maybe she was almost over the anger stage surrounding her mother's betrayal and that she needed to nourish her basic, primal need to reconnect with that person who had been her childhood fountain of attachment. Maybe right now Frida was her "ex-mother," but Olivia felt it might just be okay to make Frida her mother again. Yes, rebuilding her relationship to mamma was important.

But the most immediate goal was the current crisis, the very lethal threat presented by what the odious Greta was telling the judge. Olivia remembered that she had promised Gabriela she would never fail her, never leave her. With just that one little memory, she started searching her horrified heart to bring forth even the smallest bit of moribund determination to fight back.

"Anything else on that home visit, Miss Haroldson?" inquired Judge Silleni.

"Yes, another disturbing find. In the bathroom medicine cabinet, there were all sorts of medications, including antidepressants and birth-control pills. Incidentally, the contraceptive pill for the day had already been removed. Let's keep in mind that Miss Cervantes claimed she had no husband and no steady boyfriend."

The judge then asked Greta, "Very well. Any final words?"

"Yes, Your Honor. I would like to add that the report filed with our office indicated that Miss Cervantes was contemplating using her daughter Gabriela for the sexual pleasure of her men and would be charging extra for it. You have the report on the bench. I have nothing more at this time, Your Honor."

"Now, Miss Cervantes. You heard the accusations by DSS. Please respond."

She felt buried under piles of trash accusations — where to begin? "Thank you, Your Honor, for the opportunity to defend myself and my daughter. First of all, let me say I do not have a perfectly clean house, but I do my housework every day. As I told Greta Haroldson on the day of her visit, the green lines on the bathtub are due to the metal from the copper pipes all over the building. One would need an electric sander to remove those stains. But otherwise, our house is clean.

"Another thing that Miss Haroldson alleged is that I bring men to my apartment for sex. That is absolutely false. However, I must explain something because she mentioned that my mattress smells like semen. As I told Miss Haroldson at that time, I have been the victim of repeated rapes by the same man, Bull Garcia, for a long time now. He is in charge of collecting the monthly rents in our building. He made it a habit of collecting my rent at night, and if I did not have the complete amount ready, he would force himself on me. He threatened me with eviction if I did not comply, so I felt I had no choice but to comply…"

Judge Silleni interrupted her, "Miss Cervantes, did you file a police report concerning the rapes?"

"No, Your Honor."

"Did this Bull Garcia threaten you in any way?"

"No. Well, what I mean is that he said if I did not pay the full rent, the owner of the building would seek to evict my daughter and me."

"Did he force his way into your apartment?"

"No, he did not."

"Did he tie you up, cover your mouth, or otherwise physically force you into submission?"

"No, he did not."

"Did you fear for your life before, during, or after the rapes?"

"No, I did not."

"Is it true you were taking contraceptive medication at the time of the home visit by Greta Haroldson?"

"That is correct."

"If you have no husband and no steady boyfriend, why then were you taking contraceptives?"

"I know it does not sound good, but I just knew that Bull Garcia would again force himself on me, and I did not want to get pregnant. That is the God-honest truth, Your Honor. Please believe me — I have very limited choices in my life!"

"So you were planning on getting raped again?"

"No, I was not planning it, but I knew it would happen again!"

Olivia knew the judge was not believing it had been forcible rape. She was feeling very uncomfortable at the idea that nobody seemed to believe that she was a victim of repeated rapes by this horrid man, this dirty Bull Garcia. But was it possible that it just was not rape even if it had been very unpleasant for her? Could it be that, to ease her moral guilt at acquiescing and submitting under minimal persuasion and monetary threats, she had to call it rape? Did she submit for economic reasons and not because of threats to her life?

Well, she knew she had to resolve this moral conundrum in her head and heart, but right now, she had to pay keen attention to the judge, who appeared to be not persuaded by her defense. The judge was silent, looking sternly at Olivia, perhaps expecting her to continue.

"As I was saying, concerning my mattress, the repeated rapes are why it may have some residual semen smell. I just want to make it clear that what Greta Haroldson said is not true. In fact, it is a lie. I did not and do not bring men into my bedroom for sex. Only Bull Garcia has been in that bedroom, and that was when he was raping me."

Greta Haroldson's nostrils flared upon hearing that Olivia was accusing her of lying.

"Please continue, Miss Cervantes," urged the judge.

"One other thing that Miss Haroldson said that is also false is that she implied that the urine stains on my daughter's mattress are hers and that, therefore, they are indicative of physical or sexual abuse. Those stains are not my daughter's! Greta knows full well that at that home visit I explained to her that we bought that mattress used, at a garage sale, and it already had the stains on it. Her declaration here was not entirely honest, Your Honor."

Now, Olivia had implied that Greta Haroldson was a liar *twice* — and in front of the judge! Greta couldn't wait for the declarations to move to the testimony of the experts — the physician and the clinical psychologist. At that point, Olivia would be totally destroyed — in pieces.

"And, finally, Your Honor, I would like to add my comment to what Miss Haroldson said about my bathing my daughter and causing her to feel tingles in her private area. First, I must say that I bathe my daughter in a perfectly normal manner, and I treat her private parts just like any other parts of her body. If she, in fact, did feel tingles, it was purely accidental or unavoidable. When Miss Haroldson was there, she told me to step outside of my apartment so that she could interrogate my daughter without my being present. My understanding is that interrogations of a child should be recorded and with a family attorney present, but this was not done. As for the accusation, I want this to go into the record: Greta Haroldson enticed my daughter to answer the way she did by stating that she, Greta Haroldson, would get tingles in her own private parts when her own mother would bathe her when she was a little girl. Greta wanted my daughter to respond in that manner and she did everything she could to manipulate her. It is a travesty for her to say that she cares about children. If I am being investigated for causing tingles, then I suggest we also investigate Greta Haroldson's mother. Who knows what else she might have done? That is all I have to say at this point, Your Honor."

Greta could not recall when she had been more angry than she was at this hearing. She absolutely detested, hated, and wanted to destroy Olivia more than ever. Whatever minimal amount of fairness she might have had in her heart at the beginning of the hearing was now gone. There were a few other tools she had in store to use against Olivia and her "immigrant mongrel kid," as she called her.

"Very well. Miss Haroldson, I understand you have the testimony of two professionals who conducted evaluations?"

"Yes, Your Honor. The first one is Dr. Manuel Hinojosa, clinical psychologist." At that point, the psychologist stood up.

"Dr. Hinojosa, you may begin your testimony."

"I interviewed Olivia Cervantes in my clinical office and found her to be very guarded, as if she was hiding something. She also was hostile, and I could even say that she showed some basic traits of paranoia. When asked about the history of her family of origin, she became very defensive, and I could see why. There is a lot of conflict and plenty of sexual family secrets in the Cervantes family line. Unfortunately, Olivia exhibits considerable confusion about her relationship to a mother figure, given that she was raised by an aunt who never married. Apparently, Olivia was sent away to live with this aunt because the mother had very low financial wherewithall. This has caused considerable confusion in her psyche. It goes without saying that this confusion can transfer easily to her relationship to her daughter Gabriela.

"In the second half of the interview, I administered some mental tests to Olivia, and the results buttressed the impressions I got from the initial interview with her. Olivia's intelligence is above average but with low skills in mathematics. She tends to be sexually flamboyant and provocative, and exhibits an elevated degree of hysteria and perhaps delusions.

"I also interviewed child Gabriela Cervantes, age five, and administered the standard assessment tests and protocols. Her intelligence is highly above average — she scored a 131 on the Wechsler scale for children. Nothing else was extraordinary. But there is a part of the interview I wish to highlight.

"When I asked her if she had ever been touched in her private parts, she became very quiet. After I repeated the question several times, slowly, she started to divulge some very disturbing information. She revealed to me that yes, she had been touched and that it did not hurt. She said she had been very scared when it happened. The next part is even more disturbing, so I made sure I wrote verbatim notes of what transpired.

"I asked the poor child, 'Where was your mother when this happened?' And her answer was, 'She was there. She told me to let him touch me.'"

Judge Silleni was visibly perturbed, or, at least, he pretended to be, while Greta voiced a painful "Oh, my God!" to drive home the calculated impression that what they had here was a sinister case of child sexual abuse.

Dr. Hinojosa continued. "Given the overall results of the various protocols I administered to mother and child, it is my professional opinion that Olivia Cervantes presents a grave danger to her daughter, and I highly recommend that she permanently lose legal and physical custody of the child."

Greta was secretly ecstatic. Dr. Hinojosa had done everything that Greta Haroldson had ordered him to do, driving a lethal nail into Olivia's coffin. Greta exchanged subtle glances of approval with the psychologist from hell. He knew he had a fat check coming and a lifetime guarantee of other cases and assessments, if he did exactly as he was told. Secretly, he pitied his colleagues who still naively believed they were ethically bound to report psychological testing results exactly as determined by standardized scoring protocols. *Stupid fools!* he thought.

But Olivia was devastated. Permanently lose legal and physical custody of the child? But that was her daughter! She carried her for nine months. She bore her, and cared for her all these years. If Olivia were a bad mother, Sonia would have said so. Her babysitter, Paloma, would have said so. And the opinionated Mrs. Brunswick would certainly have said so, and given her a lecture to boot. Olivia felt that her load was too much — she was being crushed by the weight of her almost impossible situation.

The judge gave Olivia the chance to comment on the psychologist's report. "Miss Cervantes, would you care to comment on the results of the psychological evaluation, as presented by Dr. Hinojosa?"

She thought about that, but felt, *What's the use?* She gave it a feeble try. "For the record, Your Honor, I would like to state that Dr. Hinojosa is a devious and callous man who will twist the evidence to appear more helpful to the DSS allegations. What my daughter was referring to when she said she had been touched was the examination that Dr. Krodovic performed on her. Yes, I was there, and I asked her to let the doctor do his work. I explained this to Dr. Hinojosa at the time of the assessment, but for some reason he has failed to bring that up in front of this court. And irrespective of what the psychological tests may show and irrespective of the level of competence of this hired gun who calls himself a psychologist, I am a good but imperfect mother and the best mother my daughter will ever have and will ever want. DSS can never change that, no matter how many professionals they pay to tear me down as a human being and as a mother."

"Very well. Thank you, Miss Cervantes. Now, Miss Haroldson, I understand you also have the results of a vaginal physical exam done by a physician."

"Yes, Your Honor." Greta motioned the doctor to proceed and was dying to see Olivia's expression when the doctor presented his findings on the supposed purity of her "mongrel kid." The doctor's report would seal the victory for DSS.

"My name is Rogo Krodovic, MD, Your Honor. I performed a standard physical examination of all external vaginal structures on child Gabriela Cervantes, age five. Some external minor irritation was observed, probably due to patient not wiping thoroughly after urination. There was no evidence of disease or of digital or penile penetration. General Impression: Normal and unremarkable. There is nothing else to report."

Greta Haroldson was livid but could not say anything. She felt like tearing that damned doctor to shreds! And the judge, too, he seemed unprofessionally surprised at the doctor's finding of no evidence of penetration. He gave Greta a puzzled look, which she acknowledged in a similarly subtle manner, so discrete, in fact, that nobody else in that courtroom noticed anything, least of all poor, anguished Olivia.

"Miss Cervantes, would you care to comment on the doctor's report?" asked the judge.

Olivia had sensed that the doctor had been on some malevolent track when he started the exam on Gabriela that day at the clinic, and maybe, just maybe, her emotional blowup had put the fear of God in his heart and he had decided to report truthfully on the results of the exam. Or maybe the doctor truly was some sort of reprobate or socially acceptable pedophile who worried about Olivia's threat to bring that subject up at a hearing. It also did not escape her attention that the doctor, contrary to his threat at the time of the exam, did not now accuse Olivia of having been intrusive and hostile at the clinic.

"Yes, Your Honor, thank you. I have always taken good care of my daughter, so I knew that a physical exam would reveal nothing extraordinary. However, I would like to add that the exam itself is a very traumatizing experience for young children, and I would hope that the Court would take it upon itself to devise a better method of determining if there is physical evidence of sexual abuse in future cases.

"More generally, Your Honor, if you feel there is something wrong with me and the way I mother my daughter, and if you truly have a heart-felt concern for children, as you, DSS, and the professionals present here profess, then I plead with you to help me at home, with my daughter, by providing a social worker who can re-train me to be a better mother. Taking my daughter away will only traumatize her irreversibly and beyond any harm that I might have inflicted upon her. Paying a social worker for a few hours a week will be more economical than paying a foster family full time for the care of a child. Besides, a foster family can provide a bed, food, and nice clothes, but they cannot provide motherly attachment love. I am my daughter's only mother — I am the only mother my child will ever need. Thank you. I have nothing more to add at this point, Your Honor."

Unmoved by her begging appeal, the judge with the dour face pledged, "Very well. I will review all the evidence and will issue my decision in about two weeks. This hearing is now adjourned." With a peeved expression, he hurriedly walked out of Courtroom 8 and into his chambers, as if he was totally sick of listening to stupid family problems. But he tolerated that initial unpleasant part of the whole process, because, later, he would be returning as Master Judge of the Universe and would be issuing his decision on what his court would be doing about Olivia and Gabriela. It would be almost orgasmic, this feeling, this sense of ordering, with the full force of the state, what would happen to mothers, fathers, and children. It was far superior to sex or even a cocaine high.

Poor Olivia just sat there, spiritually exhausted. She felt like she had done battle with a whole army of evil enemies bent on taking her daughter away. If she got up now, her knees might give out from under her, so she waited.

But Greta was not exhausted. She was almost spewing green bile from her anger — no, rage — at Dr. Krodovic. While still in the courtroom after the hearing, she approached him and carefully whispered, "No damned signs of sexual abuse? What the hell is wrong with you? Didn't you do what you were supposed to do?"

He looked around nervously and whispered back while fiddling with his papers to draw attention away from the conversation. "No, I didn't. I had everything ready, but the mother was watching me throughout the whole examination. It was too risky to do it in this case. She would easily have seen it."

"You knew damned well what you were supposed to do and why. In the past, when hostile parents have asked for a second medical opinion, your simple medical procedure saved our case when the second physician concurred that there was evidence of tearing of the hymen. It is quite simple, and the damned kid would never know, would never miss it, so why couldn't you manage the meddling mother?"

"You weren't fucking there, Greta!" fumed the visibly irritated doctor.

Greta had already made the decision that Gabriela would be taken away from Olivia, no matter what any professional evaluation showed, so she was boiling mad inside at the evaluation that the doctor had presented to the court. "Not only did you not do the procedure you've done hundreds of times, but, this time, you even said in your report that everything was normal. This is very bad for our case. I'll see to it that you never again do any exams for DSS. Or anywhere else, for that matter."

The doctor looked her in the eye and fired back, "As if I give a damn anymore. I'm 60, and you're 27 — I'm near the end of my career, and you're just a few years into yours. If you cancel my assignments, I will let the media know the terrible thing I have been doing to these young girls under your orders, so you will have a hell of a lot more to lose than me. So go ahead and shut me down, and we'll see what happens, you arrogant bitch."

Greta, too, looked around to make sure no one was within earshot, and she retorted in a self-assured and scornful manner. "I don't think you would do that, my dear mercenary doctor. It would make more sense for you just to lose half of your business, which is what I estimate DSS involves, than to incriminate yourself with the media. You're just bluffing, you chicken-shit flunky physician. Nobody would ever believe that a silky white person of my high caliber would be involved in your sick and depraved scheme."

"*My* sick scheme, Greta dear? Years ago, I knew that one day our nefarious relationship would come to this. So to protect myself, I made secret video recordings of all our meetings at my office, including the one where you ordered me to write in my report that the Gonzales baby had gonorrhea when, in fact, she did not. Your image and your voice and your instructions about what I needed to do to those young girls during the vaginal exams are all crystal clear for the world to judge. I know I'm guilty, but do you still think the media, the public, your boss, and the district attorney will think you are innocent? You and DSS would be at the center of a huge nationwide scandal, Greta dear, and you can bet it would be followed by an avalanche of million-dollar lawsuits by the affected families and their children. You would be in no mood to wear your bright-colored dresses or high-heel shoes for the next ten years. Picture that, queen bitch."

Most of the people in the courtroom were gone, and that was good because Greta turned pale upon hearing Krodovic's words. With passion, Greta detested losing the upper hand in a power play, and she had just lost what she considered would be a deliberately humiliating move against the doctor for his failure to do as he was told in the examination of Gabriela. But to save some face at the moment, she felt she had to at least minimize the impact of his strategic defensive move. "Okay, doctor — you've made your point. We will continue as always, but make sure there are no more failures in the future. They disrupt the pace of our cases."

Greta Haroldson did not wait for the doctor's response — she went out the courtroom door quickly. Her blood was boiling as she briskly walked the courthouse corridor, her high heels clicking rhythmically against the marble floor like the sound of a metronome set at allegro tempo, and echoing like staccato notes in the cavernous hallways. Her mind was already plotting how she could get hold of those video recordings and how she could destroy Dr. Krodovic for daring to oppose her like he had just done and for failing to perform what he was clearly instructed to do on Gabriela while she was on the examination table. He had placed Greta's whole custody case in jeopardy!

How dare he! There are plenty of other doctors on contract already well versed on the special requirements of DSS who can take over the caseloads — they know what they must do so that DSS wins the case every time. They are cooperative — and they know who's in charge of their paychecks. Heck, even our

DSS-selected judges know what DSS wants and what they need to do to continue the DSS-sponsored stream of massive and influential political support at election time. We make all that possibile! Yes, these judges all cooperate, maybe for the money, some because they have their own subconscious personal vendetta against families and their brats, and others because we have uncovered scandalous personal information about them that will unexplainably become public if they do not fully cooperate. Judges, psychologists, sheriffs and their deputies, physical therapists, teachers, psychiatrists and psychotherapists, independent social workers, nurses, and physicians — they all cooperate in various degrees, if they know what's good for them. But now, Dr. Krodovic has suddenly turned cocky and has threatened to bring down our entire well-oiled DSS system. Sure, our critics and ignorant parents say it's nothing but bribes, subversion, violations of the law, cruel disinformation, secret pediatric medical interventions, falsification of medical records, and political manipulation. They can talk and cry all they want, but we have a mandate by the state government, and our high level of professionalism makes us at DSS uniquely qualified to carry out our mission. We know what's best for families and the kids they produce, so nobody — I mean nobody — can tell us what to do. That is why this Krodovic bastard will pay dearly. Whatever it takes, he must be stopped before he ruins a good thing. I will make sure of that, Greta thought, as she walked out of the building.

CHAPTER 22

On Friday, Olivia woke up late and missed work. Gabriela had gotten up on time and played with her dolls and did some crayon coloring, but her mother, exhausted from the previous day's ordeal, had slept for 15 hours straight. For most of the day, she felt disoriented, totally preoccupied with the judge's decision looming over her life. As if that were not a huge burden in and of itself, she also had to contend with the inner storm of swirling feelings over her mother Frida and the revelation about her grandfather being also her father. It is at a time like this when a grown woman, out on her own, can be so overburdened by anxieties and life preoccupations that she needs the emotional and spiritual support of her mother — someone who truly understands her pain and can take over some of it to make life easier. At the very least, a mother's hug imbues the grown daughter with the sense of security and love she felt when her mother hugged her during those times when she came running to her as a little girl with a bloodied knee from a playground fall. Her mother couldn't cure the cut, but she definitely made it feel better, at least well enough to give the little girl courage to get back onto the playground and try that jump again.

But poor Olivia was deficient in that. She didn't have the supportive memories of her mother having helped her lovingly when she cried as a little girl, so, now, as an adult, it was not in her repertoire of survival skills to feel she could count on that fountain of attachment, love, and support. Worse, she didn't know that she didn't know. Maybe that great unmet need for a basic attachment figure, one who could rescue her from the pain and hardships of everyday life, one who could hold her and say, "You're safe now, sweetheart — you're with me," had, unbeknownst to her, surreptitiously sabotaged the few relationships she had had with men. Her possessiveness, jealousy, and dependency — normal hallmarks of a two-year-old solidly bonded with her mother — were totally counter-productive in her romantic relationships, but she just blamed the men and thought it was they who never quite understood her needs.

She was beside herself, so, at the end of the day, she called Sonia. "Hi, Sonia — it's me. Do you have a minute?"

"Sure, Olivia. How did it go at that hearing?"

"Horrible, Sonia. They accused me of being a prostitute ready to rent out Gabriela for sex. The psychologist said all sorts of terrible things about my mental health. The pediatric doctor was the only one who said nothing negative. He said there were no signs of sexual abuse concerning my daughter. What a nightmare it all was!"

"What now?"

"The judge said he would issue a decision in two weeks."

"What kind of decision are we talking about?"

"DSS wants to permanently terminate all my parental rights, Sonia!"

"Oh, my God, Olivia — that would be tragic! I know how I would feel if that happened to Esther and me. Have you ever figured out who filed that report to DSS?"

"Like we said, Karl Williams or Bull Garcia. Can't figure out who else."

"So what are you going to do if the damned judge decides against you?"

There was a long pause. "Sonia, that would be the end of the world for me and for my daughter. They would never allow me to see Gabriela, ever. I would have to kill myself."

"No, Olivia — don't say that. It's understandable, but there has to be another way."

"I am desperate. Can't eat right. Forget what day it is. It's affecting my relationship to Gabriela. It shouldn't be this way, Sonia. Please help me!"

But there was almost nothing that Sonia could do. She knew the stories about DSS revenge against any individuals who dared appear in court to provide positive testimony or support to any parents already in its crosshairs, and Sonia had her own daughter Esther to worry about. Regrettably, one lamentable secondary effect from the callous tenacity and vengefulness of DSS in fighting its court cases was that it turned citizen against citizen and friend against friend, each and all reduced to the lowest common human denominator: The will to survive under the threat of terror of losing one's kids to the state. "Look, Olivia, I am really sorry you and Gabriela are in this situation, so I will think about possible strategies for you. I have the feeling that you and she will be okay, but, for the moment, don't do anything that will further infuriate those sadistic bastards — okay?"

"Thanks, Sonia; it's really good having a friend like you."

Now Sonia was feeling conflicted again. What if DSS had tapped Olivia's phone to get more damaging information? What if DSS found out that Sonia was offering help? What if DSS had interviewed Bull Garcia and he reported that he believed that Olivia had sent Sonia to beat him up? She had stuck her neck out to help Olivia with the Bull Garcia problem, but now it looked like the big favor had left Sonia vulnerable to DSS threats of incarceration or, worse, limitations in parental rights! Sonia was relieved when Olivia changed the subject of conversation.

"What's the latest with the plan for Carmelina?"

"We think it's good news. He called several of us and Carmelina into his office and offered a counter-proposal. He will put a specified amount of money into a special account for Carmelina and will distribute ten percent of the company stock to the workers. We are not allowed to discuss dollar figures with anyone, but it sounds like a good deal for everyone. Carmelina is certainly happy with the offer."

"Yeah, that sounds okay. Sending the creep to prison would not accomplish anything for her. She's gonna need money to take care of that baby. Besides, now that the workers will own ten percent, he might think twice about mistreating them."

"That reminds me. He also agreed to remove all the microphones in the work area and all the cameras, except the ones pointing to the doors."

"Great job, Sonia. Well, I'll let you get back to your family. Thanks for listening."

Later on that evening, Olivia got the yearning to see Frida again and asked her over the phone if it was okay to visit her on Saturday. Frida agreed, and, so, Olivia and Gabriela took the intercity bus to Dallas early on Saturday.

"Hi, Frida — good to see you again!"

"Hi, Olivia — come in, please. And hello to you, my pretty little girl," raved Frida as she took Olivia and Gabriela into her arms. With each new visit, they all were feeling progressively more comfortable with one another. Frida had already prepared lunch for the three of them, something that turned out to be quite enjoyable. Afterwards Olivia asked Gabriela to go play in the enclosed backyard while the two women had coffee by the window overlooking the play area.

"Mamma, I've got a serious problem."

"Maybe if you told me about it, I could cut it in half for you."

"I've already told you that someone had reported me to DSS back there in Houston. This past Thursday, we had the court hearing in front of a judge, and people there were telling all sorts of lies about me. It doesn't look good — I'm afraid they might take Gabriela away from me."

"Didn't you tell the judge they were lying?"

"Of course, but I think the judge had already made up his mind. He said at the end that he would make a final decision in two weeks. That's all the time I have left to find a solution or something. I feel bad asking you for moral support when you and I have not yet fixed the mess our relationship is in."

"Is it really a mess, Olivia?"

"When I think of how much I suffer just at the thought of losing Gabriela, and then I think of how you willingly abandoned Benito and me, I cannot help but conclude that you really did not love us at all. There is no force on earth that would make me willingly abandon my daughter — no force at all! Ever!"

"I don't know if you are looking for me to say that I did not love you, or if all you want is the opportunity to again talk about your hurt."

"The truth, Frida — the truth."

"If there is a truth in this matter of love, Olivia, I do not know it. But one way to look at it is that my feelings of terror and desperation were far greater than my love for you on that fateful day. It doesn't mean I didn't love you — it means my love was buried by intense shame and depression. I took action on that day, willingly — nobody forced me. My shame and depression permanently obliterated my position as a loving mother — I know that now. I understand your rage because of what I did."

"So am I a hypocrite for asking you for help when I really have mixed feelings about you?"

"No, Olivia — you are a daughter in need. I failed in the past, so I am in no position to say you are a hypocrite."

"Thanks, mamma — I needed to hear that."

Later in the conversation, Frida divulged to Olivia that she had some money stored away in a secret spot in her little house and that Olivia was welcome to use it if it could help her case. Olivia declined but invited Frida to return the visit to Houston sometime soon. Frida said she would be happy to do that.

Before Olivia and Gabriela left, Frida told Olivia, "Besides offering you the money, I don't know what else I can do to help you with the DSS problem, but if you think of something, just let me know. You can count on me from here on, sweetheart."

CHAPTER 23

It was the morning of the following Saturday when Armageddon came to Olivia's life. The phone rang in her small apartment — it was Jason, in a frantic tone. "Olivia, grab Gabriela, and get out of your apartment now! Not in five minutes, but now! Get out *now!!*"

"Jason — hold on. You are scaring the hell out of me. What is going on?"

"There is little time for details. My contact in district court just informed me that Judge Silleni has ruled to permanently remove Gabriela from your custody. Greta Haroldson and two Sheriff Deputies left the downtown district court about ten minutes ago, heading for your apartment. Olivia, if they take Gabriela, you will never, ever see her again!"

"That is terrible, Jason. Why does that odious Greta want to take my daughter? This is not right! I've done nothing wrong! I love my daughter!" Olivia was now almost hysterical with panic.

"No time to consider that point, Olivia — we have an emergency here."

"But Jason, I cannot just run away — I have to follow the law and maybe file an appeal later. Right?"

"Olivia! Listen to me: There is no time to consider all the options!"

"No, Jason, you listen to me. I have never broken the law. I have never run away from the police, especially when I've done nothing wrong!"

"But this is an extraordinary situation, where you have to take action to defend your daughter. If they take Gabriela, your chances of seeing her again are near zero! Do you hear? Near zero! These sadistic people do not necessarily follow the law — they have their own rules, but they use the rule of law against powerless parents like you. Your daughter's entire future is in your hands at this very moment in time! Open your eyes — you are at a crossroads,

Olivia, pretty much as your mother was back in 1982. What are you going to do about that? Make your decision now!"

Olivia seemed frozen by panic and terror. Suddenly she remembered what Don Chago had advised her several days back: "Be prepared to take action outside the normal course if the hyenas are unleashed." Was this it? Had the hyenas been unleashed? She was trembling with nervousness and panic and sweating profusely. Gabriela started to cry silently.

"Jason, please help me! I'm confused. I don't know what to do!"

"We've used up precious minutes arguing about it. They'll be at your apartment in less than five minutes. Grab Gabriela, and get out of your apartment *now*! Call me when you are in a safe place."

Click.

It was a conflict of incredible magnitude in her heart. She wanted to save her daughter, but she did not want to run from the police. She wanted to do everything according to the rule of law. Just then, Gabriela clung to her and said, "Don't cry, mamma — whatever it is, I will protect you, mamma. I love you." Olivia realized that even Gabriela understood the concept of protecting against all evils those whom one loves. She also realized that Frida had buckled under intense emotional pressure due to her history, and the result was a tragic life for her two children. Was Olivia going to let DSS and the judge's self-serving ruling change the course of history for her and Gabriela?

She grabbed her purse and a small box with all her legal papers. She then turned off the television and went out the door of her Apartment #207 with Gabriela in tow, not knowing when or if they would be returning or how soon. She had opted to push back on the wheels of destiny under the control of the state.

They were still on the second floor landing when, between the trees, she could see Greta's DSS-issued brand-new Ford Crown Victoria sedan screeching to a stop in the apartments' parking lot adjacent to Bissonet Street, near Beechnut. Dressed elegantly as always in five-inch heels, she was accompanied by two sheriff deputy cruisers. The gorilla-sized officers got out of their cars with 12-gauge shotguns in hand. *Maybe Jason was right*, she thought: *They're not here to help us but to hunt us down.*

Olivia decided to walk toward the back stairs since the main stairs were already compromised. Briskly they walked down and onto the back area of the apartment buildings, as Greta and the armed deputies knocked forcefully on her door.

"Olivia Cervantes, open the door. This is Greta Haroldson from The Department of Social Services. We have a judge's order to permanently remove your daughter Gabriela Cervantes from this apartment and from your custody. Open the door immediately!"

If Olivia had been in the apartment, she would not have had ample opportunity to open the door, for no sooner had Greta finished with her warning when one of the deputies chambered a lethal 12-gauge 00 round into his semi-automatic pump Remington and blasted the door away. The two deputies ran in, stepping over a million wood splinters that had been the door, with Greta behind them, moving and pointing their shotguns in SWAT fashion, as if hunting down some deranged psychotic serial killer. "They're not here," yelled one of the deputies.

"The television is still warm — they can't be far away! They are now fugitives! Let's get them!" she commanded.

Unfortunately for Olivia and Gabriela, Greta had a good panoramic view from the one of the corners of the second-floor landing, and she spotted them making their getaway through the back area of the apartment complex. "They're in the back courtyard — quick!" she yelled at the deputies as they ran down the stairs and to the back of the buildings. Greta opted to get back to her car and go around the block. And, as was her habit in situations like these, she took off her high-heel shoes in her car, for she anticipated doing a lot of quick accelerating, maneuvering, and braking in this hunt. "This immigrant bitch and her mongrel are not going to get away from the law," she muttered as she put the powerful interceptor V8 engine in gear.

Olivia almost vomited in panic when she saw that the two huge deputies with shotguns were now coming at them about one block behind. She was holding onto Gabriela's hand for dear life, as the poor child was panting in her attempt to keep up the desperate escape pace. At one point, Gabriela missed a step, and her right knee dragged on the pavement for an instant, yet long enough to draw blood. She started crying both from the pain and the fear of being chased by men with shotguns. Olivia stopped for five seconds, rubbed some of her saliva on the wound, and said, "I am sorry, sweetheart — this is all I can do for now. We must keep on running."

As they ran across the street onto the next block, Olivia caught a glimpse of a screeching car that had just made the corner — it was Greta Haroldson's sedan, barreling toward them at enormous speed and with its engine roaring; she had an ugly, bloodthirsty look on her face. It gave Olivia the chills just knowing that this fiendish and tireless woman with unlimited determination was after them and that she would probably stop at nothing to get Olivia's daughter. Greta, with a judge's order in hand, to remove a child from his or her home, was a formidable threat to any parent, and the official order changed her bellicose and malignant personality for the evil worse.

Olivia felt so helpless, so vulnerable, so alone in this titanic effort to save her daughter. "God, please help me, I need you now more than ever! Please! I beg of you. I need to save my daughter!" She thought it would have been good to have mamma by her side.

Reaching the sidewalk on the other side, she and Gabriela went into a five-story apartment building; luckily, this one had various entrances, so the deputies, who were now only about 20 seconds behind, lost track of them when they entered the building. Fuming, Greta opted to go around the block to cut them off.

Olivia and Gabriela sought refuge in a broom closet to catch their breath — both were sweating profusely from the running and from the terror of being chased. Especially Olivia, for she knew that, whatever her problems were before she ran, now they were multiplied ten-fold in the eyes of the law. Not only would she lose Gabriela, but she probably would end up in prison for opposing the orders of the law — that is, the orders of the infallible judge. If she had had any naive idea of filing an appeal against the custody orders from the judge, that would now be practically impossible.

Then she had another terrifying thought. *Why did these deputies carry shotguns? Was Greta Haroldson armed? Was the blast I heard from the rear courtyard of the building a detonation from one of the shotguns? Did they shoot at our door? What if I or Gabriela had been on the other side of the door? Did they even care about that?* Contemplating some possible answers to those questions made her think that Greta and her deputies were there to serve the orders, to win, to show the force of the state, even if they had to step over cadavers in their zeal to serve.

She used her skirt to wipe Gabriela's face and nose in the dark closet. "Listen to me carefully, sweetheart. Things will be okay, but we have to find a way out of here and away from these bad people. I know it's hard and that you are tired, but no matter what, you do your best to run fast with me — okay?" Gabriela was trembling, but she whimpered and nodded in agreement.

Olivia could hear the deputies running and cursing not too far from her dark closet. It would be a matter of less than a minute before one of them would open their door. It would be the end of the world. She had to get out now.

So she opened the door just a crack to get a peek, and the deputy at the end of the hallway spotted her. "Larry — over here. West hallway. Hurry!" yelled the deputy. With Gabriela firmly in hand, Olivia swung the door open and they both ran for dear life as the heavy footsteps of one deputy closed in on them. In an instant, the second sheriff's deputy appeared at the other end of the hallway, cutting off what Olivia had hoped would be the escape exit. Her heart almost stopped with an agonizing sense of failure and doom. But she looked around desperately for an alternate escape — boots closing in. There was a door marked LAUNDRY ROOM — *CUARTO DE LAVADO*, so she turned the doorknob, but it was locked. Olivia's stomach was in knots and acid, as she felt this was the end, but she could hear women talking behind the door, so she knocked frantically to get them to open the door. Apparently it was always locked, but residents could use their apartment keys to gain entrance. Those few seconds seemed like forever to the desperate Olivia, but, finally, the door opened. With one of the sweaty deputies a mere ten feet away, they entered the laundry room and slammed the door shut. As the deputy repeatedly hit the heavy metal door with the butt of his shotgun and yelled, "Open up, this is the Sheriff's Department! Open up!" it dawned on Olivia that they might have entered a dead-end area. There were five women in colorful South American dresses doing their laundry — looked like Guatemalans — and they were scared, all huddled now; maybe they should not have opened the door in the first place, they were undoubtedly thinking. The angry banging on the door continued, and it got louder; Olivia's quick perusal of the small laundry room revealed no other exit. It was just a matter of time and the public servants would be blasting away this door, too. Olivia pleaded with the women, "For the love of God, please help us — they are after my baby!" All five women instinctively set their eyes on terrified Gabriela. Who wouldn't want to help this child whose mother was already doing everything in her power to flee from her tormentors? Each and every one of the Guatemalan women there knew at least several mothers from their country who had suffered confiscation of their children in Houston. Maybe it was just cultural differences in child-rearing, or perhaps something more sinister, but it destroyed families who had come to the promised land to find work and seek happiness. Some children were returned after years of court battles and undetermined abuses in foster homes, too late to undo the permanent social and psychological damage. Others were never seen again, even after interminable petitions to the courts.

The banging on the door stopped; were they getting ready to blast their way in? Olivia and Gabriela had only a few seconds left, and it would all be over. Just then, one of the women pointed to Olivia a spot behind several large trashcans where people placed empty detergent boxes and all the lint from the clothes dryer plastic filters. There was a small door that covered the subterranean crawl space for all the drain and water pipes in the laundry room. "Go in there, follow the pipes. They lead to the outside of the building. When you come out, go right. There are usually one or two taxis there. We will try to delay these gringo bastards. God be with you, sister. Take care of the little one," said Esperanza, about 50, wearing a bright yellow cotton dress with red-flower embroidery.

"Thank you so much. God bless you, too."

Esperanza quickly closed the door behind them and put the trashcans back in place. No sooner had she done that when two enormous blasts ripped apart the door latch and lock, but not the entire steel door. Two very angry deputies rushed in as the five women cowered together near the base of one of the clothes dryers. In a few seconds, they had searched the small area and then looked, almost accusingly, at the women. They all pointed to a partially open window, which, even when fully open, was still too small for a person to crawl out of. But since Olivia and Gabriela were nowhere to be found in the laundry room, the deputies had to conclude that, in their moment of desperation, they had squeezed out the window, no doubt with cuts and bruises as a result. "This leads to the southeast courtyard. They mustn't escape! Let's go!"

Meanwhile, Olivia and Gabriela were crawling on their knees as fast as they could, following the water pipes and getting cobwebs all over their faces — too desperate to care if there were spiders on them. It was a good thing that the earth was soft and moist, given that Gabriela had that nasty cut and scrape on her right knee, Olivia thought.

After they had rounded two corners, they saw the light ahead, although there was some type of obstruction there. As they reached the end, Olivia discovered that there was a half-door, but, in no time, she located the inside latch by touch alone and was able to open it. She got out first and then helped Gabriela get on her feet. There was no sign of the damned deputies. Olivia wanted to breathe a sigh of relief, but maybe it was better to get inside the taxi first. As instructed by Esperanza, they went to the right and quickly reached the corner of the building, where they made another right. Yes, the taxis were there, but so was the hated Greta Haroldson! She had suspected that Olivia might want to grab a cab to quickly get out of the area, so she just stood there and waited for Olivia and Gabriela to come to her. It had been a very shrewd move on her part.

Greta had placed herself strategically close to the corner of the building so that, by the time Olivia saw her, it would be too late. And it was! Greta grabbed Olivia by the wrist, twisting it in the process. She said with a smirk, "You are done, Olivia. You will end up in Huntsville prison, and your immigrant mongrel will be taken away, forever!"

Somehow, Greta's twisting of her wrist made Olivia lose all the fight in her, for she stopped struggling and turned almost limp, as a bird does when a cat has it by the neck. Gabriela had never seen anyone treat her mother that way, so her fiery little heart sprang into action. "Stop hurting my mother, you ugly witch! Let her go!" she demanded. And, with that, Gabriela landed a powerful kick on Greta's left shin, something that made Greta reflexively release Olivia and buckle over with pain. It was far more painful and difficult to balance because Greta was back into her five-inch high heels.

But Olivia was frozen in time, just standing there, not knowing what to do. Should she try to help Greta, who was now keeled over in pain? That is what she started thinking, but Gabriela set her straight. "Come on, mamma — we have to get to the taximan!" she yelled, pulling Olivia by the hand. "Come on, mamma!"

Once in the cab, Olivia told the driver. "Quickly, sir, she's trying to take my daughter." The cabdriver, a dark-skinned man with very prominent Indian cheekbones, was from Ecuador; he had witnessed the way the white woman had talked to Olivia and her daughter, and he did not like it. He knew what had to be done.

"Sure, *Señora* — where do you want to go? I take you." he asked as he quickly sped away.

"Anywhere, just away from here," cried Olivia as she hugged Gabriela intensely, as if she would just fly out of her arms for some unknown reason. Both of them were still breathing hard and had many cobwebs in their hair.

"*Señora*, I take you — can I suggest something? It seems to me that the white lady back there noticed my cab number, so in no time, they will be tracking or following us. If you want to get away from them, I suggest I drop you and your child at the Fiesta Store parking lot. Then you can take another cab wherever you want to go — okay? I take you there."

"Yes. Thank you for suggesting that."

Two minutes later, he spoke again. "*Señora*, if these bad people catch up to me later and question me, I don't want any trouble, I have a family, just like you. So I will have to tell them I dropped you off at the Fiesta Store. But, from there, they will quickly figure out which other cab you took, so ask him to drop you off in the downtown area. Walk a few blocks; then take a third cab. And the third taxi — don't have him drop you off exactly where you are going. Nearby is better. But I take you to Fiesta Store now."

"That's very nice of you to advise me. What is your name?"

"Cristobal, like the explorer. I am from Quito, in South America."

About ten minutes later, they arrived at the Fiesta Store on Bellaire Boulevard; Gabriela was falling asleep from exhaustion. Olivia cleaned her knee wound that had gotten caked dirt on it. "How much is it?"

"Nothing, *Señora* — I want to help you. Go into the Fiesta Store through this door, and come out a minute later through that other one way over there. I wish you and the baby well."

"Thank you so much."

While in the huge store, Olivia went into a private booth to call Jason. "Jason? Oh, thank God! We just went through the most horrible experience of our lives! Sheriff deputies with shotguns have been chasing us! Greta, too, in her car! They blasted my door and the laundry room door as well! We are terrified, Jason! Help us!"

"Calm down, Olivia, calm down. Are you both okay?"

"Only terrified to death, but not hurt. Jason help us — help us!"

"Where are you now? Are they nearby?"

"I don't think they are here. We took a cab — no, a taxi. Sorry. We are at the Fiesta Store."

"Which one, Olivia? Which one?"

"Oh, sorry, the one on Bellaire Boulevard."

Jason was silent for a few seconds; then he came up with a plan. "Listen carefully. Take a taxi east on Bellaire Boulevard. Tell the cab driver you want to go to the pharmacy two blocks east of Renwick Drive. Get out there, and make believe you are going into the pharmacy, but wait until the cab is out of sight. Continue walking two more blocks east on Bellaire, until you get to Chimney Rock Road. There is a big public parking garage there. Go to the department store that connects to the garage — it's called Maxwell's — and enter the garage from there. Wait for me in Basement Level 3. Is that clear?"

"Are they sending me to prison? Are they really taking Gabriela from me? Will I be able to see my mother Frida again? Jason, I am terrified!"

"Look, I don't have any answers for you, but I can tell you I will help you to resolve this one way or another. Now, get going to that garage!"

Twenty-five minutes later, Jason drove his car to Basement Level 3 and spotted them in a corner, away from the elevators. Olivia and Gabriela got into the front seat, and Olivia broke down in almost hysterical crying. "Jason, Jason, I am so happy to see you. Oh, my God, I thought they were taking us away." He hugged both of them for the longest time and tried to calm them down.

"Things will be okay. Calm down, calm down. I will help you. Right now, we have to get out of here and figure out what to do."

He was being positive for their sakes, but, deep down, he knew he was now fully involved in helping fugitives escape the law. It was unavoidable for him to think of his stake in all this. His freedom, his career, and his financial solvency were all at stake. Never had he felt so vulnerable as an adult. Given the long arm of the law, their efforts and risks could all be for naught.

To lose any possible tail, he drove around aimlessly for about 30 minutes and then headed for his house in North Houston. Once in the area, he asked Olivia and Gabriela to crouch so that neighbors would not see them. He closed his garage door before everyone got out of the car.

He gave them something to eat and drink, and then they had to shower. The clothes they had been wearing had to be discarded because they were torn and unwashable. Jason gave them some of his clothes and underwear, re-sized with safety pins, to make them fit more comfortably. He told them he would go to the department store shortly to get them appropriate clothing. Olivia used the various first-aid items in the medicine cabinet to dress Gabriela's knee cut. Then it was time to consider their very difficult situation.

"Jason, thanks for urging me to leave my apartment on time. That was the right thing to do. But now I feel lost — we are being hunted down, I can't go back to my apartment, and what about our belongings and Gabriela's toys?"

"Olivia, put it in perspective. If DSS had Gabriela at a secret location now, would you gladly give all that up to get her back?"

Yes, she would. We all lament about the things we don't have and wish we did. Jason had chosen the right perspective for making Olivia count her blessings in still having Gabriela with her. "I have lost all perspective, Jason. Our lives are upside down. I am disoriented. Can this be fixed?"

"I have no idea why Judge Silleni ruled against you, but I do know that he has a track record of ruling in favor of DSS about 95% of the time. He must have a personal issue with families, or kids, or maybe he's a pedophile, and DSS has the goods on him and has threatened to make that public — I just don't know. Appeals won't work either, because that means they will have full custody of Gabriela while the appeals go through the system. That will take years. We also have to contend with what they will charge you with for fleeing. To make it worse, they will use that to further show at appeals hearings that you are totally unfit to be a mother."

"So, what are you saying?"

"There is no solution in working within the system, Olivia. That is why, after careful thought, I urged you to run from your apartment with Gabriela. I would not have ever forgiven myself if I had not warned you."

"Thank you, Jason. But now what? How are we ahead now? No home; all our belongings are irretrievable. I certainly can't go back to work."

"I'll remind you again. You ask how you are now ahead. You have Gabriela with you. Is that being ahead?"

"Yes, you're right. Forgive me — I'm just feeling lost."

"You are in crisis, but try to stay focused, and don't make any irrational decisions."

"I feel that Gabriela and I are now in some type of purgatory or limbo. How do we get our lives back, Jason?"

"You don't," he said softly, after a slight pause.

"What do you mean by that? I thought you were my friend!"

"Calm down; I am your friend, and it's my unpleasant job right now to help you see reality because you are having a hard time with it."

"Okay, I'm sorry. So, what do you mean by that?"

"You cannot go back to your old life because the judge, the Sheriff's Department, the Police Department, and DSS will hunt you down and take Gabriela. If you willingly turn yourself in, they will take Gabriela. You cannot appease these bastards! You cannot win against their system. Your life, as you know it, is over. The state has the absolute power to change the course of history for families, for parents, and certainly for helpless children. This is what we are talking about."

"But Jason, what am I supposed to do? Gabriela needs to start school in three months, and I have to work to support her. What do I do?"

"Mexico."

"What?"

"I've given it a lot of thought, Olivia. Unfortunately, I don't think you have much choice. These bastards are relentless, and, if you stay in this country, they will get you sooner or later. Maybe in a day, or a month, or a year. Can you live like that? Could you have a normal life wondering if DSS went to the school that day to snatch Gabriela? Teachers would have no choice but to let the omnipotent state officials have her. You would never see her again. Just thinking about that possibility — every day — would be a chronic nightmare in your life — a terror that one day would surely morph into an insufferable and tragic devastation in your life and hers when they eventually find her and take her away. There is no other way — you have to take her and run to Mexico, Olivia. They can't get you there, as much as they would enjoy doing it."

Olivia was silent for the longest time, contemplating their future. "And my mother, Frida? I was just starting to repair our relationship. And Sonia and the rest of my friends? Poor Mrs. Brunswick."

Jason must have been getting a bit exasperated with Olivia's inability to see the seriousness of her situation, because he retorted, "Olivia, do you have a better plan?"

CHAPTER 24

That Saturday night, Jason fixed one of the bedrooms so that Olivia and Gabriela could sleep together. After about 30 minutes, Olivia joined him in the study.

"What are you working on, Jason?"

"It's an article I have to turn in tomorrow. Couldn't sleep?"

"Been doing a lot of thinking about the sermons you gave me earlier."

"I take it that Gabriela is asleep?"

"She's exhausted from all that running with the gun-toting maniacs after us."

"What have you decided to do?"

"I have to come to terms with my reality. They're after us, and we cannot possibly win any confrontation — legal, moral, or otherwise. They have all the resources of the government at their disposal. Gabriela and I are no match."

"It seems you are making progress in the right direction."

"But if we did it — go to Mexico — how would that work? We just cross the international bridge at Laredo and start a new life in Nuevo Laredo, Mexico? Just like that?"

"Yes, but two words of caution. I would say you probably should go all the way to Mexico City, just to be on the safe side. We also have to consider what DSS might be thinking. Have they considered that you might try to leave the country?"

"There is one thing that worries me about you, Jason."

"Okay, what is that?"

"Here you are, telling me in cold, calculated terms that, to survive, I must leave this area and go a thousand miles away."

"Somebody has to have a cool head about looking at your situation."

"It's not that."

"Well, what is it?"

"It does not seem to be affecting you that soon we will be very far from here."

"Oh, I see."

There was a long and awkward pause in the conversation. "Look, Olivia. I told you that I felt we were on the right track in our relationship. Now, these series of crises have come between us. We cannot hurry the normal development of a relationship just because circumstances may call for it. It would be a recipe for trouble."

"But, how, Jason? How would that be trouble?"

"Do you want me to spell it out?"

"Well, yes," she blurted out, giving the impression she was not really sure.

"Ever since I met you, you have been in various stages of crisis, but, in spite of that, I like you, your face, and the level of determination you show for fighting against DSS. My knowing you and liking you is no problem. The problem is, in my view, me."

"I don't understand. You are no problem. I already told you I am falling in love with you, damn it."

"I am the problem, Olivia. I am the problem because your chronic state of neediness may color your eyes and how you see me. I am not sure you see my total personality; you see me as a kind person, as a fountain of moral support. Maybe if your life was more relaxed now, you would not really like me as a total person."

"So you want me to beg?"

"Where did that come from?"

"You are Mr. Cool, looking at all the angles, and I am the foolish romantic falling in love just for the hell of it."

"No, Olivia, no — that is not what is going on. I care about you as a person, not as a romantic or sex partner. You have already suffered a lot in your life, and I would not want to add to that by starting a romance with you on the wrong foot, something that will lead to pain later on."

"So, you're the type who calculates all the math before you fall in love — for you, it's not in the heart but in the mind?"

"You could say that."

"I can see why, at your age, you are still not married."

"That sounds to me like an insult — a personal attack. Have I ever insulted you, Olivia?"

"No, you haven't. I am sorry — you are right."

"Look, I've told you before — let's just see what happens. I like you, I admire you, I respect you, and I do not wish to put the brakes on our budding romance."

Yeah, sure, she thought, *when we are going to be one thousand miles apart. Fat chance.*

"Okay — back to Earth. What about my mother? What do you suggest?"

"It's clear to me that, if you wish to continue repairing your relationship, then she must join you and Gabriela in your odyssey."

"But she has her own life in Dallas."

"Forgive me for saying this — but, *what* life?"

At that point, both Jason and Olivia moved from his study to the kitchen. Jason had already started the coffee brewing and served cups for both.

Jason added, "I think this development of running to Mexico will give you and your mother a wonderful opportunity to rebuild your lives together. Besides, you've said before that Frida loves to hold and talk to Gabriela. Your daughter needs a grandma — someone who can love her without the contamination of strict discipline. Frida needs a granddaughter — someone to love so she can redeem herself from the failures of the past. And you and Frida need each other — you need Frida to finish mothering you."

What Jason had just said made sense to Olivia, but she was scared at the thought of moving all the way to Mexico City with no job and no money. Jason knew this. He handed Olivia an envelope with several thousand dollars. "This will help all three of you survive in Mexico for several months while you find a job. Besides, Olivia, if you get into a snag, you can always call me, and I will wire you more money. I expect you to be responsible."

Suspicious as always, Olivia didn't know if Jason's generosity was actually an attempt to get rid of her or simply the actions of a kind man. How can you facilitate the running away of someone you care for? She still had a lot to learn.

"Thank you. You are very kind. So tell me, Jason: When do you think we should go to Laredo?"

"As soon as possible. I imagine DSS and the deputies are checking all possible places where you could be hiding. They're contacting all the people you know. Maybe they've even thought that you might make a run for it to Mexico. The sooner you go, the less time you give them to make interception plans."

"Do you think they might be waiting at the Laredo International Bridge?"

"Don't know, but you'll have to case the joint first before you make any attempt to cross. Having Frida with you might be a good idea, since they will be looking specifically for a young woman with a five-year-old child only."

That same night, Olivia called Frida in Dallas and explained her crisis situation. "I'm sorry, mamma, but there is no other way. DSS and its deputies have shown they can be pretty vicious. Gabriela and I must go to Laredo within 24 hours and, from there, to Mexico City. I would like for you to be part of that."

Even though Olivia was asking Frida to join them, she was doing so in the hope that they could iron out the resentments Olivia still had in her heart. Great strides had been made in the numerous visits she had made to Dallas, but the relationship was still far from what could be called a normal mother-daughter one. In fact, Olivia had not forgotten Jason's admonition to never forgive a serious moral transgression, and Frida's abandonment of her two children in 1982 was such a violation of moral duty. So was there a true and realistic hope of normalizing relations with Frida, or was that just a flimsy pipe dream based on Olivia's primal need to relate to a mother, especially when Olivia seemed to be going from crisis to crisis?

"Olivia, how will I support myself in Mexico? Here I have a list of steady clients."

"I imagine you could start the same little business in Mexico." Olivia did not want to elaborate too much because she did not want to appear that, after begging Jason, she was now begging her mother. In fact, she was getting indignant about asking repeatedly when she wanted something.

Olivia was wondering what the very long silence was about. Did mamma really have to search her soul that much? "Listen, Frida — I don't want to twist your arm, so if you can't or won't, I'll understand."

"It's not that. I was just thinking what I would do with my clients and my few belongings here. But I figure I owe it to you, even though I am afraid. I'll do it."

"That's great, mamma. Take the Intercity Bus early in the morning, but call me as soon as you know what time you are leaving, so I can take the bus from Houston about two hours later. When you get to Laredo, wait for us at the San Agustín Plaza. It's about one block from the Convent Avenue Bridge, and there are several hotels nearby with restaurants and restrooms."

After that, she called Sonia to advise her of her plans and to relay goodbyes to Rosalba, Lizbet, Glenda, Judith, Rita, babysitter Paloma, and Sonia's husband Matt. She asked Sonia to look after Mrs. Brunswick for the first week at least, and to get an alternate person for the longer term. Then she called Aunt Jenny and Don Chago. It was all harder than she had imagined.

When she finished with all her phone calls, she noticed that Jason was giving her a concerned look. "What?"

"It just occurred to me that DSS might have tapped Sonia's or Aunt Jenny's line. Maybe I'm being too paranoid, but, then again, who would have thought you would end up running from deputies blasting doors away?"

"How can we know?"

"We'll know in the morning when I take you to the bus terminal. I will go in alone to case the terminal before I say it's okay. Frida will probably call later tonight to let us know what time her bus leaves Dallas. Then I'll call the local terminal to get the time for one leaving for Laredo about two hours later. I'll wake you both up in the morning. Now, get some sleep."

Jason had been working on his article for one hour that night when the phone rang; it was Frida. In a quavering voice, she asked, "Hello, young man — may I speak with Olivia, please?"

"Is this Frida?

"Yes, I am Frida, her mother."

"Hi, Frida. My name is Jason McDougall, I am Olivia's friend. But she and Gabriela are sleeping soundly right now. Are you calling to give us the time your bus leaves Dallas tomorrow morning?"

"You must be that 'Jason' young man she talks to me about. She has told me several times that she is madly in love with you but is afraid to make you fully aware of it."

"Well, we are friends right now — that's all."

"Now, do you know why she is afraid to tell you outright about that?"

"Well, no — I don't."

"I will tell you, Jason. She keeps telling me that you are an outstanding man with very high principles and that you are an intellectual. She loves you, but she doesn't want to tell you because she is deathly afraid of your rejection. She says that, standing next to you, she is no more than a dog in comparison. That's sad — that she feels that way — but that's what she has said. So now I've told you — now you know."

"Frida, what time does your bus leave for Laredo tomorrow morning?"

"Six o'clock. I'll be on it. Make sure all three of you arrive early for your bus so you can sit together."

"Oh, no — I won't be going. Only Olivia and Gabriela."

"Why is that? Why aren't you coming?"

"Not easy to explain, Frida. It's complicated."

"Does she know that? It will break her heart."

"She knows — we talked a bit about it."

"Olivia has never been in love, young man. You are the first."

"Listen, Frida — I've got to get back to my writing. Good luck in Laredo and then in Mexico City. Have a safe trip."

Jason did not feel too comfortable with what Frida had said. In truth, he was not actually rejecting Olivia — he was being cautious and felt it was just too soon to be talking about a relationship. He always liked to measure things properly before taking action, like making sure statements were real and accurate before writing them down as part of a *Houston Chronicle* article. He figured he had gotten ahead in life by not making any decisions that could wait for more timely information.

Before going to bed, he determined that the bus company had an 8:10 morning bus to Laredo, so he set his alarm clock for 6. He really felt sorry for Olivia and Gabriela, whose lives were being so drastically changed by the events of the last few months. And who knows what fate awaited them in Mexico City....

CHAPTER 25

In the morning, Jason drove them to the large bus terminal at the corner of Richmond Avenue and Sage Road, just southwest of the downtown area. As a precaution, he parked one block away and walked alone to the terminal, asking Olivia and Gabriela to crouch down just in case some official was patrolling the area. In the departures area, there already were fifteen buses loading passengers and baggage — but nothing unusual there. Inside the huge terminal, there were hundreds of people with makeshift baggage made out of boxes and rope baskets, heading out to San Antonio, St. Louis, New Orleans, Chicago, Milwaukee, Kansas City, Laredo, Miami, and even New York City. Some were going to visit families, others were looking for a better job, and still others were maybe getting away from a life that just hadn't panned out in Houston.

Jason nonchalantly looked around, trying to spot any law-enforcement officers, uniformed or even undercover, sitting like private eyes, inconspicuously reading the massive Sunday edition of *The Houston Chronicle*. Would Greta Haroldson actually show up for something like this? She would surely stand out like a flashing neon sign during the 1977 New York blackout. But, no. No uniforms, no private eyes, and no neon sign. Seemed the coast was clear.

He went back to his car and returned with Olivia and Gabriela, although he still kept a keen eye out for anybody paying undue attention to a mother and a small child. He bought the one-way tickets to Laredo for them and joined them on the departure platform. They had barely any luggage, just two backpacks with some clothes he had bought for them. He kissed Gabriela on the forehead and gave her a hug. "In Mexico City, Gabriela, you'll have a lot of fun. Ask your mamma to take you to see the pyramids — and the giant tarantulas at the Chapultepec Zoo. Don't worry, they won't bite — you can

185

hold them in your hand!" Then he turned to Olivia. "I'm sorry we didn't have more time together, Olivia, but at least you'll have Gabriela and your mother. Good ingredients for a better life. You will do okay."

She looked at him like a forlorn puppy. "Come with me, Jason. Let's start a life together. I know I'm less than half the woman you deserve, but I can improve. I can read more and learn about culture, about politics. I promise never to interfere with your work. I will settle for just being in the same room with you, even if you never touch me."

Those were hard words for Jason to hear, because he knew they were coming from Olivia's heart at great risk of the dreaded rejection she so much feared. He surely did not want her to raise her hopes, when there was no chance of his joining them to make a family. But he had his standards about relationships, and, so far, he had not made any big mistakes in that area. It was a simple but unfortunate case of two people being at different stages of their lives when they met. "Olivia, don't say that — please. Don't put yourself down. You are a wonderful woman, but we are in different worlds, and it just wouldn't work out. Once your life settles down in Mexico, you will be meeting many eligible men who can make you happier than I ever could. You'll see."

"That's okay, Jason — you don't want me, and I don't have the beauty or the charm to make you love me — that's all there is to it. I wish you the best in your life, and thank you for everything." She took one step forward, and, with her dainty index finger, she wiped one running tear from her cheek and transferred it to his lips. "You never even kissed me, but now you have tasted my tears."

Jason stepped back from the platform as the buses started rolling out, one by one, all going in different directions. The bus terminal was not far from Highway 59, the one they would be taking southwest to Laredo, so, in no time, their bus was cruising at highway speed. It would be in Laredo in about five hours, counting a short break in Victoria, the halfway mark.

He went back into the terminal waiting area to check again for possible DSS spies who would report if they had seen Olivia and Gabriela. Nothing seemed out of the ordinary, so he left the area.

Driving back to his home, he reflected on the whole chapter of his life he had just spent knowing Olivia and Gabriela, and the brief phone conversation he had with Frida the previous night. He philosophized that, in life, one has to stick to the principles which have minimal risk, even when one occasionally does not feel like it. It was merely a matter of discipline — and maybe a little luck, he conceded. That is what perhaps made him a desirable man in the eyes of Olivia. If he did not follow those rules, he felt, maybe he would just be like any other lustful man to Olivia. Or maybe none of that mattered anymore, now that she was out of his life. When he got home, he continued writing the article that would soon be due on his editor's desk.

Maybe he had left the bus terminal too soon, for, two hours after Olivia's bus had left, three deputies showed up and spoke to the departures manager. After exchanging some unpleasant words, the manager took them to a back room where all the security video recordings in process were kept. They quickly zeroed in on the 8:10 bus that had left on time to Laredo and compared the video images to enlarged photos they had brought with them. They had a match!

Immediately, the leader of the three got on the phone with Greta Haroldson, who, at that time, was at a terminal of a different transportation company, scouting the imminent departure of a bus also leaving for Laredo, but via San Antonio. "Greta, we have a positive identification. The woman and the kid boarded the 8:10 bus to Laredo. The departure foreman recognized the photos, and the security video confirms it. They are two hours ahead of us. There is no way we can catch up to and intercept that bus. So I suggest we cable the arrest orders to the Texas Highway Patrol station in Victoria. They have several cruisers on the road for 100 miles on either side of their headquarters; the interception and arrest should be easy. Just give the word."

"No way! Absolutely no fucking way! I want to be there at the arrest of this insolent immigrant, and I will rejoice when I finally take away her half-breed kid." Then, she lowered her voice somewhat. "Let me ask you, sergeant. Do you have any small kids?"

"Sure do, Greta. We have two — but what does that have to do with this case?"

In the most vile tone possible, she added, "If you know what's good for you, sergeant, do not, under any circumstances, ask the Texas Highway Patrol for help! I will take care of this problem, damn it. Is that perfectly fucking clear?"

Despite Greta's outward hostility toward the sergeant, she inwardly did agree with his assessment that there was absolutely no way to drive from Houston to catch up to and intercept that bus before it reached Laredo. Immediately, she called her DSS supervisor Antonio Guerra, who was at a child-welfare conference in The Bahamas, and explained the situation, cunningly leaving out the possibility of asking the Texas Highway Patrol for arrest assistance. "However, at this point, there is only one way to arrest this fugitive and place the kid in safe hands with DSS."

"Greta, I trust you. What do you suggest we do?"

"I need for you to immediately authorize the use of a private business jet to take me to Laredo at once. I will be there waiting for her at the terminal when her bus arrives. Will she be in for the shock of her life!" She said it with such heartfelt gusto that one could imagine that Greta could even taste the blood of her fleeing prey!

"But, Greta, that's an expensive proposition. There has to be some other way."

"But there isn't!" She had to control herself because of the rage she was starting to feel. *How dare he question my judgment! I am never, ever wrong!* "Look, I do what needs to be done to justify continual increments of your mega-budget proposals. Every year, the state budget committee approves higher amounts — no?"

"Well, you do have a point. Very well. I will call our contact at Hobby Airport. You get yourself to Laredo, and let me know when you have her and the kid in custody."

"My pleasure serving you, boss." Very few people dared to say "No" to Greta.

In less than 45 minutes, Greta Haroldson was racing through the blue Texas skies in a Bombardier Learjet at 500 miles per hour. Using that aircraft for only one passenger — and on such a short flight — was a bit of an over-kill, since it was designed for transcontinental travel. *But, what the heck,* she thought, *I am worth every penny of it.*

Ninety minutes after taking off from Houston's Hobby Airport, the Bombardier was touching down at the Laredo International Airport in the northeast part of the city. Greta looked at her watch and calculated that Olivia's bus was due to arrive at the downtown terminal in less than 30 minutes — which was cutting it too close for comfort but a lot better than asking the Highway Patrol to assist her and thus denying her a personal on-the-spot capture and victory over Olivia.

At the airport, she called the sheriff's department and asked them to meet her four blocks from the downtown bus terminal, which was located at the corner of Hidalgo Street and Salinas Avenue. They offered to go directly to the terminal, so as not to risk having the bus arrive before Greta and the deputies, but, again, she vehemently opposed that plan.

Greta grabbed a cab and told the driver to hurry to the downtown area. She was restless in the back seat of the cab — leaning forward, never once resting against the cushiony back of the seat. She wanted to catch every glimpse of the landscape and the buildings as they whisked by, bringing her closer and closer to her victory. Greta was like a salivating wolf eye-balling a baby deer next to its mother.

After a few minor delays due to traffic congestion, Greta's cab arrived at the assigned street corner. There were two sheriff's cruisers already there, waiting for her. She paid the cab and quickly got into the head deputy's car. "Quick, we have to get there," she ordered as if she were the Sheriff herself. It was only four blocks, so the two cars arrived there in less than a minute, screeching their tires to a halt on the entranceway and effectively blocking any buses from leaving the lot, just in case. Greta told the deputies to talk to the arrivals foreman while she checked the buses herself. Much to her dismay and fury, she saw the bus from Houston already parked on the platform, and it looked like it had been there a few minutes already. Passengers were milling around, many picking up their boxes and baskets from the compartments in the lower sections of the bus. With great expectations, she then went inside the bus — no Olivia. But Greta could swear she smelled Olivia's cheap perfume — you know, the kind the attendant lady at the bakery has on display, as a sideline business to supplement her low wages. Or was Greta's intense and overriding obsession to capture Olivia and take her daughter away causing her to hallucinate about such matters?

Back on the platform, she started to perspire profusely and was trembling with rage. "Hey, did you happen to see a woman of about 27 or 28 with a small girl? She was on this damned bus," she asked a group of people. The passengers, all Hispanic, did not like the idea of an angry *gringa* cursing while asking, in a commanding manner at that, for a favor, so they independently but unanimously played dumb, even though all of them remembered Olivia and her little girl, because, back in Houston, Olivia had boarded the bus in tears.

After checking the bathrooms and all other areas of the terminal, Greta concluded that Olivia and Gabriela were already on the streets, so it became imperative to post deputies at both downtown international bridges into Mexico immediately. The bridge closer to the terminal was the Convent Avenue International Bridge, and that was about six blocks away. Still fuming, Greta decided to hit the streets, on the lookout for her targets.

But Olivia and Gabriela did not walk directly to the bridge, for they had to meet Frida somewhere at San Agustín Plaza, which was a bit farther. When they got there, they found Frida, wearing a colorful one-piece Mexican Indian cotton dress, already comfortable on a park bench with her one small bag. "Hi, mamma — nice to see you again. It's so odd to meet with you in Laredo!"

"Oh, Olivia, I am glad you two got here with no problem. I was fearing that those terrible people might want to hurt you or something." Frida hugged and kissed both of them and made room on the bench so everyone could sit. There were many people busily walking from any number of entry points on the plaza to the southwest corner, the one leading to the bridge, each carrying his or her own personal story that brought them to that point on that day. Certainly Frida and Olivia had a complex one to tell.

"You know, Frida, I am really scared about what we are doing, even though I know there is no other way. I sure hope that you and I will be able to get along, given what has happened in our past."

"We are all wounded warriors, Olivia. Every year that I lived alone in Dallas, I died a bit because of what I had done to you and Benito, rest his soul. But since you showed up, I feel there is hope of making things better. It's all a long chain of pain and suffering. I am sure my parents were hurt by someone, and they hurt me. I, in turn, hurt you. You are the judge if you have hurt your own child. And who knows where it all began?"

Those last few words scared Olivia, for she knew she had not been a perfect mother. Was she being a hypocrite for damning her mother's behavior when she herself had rejected Gabriela that night when she wanted to sleep in the bed with her? Hadn't she called her daughter a pig? More disturbing, was Gabriela herself now carrying the seeds of future rage and resentment against her own mother for those violations of moral code? Would Gabriela later blame Olivia for the traumatic experience on Dr. Krodovic's examination table? Three generations, each carrying grievances against the previous one, while, paradoxically, unable to refrain from doing that which they criticize.

"I will make every attempt to be positive about our relationship, but just keep in mind that, from time to time, I may lapse into my resentful mood. As for you, I think that, once we settle down in Mexico City, you should start seeing a therapist, not a social worker, to help you with your own self-esteem and depression issues. Then we could see another one for our joint-relationship problems."

"I think it's a workable plan, Olivia."

"Well, mamma, I think we'd better slowly head for this Convent Avenue Bridge. We have to keep an eye out in case Greta or some deputies are here. I wouldn't be surprised."

They walked the half block and got closer to the walkway leading to Nuevo Laredo, Laredo's sister city in Mexico. Just then, Olivia spotted two uniformed officers right at the walkway tollbooth. *Those two guys there don't look like immigration officers, and if they were, shouldn't they be on the walkway for people coming from Mexico? And look at those sheets of paper they're holding — could be photographs. Looks risky.*

They backtracked to the plaza and then walked six blocks east to try their luck on the second bridge, the Juarez-Lincoln International Bridge, but that, too, was under surveillance.

"It looks like they've got us cornered. I would be afraid to try either bridge; I'm almost sure those pieces of paper they're holding are our photos," Olivia told Frida, in an anxious voice.

Frida had an idea. "Look — there are many small department stores here in the downtown area. We could buy some makeup, mascara, and such to make our faces even darker. Let's get some jet black wigs, some shawls for the three of us, and let's take a cab across the bridge. The moving traffic will make it harder for those creeps to make a quick identification. Besides, it looks like they are concentrating mainly on pedestrians." It was the only plan they had, so they went for it.

Thirty-five minutes later, they came out of Laredo Clothing & Jewelry, all made up, with long black wigs and colorful Mexican shawls. They caught a taxi on Convent Avenue, just eight blocks north of the bridge, and the cabbie agreed to take them to the best *cabrito asado* restaurant in Nuevo Laredo, a Mexican delicacy that most Americans dislike. Six blocks down the road, the cab slowed down a bit due to traffic, and Olivia's heart jumped: There was the hateful Greta Haroldson standing at the corner, staring at them as if to make sure they were who they were. Then she screamed what Olivia did not want to hear.

"Here they are! I got them — I got them!" Greta approached the slowly moving cab, but Olivia raised her window on the right side of the car and locked her door just in time as Greta pulled on the door handle. The cabbie instantly thought he was being hijacked, so he locked all the doors and raised all the windows from his console.

"Please, hurry — there is a crazy woman outside!" Olivia begged the taxi driver.

The taxi was just a bit more than a block away from the beginning of the bridge, but it was just a matter of time for the deputies at the toll area to become aware of the situation, especially since Greta kept screaming, "I got them, I got them, they're mine, you hear!" as she ran behind the cab with her high heels in hand and panty hose in shreds around her feet. It was just sheer luck that traffic sped up again and the cab left Greta farther behind — by then she was more sprinting than running. As the taxi pulled into the vehicle tollbooth, the cabbie quickly paid the toll and took off to get away from the crazy lady behind. Olivia breathed a sigh of relief, but it lasted just a few seconds as she saw that Greta had finally succeeded in getting the attention of the deputies, so now all three of them were running at full speed behind the cab. Gabriela and Frida were now in tears at the developing crisis. "Mamma, why are they chasing us? It's those bad people again." There was no time to answer a thoroughly complicated question.

Traffic on the bridge was light, so the taxi was able to put more distance between it and the menace behind it, but, unfortunately, that did not last long, for soon it came to a grinding halt, as was common on every day of the week. Olivia asked in desperation, "Are we going to be stuck here?"

"Well, it looks like the customs officers have stopped a suspicious vehicle. It's going to be a few minutes."

Olivia again looked through the car's back window, and her blood turned cold as she saw that Greta and the two deputies were advancing at breakneck speed. She made an on-the-spot decision. "Well, that won't work. We're getting out right here." She looked at the taximeter and gave the cabbie a rounded amount to cover that and the toll, plus tip. "Let's go!" she shouted at Gabriela and Frida.

A few seconds later, they were running on the pedestrian walkway, but it all seemed so hopeless, since Frida could not go very fast and Gabriela seemed in a daze this time. One quick glance over her shoulder revealed to Olivia that their tormentors were a mere 25 feet behind and breathing fire from the chase. A few agonizing running steps later, and Olivia saw the bronze plate on the railing that demarcated the international borderline between the two countries. They were now in Mexico, and there were the two customary Mexican military police at attention, near the line, armed with M-16 automatic weapons. She thought it best to say something to them, in Spanish. "Sergeants, please help us. These people running behind us want to kidnap my child — they deal in human trafficking!" Instantly the two Mexican military guards blocked the pedestrian walkway after Olivia and her family had made it over the line, and, with their weapons drawn, they barked like vicious pitbulls: *"Back off! Back off! Back off now, or we will fire!"*

The ferocious action of the Mexican military sergeants brought Greta's merciless and unrelenting chase to an instant end. As Olivia, Frida, and Gabriela continued whimpering and walking toward the end of the walkway, Olivia took one more look over her shoulder. Greta and her two deputies had been stopped cold about 15 feet on the American side of the international line; all three were panting and totally wet with perspiration, but they were otherwise motionless in their abrupt and total defeat. Slowly they started walking backwards, the two deputies with almost bland faces. But Greta seemed unable to let go of the image of what had brought her enormous effort and quest to a definite and unquestionable end. That was the last that Olivia and her family saw of her. Ever.

CHAPTER 26

Going through customs was relatively fast and easy, and, in five minutes, they were on Avenida Guerrero, really now in Mexico! They walked for two blocks south and decided to sit for a while on a bench at the Plaza Benito Juarez. "Olivia, you didn't tell me I would be hunted down like a wild animal; I would have worn my sneakers and not these cheap *chanclas*."

Hugging both of them, Olivia assured, "Mamma, I believe the worst is over. I guess I will never know why DSS, that sinister Greta Haroldson, and the judge were hell bent on taking my precious Gabriela from me, but maybe that does not matter anymore. We just have to concentrate on making a new life in Mexico City. It will be hard, but I have a little bit of money that Jason gave me."

"That reminds me, Olivia. I still don't understand why Jason did not come with you. He seemed like such a nice man."

"Mamma, don't talk about that, or I'll melt in tears again. Let's get something to eat."

After a hearty meal at La Casa de Felipe Restaurante, they concentrated on finding a cheap hotel on the main street, Avenida Guerrero, since they were tired, dirty, and sweaty. Besides, it was too late in the day to head to the metropolis — tomorrow they would take the 9:15 A.M. Estrella Mariana Bus to Mexico City, far away from Houston and the threats and failed lives it now represented.

They zeroed in on Hotel Carolina, one block south of the Plaza Benito Juarez. That night, it was Frida who tucked Gabriela into bed and gently stroked her forehead and hummed her a sweet lullaby until she fell asleep.

Olivia liked that very much, and it endeared her even more to a mother she should have been loving all along, had they all had a normal life.

In the morning, they had breakfast in the hotel restaurant, going heavy on the *huevos rancheros* with jalapeños and flour tortillas. Afterwards they all had chocolate *conchas*, the women with coffee, Gabriela with warm milk. When Olivia asked the waiter for the check, he responded that a gentleman at the door had already taken care of it. "Olivia, you've been in Mexico less than 24 hours, and you already have an admirer! My God, this is fantastic! Just imagine if you had worn some lipstick!" exclaimed Frida.

"Oh, mamma, you know these Mexican men — always making passes at women." Olivia turned around anyway, to enjoy the flattery, but couldn't see the man, so she turned again to face her table. But a man was making a beeline to their table, and the waiter, now near the kitchen door, pointed to Frida to indicate that this was the man who had paid their check.

"Olivia, there is a man walking straight to our table; he's the one, the waiter said."

"Tell me — is he tall, dark, and handsome?"

"Well, he's not dark, but he's tall and very handsome. If you don't want him, just let me know."

"Mamma, I *know* you are already starting to feel better. We are on the right track," chortled Olivia.

"He's almost here." Since Frida had perhaps unintentionally added unnecessary tension to the event, Olivia was now too nervous to turn around and look. But she did not miss the expression on Gabriela's face.

The stranger was finally behind Olivia. "Do you know how many cheap hotels I had to check to find you?" She instantly recognized the voice! *No! It can't be!* She froze with a mixture of joy and apprehension.

Gabriela jumped from her seat and ran to hug the man. "Jason, Jason — why did you get so lost?"

Frida was amazed that she had not picked up on it sooner. "This is Jason?"

"Yes, grandma — he's the one who's going to marry mamma. He was just lost for a while."

Gabriela's innocent "just lost for a while" remark was an on-target description that best fit what had happened to Jason McDougall and his hesitation in accepting Olivia's anxious but heartfelt invitation to join her in making a new life in Mexico.

She had been caught off guard and was still frozen on her seat, not knowing how to react, not able to turn around. She was anxious, embarrassed, afraid, confused. Jason was standing behind her, not wanting to intrude on what he figured was a difficult situation for Olivia. He bent over slightly to smell her shiny and fragrant hair. "I can tell you are still using that banana-watermelon perfume, but if your offer still stands for us to make a life together, I guess I could get used to it."

Olivia jumped up and swung around so quickly that her long hair created a beautiful and shimmering arc around her. "Yes, Jason — that offer still stands, and I want you forever!" Her eyes welled up with tears as Jason took her in his arms.

Frida waited a bit for the next part but then had to give them a push. "Olivia, if you don't kiss that man right now, I will!"

And, for the first time ever, Olivia was kissed in a truly romantic and genuine manner. She knew in her heart that this kiss was different, for it was the only one that had ever touched her soul; she knew that she could not have found a better man, or Jason a better, more determined woman. She was happy, she was exhausted, she was all tears.

"By the way, Olivia, your kiss tasted like chocolate *conchas*, so you won't mind if I order one, will you?" asked Jason.

With Jason's arrival at the table, the family was now complete. There was no other mother like Olivia who had fought harder or more valiantly to save her daughter against incredible odds, no other mother like Frida who had to develop courage out of the nothingness of an empty heart to face her grievous moral failure and the memory of a depraved childhood, and no other young daughter like Gabriela Cervantes who simply provided her mother with much-needed company and a warm little hand while the nightmare was raging in full force over their lives.

THE END

www.ingramcontent.com/pod-product-compliance
Lightning Source LLC
Chambersburg PA
CBHW060935180626
46817CB00004B/1566